DUKE IN NAME ONLY

The Entitled Gentlemen, Book Two

by

Caroline Warfield

Dragonblade Publishing, Inc. is an imprint of Kathryn Le Veque Novels, Inc.
P.O. Box 23
Moreno Valley, CA 92556
ceo@dragonbladepublishing.com

Produced in the United States of America

First Edition June 2023
Trade Paperback Edition

ARE YOU SIGNED UP FOR DRAGONBLADE'S BLOG?

You'll get the latest news and information on exclusive giveaways, exclusive excerpts, coming releases, sales, free books, cover reveals and more.

Check out our complete list of authors, too!

No spam, no junk. That's a promise!

Sign Up Here

www.dragonbladepublishing.com

Dearest Reader;

Thank you for your support of a small press. At Dragonblade Publishing, we strive to bring you the highest quality Historical Romance from some of the best authors in the business. Without your support, there is no 'us', so we sincerely hope you adore these stories and find some new favorite authors along the way.

Happy Reading!

CEO, Dragonblade Publishing

Additional Dragonblade books by Author Caroline Warfield

The Entitled Gentlemen Series
Duke in All But Name (Book 1)
Duke in Name Only (Book 2)
An Unlikely Duke (Book 3)

The Ashmead Heirs Series
The Wayward Son (Book 1)
The Defiant Daughter (Book 2)
The Forgotten Daughter (Book 3)
The Upright Son (Book 4)

Dedication

For messy, complicated families everywhere, including my own.
Bound together by tangible love, compassion, and generosity, may they
all find their own way to strength and unity.

CHAPTER ONE

Along the Upper Mississippi
November, 1818

"SO, WHO ARE you really?" demanded the ruffian at the rear of the canoe paddling through the changing currents of the Mississippi River. He spat over the side and grinned, gap-toothed, at his helpless passenger.

Wet, wounded, and weary, Phillip felt no humor whatsoever.

I'm the damned fool who walked away from the greatest house in Dorset, an army of servants, and great piles of money only to get bamboozled, robbed, and beaten into the bargain. Stupidity hurt worse than the bruises. The seeping wound in his side stuffed full of moss by his unlikely rescuer was another matter.

"I told you," he groaned, his voice shaking with cold. He'd blurted out more than he should have in his delirium.

"Yer feisty for a man with nuthin' but the shirt on his back at the mercy of a stranger's kindness. Say the other again then. I need a laugh, and you sure as hell aren't pulling your weight any other way," the uncouth boatman demanded. A great mountain of a man, he smelled as foul as he looked—dirty, unshaven, dressed in filthy buckskins, with a nasty scar down one cheek.

Fair enough. Phillip sighed and forced the words drilled into him from his youth through shivering lips. "I am Phillip Roland

George Arthur Tavernash, Sixth Duke of Glenmoor, Earl of Wentworth, Viscount Gradington, Baron Walsh."

The boatman let out a bark of laughter so strong it rocked the boat. "Well, Artie, you're entertaining. I'll give you that. Folks may pay money to hear you say it with that fancy accent of yours. God knows you're gonna need it."

"What's your name then? Perhaps I'll laugh," Phillip said, his voice growing weaker.

His companion didn't answer. Experienced travelers told Phillip to expect the water of the great rivers, both the Ohio and the Mississippi, to be treacherous. No one warned him about pirates and swindlers.

The boatman put his back into his work and, with astonishing skill, neatly avoided a floating log that threatened to collide with them. He maneuvered the canoe through swirling eddies, slid around into a calmer channel, and guided the canoe south with the current.

"Luke Archer," the ruffian replied a moment later. "The one you can thank when I drag your worthless carcass ashore." He said nothing else, or if he did, Phillip didn't hear it.

Several hours—or perhaps days—later, sharp pains brought him to awareness as he was dragged from the canoe, thrust over the man's shoulders, and carried a short distance.

"Nan! Get yourself over here. I brought you a wounded duck!" his rescuer shouted as he dropped Phillip to a rough floor. Heat enveloped Phillip before, blessedly, the world went dark again.

NAN ARCHER PULLED her hands from the mound of bread dough she was pounding and nodded to Sal to take over. All taverns required daily bread, and Archers' Roost was no different. Situated on the west bank of the Mississippi River, thirty or more miles north of the confluence with the Ohio River, on the edge of Cape Girardeau in Missouri Territory, it did steady business from settlers and river traffic alike. She sighed and wiped her hands at the dry-sink. She hadn't expected—and didn't relish—a visit from her oldest brother.

She followed his voice into the public room with a frown. "Luke Archer, do y' have to bellow like a heathen? Can't you just—"

Nan stopped short. A man lay sprawled across the floor of her tavern. Sprawled and bleeding. She grabbed a clean towel and fell to her knees at his side. "Some duck," she murmured.

A handful of customers, huddled by the fire against November's chill, stared at them.

"Nate! Fetch me a beer," Luke bellowed, earning a glare from his sister. Their youngest brother, Nate, who had anticipated him, handed him a mug.

Nan pulled the mass of moss from what she could see was a stab wound, grimaced, and replaced it with the towel. She grudgingly noted Luke had done a decent job of slowing the bleeding, but the blood continued to seep. She pressed the towel down and felt a faint but rapid heartbeat.

"Is he dead?" Nate asked, staring at the man.

"Wasn't when I hauled him out of the canoe," Luke said, drinking deeply.

"He will be if we don't get him warm quickly. The cold is killing him faster than his wounds," Nan said. "Did he give you his name?"

Her brother scratched the stubble on his chin. "Artie," he answered. "Called hisself dook."

"Someone build up the fire. The chimney will warm the upstairs," Nan said. She called for Nate and Baptiste, their man of work, to carry the wounded man up to the spare room she kept for visiting brothers. She couldn't afford to give him one of the rooms for paying guests out back. She glanced up at Luke. "Dook?"

"Dook. Duck. Something like that."

Duke? Nan studied the ragged shirt and torn trousers on the injured man. *Can't be.* She rose and wiped her hands as Nate and Baptiste lifted him. "Where'd you find him?" she asked.

"Just above Kaskaskia. On the east bank. That flat spot where the river turns south again," Luke replied, downing his beer and going behind the bar to pour another.

"Odd." Nan put a hand to her neck in thought.

"Yep. Don't expect pirates along that stretch. Too much civilization." Her brother spat into the corner.

"Must you treat The Roost like a midden?" she growled. "We have a spittoon." Luke ignored her as he always did. She pulled her temper in check and followed the men. The wounded man, whoever he was, needed help. "You think river rats did this?"

"Don't you?" Luke followed her up.

"If those gangs operating over by Elizabethtown are moving their operations over here, it could mean trouble," she said over her shoulder. The entire stretch of the Ohio River south of Illinois Territory was riddled with outlaws, pirates, and lawless towns. Elizabethtown, on the Illinois side of the river, lay just west of Cave-in-Rock, a notorious den for pirates.

Towns on the Upper Mississippi, north of where the Ohio River joined it, from Cape Girardeau to Saint Louis, were older, more densely populated, and far safer in comparison. Nan took comfort in that.

"Could be. But why so close to the big town and the law? Maybe they captured him over there, hauled him overland, and dumped 'em. We need to ask him," Luke said, following her.

All the way northeast through Illinois Territory to Kaskaskia? Unlikely, she thought. "If he lives," she muttered, hurrying after the patient.

They laid him on the narrow bed. Nan sent Baptiste after hot water, her herb box, and clean scraps of cotton. She sent Nate for his spare set of clothes and looked directly at their oldest brother. "Strip him to his drawers," she ordered.

Luke found the idea of taking orders from a woman amusing. "You do it. I won't tell."

She had neither time nor patience to argue. She ripped the remnants of a linen shirt from the man and handed it to her brother without taking her eyes from the face of the man on the bed. Grey skin and purple lips did not bode well for his future. Neither did the spasms in his legs.

"Stop acting like a tree stump and rub his legs to get his blood flowing." This time, Luke obeyed her, removing the man's trousers when he did. She lifted a blanket over him and began to rub his arms, trying to get blood from his extremities to his trunk.

"Smells like a dead muskrat," Luke muttered.

"How can you tell? When did you bathe last?" Nan countered, wrinkling her nose.

When Nate and Baptiste returned, Luke grabbed his beer and headed for the door. "I'll bed down in Nate's room tonight," he said.

"Not in those stinking clothes you won't," Nate called after Luke's retreating back. At fourteen, Nate valued his own space, even if it was half the size of Nan's and a wall separated it from the one they used for the stranger.

"Take your brother's place, Nate. Rub the blanket on both his legs. It will send blood to his heart and warm his middle."

"Is this what happened to Old Jacques LeClair last winter?" Nate asked.

"No one found him in time. He froze. We have a chance with this one," Nan said, working on his hands and arms. Neither arm had a break, but his collarbone appeared to have been smashed.

After a while, she took a cloth dipped in hot water and wiped his filthy face, patting it so the heat would penetrate. One blackened eye had swollen shut and a massive bruise bloomed on the opposite cheek. Blood seeped from a swollen lip. She rinsed her cloth and began to do the same down one arm.

She glanced at the hand she held and murmured, "Soft. Greenhorn hands. This one has never done a lick of work in his life." The two middle fingers on his other hand, his left, were swollen and purple. They had been broken and would need binding. She started on his chest and noted with approval that there was nothing soft about his shoulders and arms. The muscles under all the bruises were hard enough.

"Dumb one too, if he let some river pirates lure him in. Everyone knows not to fall for their tricks," Nate said. "You think he's from out east?"

"Likely. For sure, if he fell afoul along the Ohio." She sighed wearily and sent for clean water.

The man's clothes were in rags, but after feeling the material, Nan would bet two day's take that they were finer than any he'd get in Saint Louis or Kaskaskia. *Merchant? Settler? Or just an idiot out to see the country? Got more than he expected either way.*

An hour later, fully bathed and dressed in a borrowed shirt, with his wounds bound up, the patient stared back at Nan blankly. His shivering and spasms had eased. A quick probe had shown her two broken ribs. She'd have to bind them, but that would have to wait. Nan urged tea laced with rum on him; he didn't complain.

"Where?" the man asked.

"You're at Archers' Roost in Cape Girardeau. My brother Luke brought you in looking like you were mauled by a bear."

He made a soft grunt that she took as agreement. He probably felt like it, too. She urged another sip and he took it.

"Good," he whispered before drifting off to sleep.

She left Nate to watch the patient, and ordered Baptiste to see to the fire downstairs all night. She followed him. There were paying customers, and she needed to see to them before Luke drove them off, or worse, gave away her stores. Besides, she had bread to bake. Her thoughts, however, kept wandering back to the room under the rafters.

CHAPTER TWO

PHILLIP STARED AT the beams above him several hours later. His unlikely saviors had put him in some sort of attic. Memory was illusive through the pounding in his head, but he recalled being beaten and left for dead. And then… Another ruffian. He thought they'd come back to finish him.

He'd been tossed aside like a worthless piece of trash. His eyes fluttered shut. Perhaps he was.

Much later, voices woke him up. More light filled the room. Whoever it was spoke quietly, and he made out only snatches.

"Din't wake up." A boy's voice.

"…warm enough. May make…" A woman? More words then, "Still sleeping…"

"Good thing. Stunk up…" the boy spoke again.

Stunk? Do they mean you, Glenmoor? Probably. "Hello." Did a sound come out? He thought not. He tried again with effort. "Halloo…"

A woman loomed over him in the dim light. "Alive after all," she murmured. "How do you feel?"

"Like hell." Belatedly, he remembered a gentleman didn't use such language in front of a lady.

She didn't seem to notice; she chuckled. "I expect so. They worked you over good. Are you hungry?"

Phillip shook his head and screwed his eyes shut in pain when he did.

"Easy," the woman said. Her voice, rich and smooth, flowed over his tangled nerves like a tonic. She turned and murmured to the boy, sending him after something before looming over Phillip again. "I'm afraid I need to look at that knife wound. They didn't hit anything vital or you'd be dead already. Now that we have you warm, though, the wound's the biggest danger."

Knife wound? Had he seen the flash of a knife in the midst of the beating? He tried to fight back. He remembered that. His efforts were hopeless. Then pain.

Pain again. He groaned. She'd pulled off a bandage and probed the cut in his side, muttering to herself. "No redness yet. Got all the moss, I think."

"Moss?"

"Country remedy. Luke saved you bleeding to death with it," she said.

Warmth. She'd brought warm water to clean the wound. Or was it the feel of her hands that heated him? He laughed, causing a shard of pain. *At least you can still react to a woman, Glenmoor, worthless lump that you are.*

The boy returned and handed her something. Warmth turned to heat, and he jumped.

"Sorry. It's a poultice to draw any poison from the wound." Her honeyed voice settled him down. "I still need to bind your ribs. Are you up for that?" She studied his face several moments before shaking her head. "Maybe later."

She brushed back his hair. Phillip sighed with pleasure; he had always imagined a mother's touch would feel like that. He had little experience with it. "You best sleep. Sleep heals," she said before blinking, and adding as an afterthought. "What is your name?"

Phillip Roland George Arthur Tavernash, Sixth Duke of Glenmoor, Earl of Wentworth, Viscount... "Ah..." It was all the sound he could make.

"Arthur? Luke called you Artie."

It's as good a name as any. He had ample evidence to prove he shouldn't be the Duke of Glenmoor anyway. *Damn it. If I'm not the duke, who am I? That's why I set out on this ill-conceived journey, isn't it? To find out.*

She rose, leaving him bereft, longing for her soothing voice and gentle touch. "Here's Nate again," she said. "He brought the tonic."

She slipped an arm behind his head, setting off bright lights, and pressed a hot cup to his lips. Unable to speak through his pain, he gagged down something sweet, cloying, and awful.

"That will help," she said, soothing his brow again.

The light faded, and as he sank into sleep, he had one final thought. *She thinks I'm worth saving. Not worthless.*

⇶⫷

NAN CAUGHT LUKE on the landing before he could burst in on their patient. "Leave him be."

"I want to know before I leave," Luke said. "Did you even ask him who did this and where?"

"He can barely talk."

"I don't need any speech in his fancy drawl. I jist need to know if some of those river rats are moving up river."

"Why didn't you ask him when you picked him up?"

"Was hardly fit to talk."

"Still isn't. Give it a day."

Luke shook his head. "Can't. Due in Smithland in three days. I was bound there when I found your duck. Sun's high already."

"What business do you have in that hell hole?"

"Pa sent me to collect a debt. He was promised two new Kentuck flintlocks by Tuesday next."

"Can't pry himself out of that cabin up the Missouri to do his own dirty work? Or has he gone on farther west?" Nan waved a hand to shut off any reply. Their father's need to keep moving had marred her life. He dragged her across one remote hollow to another from the time she could walk until she refused to budge any further. Luke saw it differently.

"Y're here with none but Nate and old Baptiste. I need to know if the situation is turning ugly."

"You're going right into the roughest town on the Kentucky side of the Ohio River, and you worry about Cape Girardeau? When did you ever worry about me anyway?"

"Towns are all ugly," Luke muttered. He shifted. She almost thought she'd shamed him. "You're good at taking care of yourself, Nan—too much so, in my opinion—but you're a woman," he said as if that settled something.

Nan snorted.

He ignored her. "Before I leave you here with a stranger under the roof—even a beaten up one—I want some idea what is going on."

"One man gets attacked by river pirates and you think we have some sort of bandit uprising on our hands? From the look of him and what was left of his clothes, he comes from money. He's too dumb to hide it and they probably smelled it on him. Easy target. Jump him quick. Done."

Luke rubbed the three day's beard on his chin. "Probably. I'll just check if he's awake." He opened the door before she could stop him. The patient blinked back at them, probably woken by the argument in the hall. "Hey, Artie. You're alive."

Nan scurried in behind her brother. The man Luke called Artie scowled at her. She didn't blame him. Her brother probably hadn't bathed in months.

"Can you tell us who done this to you?" Luke asked.

"Scoundrel. Met him in Mount Vernon," Artie muttered clear enough.

"Mount Vernon?" The new name puzzled Luke. He turned to Nan.

"Way up the Ohio in Indiana, used to be called McFaden's Bluff," she explained. "It's gotten all civilized."

"He looked respectable," Artie muttered.

"Came down the Ohio with you?" Luke asked.

Artie nodded.

"Sounds more like a swindler than anything. Sitting upriver, setting lures for greenhorns. Satisfied now?" Nan glared at Luke.

"What'd he want?" Luke demanded. "And how'd you end up so far up the Mississippi?"

Artie choked something, but Nan couldn't make it out. "Stop it now, Luke. Leave the man be. We'll talk to him later. Get you gone."

Her brother peered over at her for a moment, came to the same conclusion, and nodded. "I'll be going cross country by way of the farm and Round Nob. Back in five days." He turned on his heels and left.

By the time she turned to Artie, he'd fallen asleep. Her curiosity, however, once awoken, would not fade easily.

CHAPTER THREE

I T TOOK THREE days before Phillip could sit up well enough to take soup without having it spooned to him like an infant. The boy, Nate, came regularly, but he stopped sleeping on the floor the previous night. He'd brought the soup and sat cross-legged in the corner whittling. Of the woman, he'd seen glimpses now and then, usually peering down at him, except when she'd bound his cracked ribs, and then he'd been in too much pain to take stock. Not so much today.

Phillip dropped the spoon back into the mug in his hand and set it on the stool by the bedside. He ought to lie down, but hesitated. He needed to ask Nate to help him ease the call of nature. Before he could, the door opened and his breath caught.

Nan Archer, his healing angel, stood in a shaft of light, giving him his first good look. He swallowed hard and groped for words. Statuesque floated to the top. Tall, proud, and generously endowed, she stood with one foot firmly planted in front of her, her back straight, and her chin high. She reminded him of the Greek statues he'd seen in Paris two years before. A goddess with glowing honey brown hair piled on her head.

"Nate, enough dawdling like a banker's daughter. Clean up those wood chips. Baptiste needs help chopping wood, and the kitchen floor won't clean itself," she said, stuffing the empty soup mug in the boy's hands as he pushed past her.

Perhaps not a goddess exactly. His first thought was that she sounded like a fishwife, but her deep, throaty voice held more authority than harshness. Perhaps a governess. The plain dress that she wore buttoned high may not have been silk, but it fell in soft folds over generous curves.

She put a hand to his head with a businesslike flick of her wrist and muttered, "No fever." She lifted his borrowed shirt without a by-your-leave and probed his wound less gently than he hoped. "No heat either. You're a lucky sod if it doesn't putrefy entirely. So far not. No need to have Nate playing nursemaid when there's work to be done. Can you talk?"

If I can get a word in. "About what?"

His martinet of a caregiver sat on the stool. "How did you come to be in this mess? You said you met a river rat up in Mount Vernon, not taking him for the swindler he was."

"Alfred Carpenter. Dressed and spoke like a gentleman," he said. *At least as the sort that passes for a gentleman in most of America.*

She tilted her head in thought, which he found charming. "Don't know the name. It was likely fake anyway. Why were you in Mount Vernon? It's in Indiana. Were you floating downriver?"

"It was a stop on my way to Kaskaskia and then Saint Louis," he said. "I had been in correspondence with the land office in Kaskaskia and—"

"You plan to be a farmer?" she demanded.

"Hardly! I plan to hold land until prices—"

"You're a damned speculator," she sneered. "I should have guessed. I'll bet you heard the United States Government began selling land in Missouri Territory cheap this year, too."

He didn't deny it. "You disapprove of making a profit?"

"I disapprove of prideful easterners driving up the price of land so hardworking locals can't get a stake. It pushes people like my pa further and further west."

Prideful easterner? What about radical rabble? He shifted in a fruitless effort to sit taller. *Who does she think she's speaking to?* He glanced at his borrowed shirt, broken fingers, and bruised arms.

She takes you for the pathetic mess you are, you damned fool.

"So, you traveled downriver in your fancy suit bragging to a stranger about your plans." One brow arched gracefully over deep blue eyes.

Phillip opened his mouth to deny it, and couldn't. He'd suspected by the time the boat reached Indiana that displaying wealth had been a mistake, but fancy? His embroidered waistcoats, silk coats, lace-adorned shirts, and emerald stick pin were in a trunk in Philadelphia in the home of Sir Charles Bagot, His Majesty's envoy. He had thought his mode of dress quite republican!

She waved away his reply, a habit of hers, he suspected. "This Carpenter. What did you tell him, and how long before he showed his colors?"

"A flat boat isn't exactly a yacht. It isn't as if we shared cigars in the smoking saloon," he said.

She snorted. "More like rum on the deck."

That she guessed exactly right didn't help his self-esteem. "Yes, and before you say it, I said too much about my plans." He scowled at the inquisitive woman. "At least I kept my belongings close. He never meddled with them."

"Didn't need to. Not yet. When did things change? Smithland?" she asked.

"Am I the only man on the planet who doesn't know the ways of the river?" he sighed.

"No. There are plenty who walk into traps. Let me guess. You docked on the Kentucky side at Smithland, and he suggested an inn. You walked right into it, right? Did he drug you?"

"I think so. I woke up in some camp. My belongings were strewn all over the ground being divided by three bully-boys." He scowled at the thought.

The woman leaned closer. "What did they look like?"

"Your brother Luke," he said without hesitation.

Her bark of laughter lightened his mood.

"Sounds about right. I wonder why they didn't just kill you

outright and take your goods."

"Carpenter had bigger game. He wanted information and papers."

Her brows drew together, and she paused for a few moments. "Land," she said at last. "He was after your land? Explain."

"You're worried about eastern speculators. You should worry about bandits in your own midst," he said. No one in Philadelphia warned him about pirates and swindlers when he set out on this reckless pursuit of adventure.

"He wanted you to sign it over?"

"That was the first plan. I refused. He laughed, broke my fingers to take my ring, and had me trussed to drag overland for I don't know how many days. One of the bully-boys left. The other two did the dragging."

"To Kaskaskia." She didn't make it a question.

"Nearby, I think. Then the beating began. He was keeping me alive but just barely."

"Did he give up?" she asked.

"Do I look like he gave up? No, he had a change of plans. Some others met us, one of them better dressed. He looked like Carpenter. He turned out to be an expert forger. They didn't need me after that."

"Is that when they stabbed you?"

"Must be. I don't remember. By that time, I was too beaten up. They threw me into the river; I washed up later half drowned. When your brother found me, I thought they came back."

She shook her head. "It sounds like a much more educated operation than the usual banditry," she said. "I don't figure they're a threat to Archers' Roost. The farm may be a different story." Her head tilted again; the gesture struck him as the habit of a woman of innate intelligence, who sorted facts before acting. He admired that.

"What farm?"

"My family's. A whole section—six hundred and forty prime acres—over in Illinois." She said it with pride that would rival any duchess Phillip had yet to meet.

Entranced, he could only gape at her, their eyes meeting. They held for a moment before she grinned and gave her head a self-deprecating shake. "Ours and the bank's, of course!"

Phillip tried to remember the total acreage he owned. Woodglen, his primary seat, had well over ten thousand acres. There were five smaller holdings. *What an odd little world this is.* "Impressive nonetheless, Miss…Archer, is it?"

"Archer, yes, but no one calls me Miss Archer. I'm Nan." She surprised him by blushing slightly before rising to leave. She hadn't seemed the sort to blush. "Get well, Artie, or whoever you are. You'll need your energy to work off what you owe." The governess was back.

Phillip's eyes widened. "I can pay you, of course."

Her amused snort put him in his place. "Not likely. Not soon in any case."

"Phillip," he said in clipped tones.

"Flip it is." She turned to leave.

"Send Nate back, please," he called after her. He couldn't reach the chamber pot on his own. That would be his first goal for healing. "Please. I need personal assistance."

Again, amusement sparkled in her eyes. He'd find it attractive if it wasn't at his expense.

"I will. I'll add it to what you owe us."

She was gone then, and the room felt unbearably empty.

NAN FINISHED WIPING beer from the rough surface of the bar and watched Sal, her hired woman, sweep up by candlelight. Exhaustion that she had been too busy to face enveloped her. The lunchtime crush had been gratifying, and so had the brisk traffic for drinks all evening. Her guest rooms were full, two or three to a room, a blessing this late in the season. She almost asked Nate to give up his little room, but decided against it. She squeezed her eyes shut.

"We're done now, Sal. You should get to bed."

Sal nodded and wandered toward the cubby behind the kitchen where she slept. Nan had considered asking Baptiste to give up his little closet back there too, but she was reluctant to put a stranger right next to Sal.

Nan's mind flitted back over the day. She had reason to be tired. Add six loaves of bread, two loads of laundry, seven trips to bring in wood, two large vats of stew prepared, and one brawl defused and you had it. *Money in the till.*

She longed for a few moments of quiet more than she longed for sleep. Her greatest joy in life came in the bits of time when she managed to read by candlelight every evening, just as it had in whatever cabin they lived in when she was a girl. When she started up the stairs, though, the patient across from her room tickled her conscience. She hadn't seen him since morning; she ought to look in.

No sound came from the other side of the wall except Nate's steady breathing in his own room. She set her tallow candle on the patient's bedside table and went to replace the one in the wall sconce that had gone out in case they needed it the next day. She didn't light it. Candles were precious.

"Smells foul, but I'm grateful for the light."

She jumped at the sound. "You're awake."

"You left me here alone all day."

She could just make out his features in the dim light. His swollen eye now opened in a thin slit. "Not true. Sal brought you food. Twice." Nan glanced at his supper bowl, scraped clean, on the table. "And I hope Nate looked in on you."

"Good lad. He helped me up. We both hope I can manage the necessary without him tomorrow."

When she moved the candle across the table, closer to the bed, he scowled.

"Don't they have candles where you come from?" she asked.

"Not tallow," he replied.

He meant beeswax, she supposed, or something even more costly like the oil lamps she saw in Louisville when she was a girl. She felt a pang. "You'll have to make do here," she growled.

"And be grateful. I am, truly," he said. "What is that under your arm?"

She set her book on the table. "As you see, I mean to read once I check on that knife wound." She steeled herself for the mockery that usually came when she claimed she could read.

It didn't come. If her claim surprised him, he didn't show it. His eyes followed her movements as she raised his shirt, and he grimaced when she probed, though she went as gently as she could. She didn't like what she found.

"You're unhappy. What is it?" he demanded.

"How do you feel?" she asked in return.

He groaned. "Still like I was mauled by a bear. Why?"

"Your skin is hot. Poison may be setting in. I need to apply another poultice. Should have replaced it this morning. Stay awake until I get back."

"Help me up."

She stopped at the stairs at his command. "What?"

"Help me up. I'll read to stay awake."

Nan hesitated. She supposed being upright wouldn't make the situation any worse if he could bear it.

He paled at the process, but he bore it, and smiled when she set him back against the pillow. When he reached for her book, she had to hold her breath to keep from telling him no. She prized books too much to trust a stranger with them.

"*Gulliver's Travels?*" He sounded incredulous.

She stiffened. "Why not?"

"Why not indeed. I know it well. How did you come by it?"

She clamped her jaw shut. *What business is it of this snot-nosed easterner?*

"I don't mean to offend. I didn't think Cape Girardeau had a library," he said.

"We do, actually. A small lending library, but the book is mine. A merchant left me that one when he had no money to pay for his room."

She left before he could pester her with more questions.

PHILLIP DROPPED THE book, sagged his head back, and closed his eyes.

Infection. The vermin may kill me yet. And what would I have to show for my life? At least Gideon will take care of Woodglen's people. The Crown will declare him duke, as they should—it's rightfully his—or dawdle until they can give it to his son. They hate admitting mistakes. When he brooded that he was the mistake, he pulled himself together, there being no point in that.

He had found the proof Gideon was no bastard in South Carolina where their father was stationed during the colonial rebellion and sent it to his solicitors to ensure the title passed to Gideon's line in the next generation. Meanwhile, he had given his brother complete authority over the ducal estates. Phillip smiled. Gideon wouldn't like it. He would do it for his son, though. He would manage things as well, or likely better, than Phillip could.

He picked up the book for the distraction and flipped through it, settling on the passages about the voyage to Brobdingnab, the story in which giants display Gulliver as a curiosity. The American west had turned out to be almost as foreign to Phillip as the lands he found were to Gulliver. *Maybe that's how I will end up. A curiosity for the entertainment of the locals.* He shut the book.

Luckily, Miss Archer interrupted his morose thoughts. He instinctively started to rise at a lady's entry, but sank back immediately. This was no drawing room, and he was incapable. She didn't notice.

She set a steaming mug on the table, a warm rag next to it, and the hot poultice on the stool, starting in on him without a word.

All business again. He tried not to let her troubled expression worry him.

She pulled off the bandages, sniffed them briefly, and frowned. She cleaned the wound careful, clucking as she did. It hurt like the devil, and for a moment, he thought he would faint. When she lay the poultice on him, he almost did.

"We've done the best we can. We'll have to watch and see," she said, straightening.

"You have to keep me alive," he murmured.

To his amusement, she took his teasing as an insult. "As I would any wounded animal—except ones for the stew pot. Why should I do more, sir?"

"So, I can pay my debts," he answered.

Her smile almost drove the worry from her eyes. "There is that. I'll do my best to make sure you do. Drink this tonic now, and then down you go."

He did as she bid, but was dizzy when she helped him lie flat.

She began to pack up her things. "Don't leave me. At least stay until I sleep," he said, reaching for her.

Miss Archer hesitated. But nodded and sat on the chair she had cleared.

"Read to me," he said. "That way you won't miss your time with the book."

As he hoped, she read smoothly with few stumbles over unfamiliar words. Her deep honeyed voice flowed over him like a warm quilt and he slept.

CHAPTER FOUR

NAN WOKE WITH a start. She'd stayed with Artie—or Flip, or whoever he was—too long and fell asleep in the chair. Night had been half gone, and her patient slept restlessly when she had found her bed. She splashed water on her face, dressed quickly, and ran downstairs to find that Sal had started the bread. Baptiste knelt to build up the fire, and Nate came in carrying an armful of logs while he held a thick slice of bread between his teeth.

"Did you check on the patient?" she asked Nate.

The boy set the logs down and freed his mouth. "Mr. T? He's still asleep."

"What did you call him?"

"He said his name was Mr. Tavernash." Nate shrugged. "Too big a mouthful."

"'E said 'is name is Philipe," Baptiste said over his shoulder.

Philipe, of course. He must have said Phillip; she heard Flip. "Sleeping peacefully?"

Nate scratched his unruly hair. "Not so peaceful maybe. Mumbling like."

By the time Nan prepared another poultice, brewed willow bark tea, and made sure all three of the others could manage the overnight customers demanding breakfast, she found her patient feverish and thrashing.

Damn.

He fought her when she tried to change his poultice and bandage so that she had to run down to fetch Baptiste.

Her old servant saw the problem immediately. "Best get that fever down,'mselle Nan," he said, holding the man down while she worked.

"We have no ice," she muttered.

"The river is plenty cold this time of year."

"Good idea, fetch water quickly. Not clean enough for his wound, but we can cool his head with it."

There was little she could do while she waited. She dribbled willow bark tea into his mouth. And prayed.

PHILLIP THOUGHT PERHAPS he had died, but his pain argued otherwise. He could hear voices, but they rarely made sense. He floundered in a world of dreams, nightmares, and confusion, both sleeping and awake for two days.

He woke once to find an old servant wiping his shoulders with icy water, murmuring to him in some sort of French patois he couldn't make out. Phillip blinked up at him before slipping back into the chaos of his mind.

Once a boy called to him, at least he thought he did. "Mr. T, come back to us." Had he run away? Had the boy? He couldn't recall. Something bitter filled his mouth, choking him. He tried to push it away, to flee.

Lost. I'm lost. The nightmare recurred over and over. He needed to find his home, only he had no idea where it was. Or what it was. Or who he was.

The only lodestar in the madness was the sound of a woman's gentle voice, calling to his troubled soul. *Miss Archer. Nan.* She came and went. He tried to reach for her several times, but could not.

Finally, he slept. At least, he thought he had when he drifted upward at last and opened his eyes to find himself in a strange place. *Did I fall asleep in one of the steward's remote shacks?*

"Are you truly awake?" The boy from his dreams rushed to his cot and put a hand on his head. Presumptuous, that. "Cool! I best fetch Nan."

Nan. Miss Archer. The river. Beatings. Archers' Roost. Memory came flooding back, most of it bad. When she came to him moments later, he knew where he was. Her hand on his brow, gently touching and brushing his hair back, wrapped him in a blanket of safety.

"It appears you aren't going to die on us after all," she said.

"I decided I'd rather not," he rasped, his voice rusty.

She turned to the boy, Nate. "There's broth in the iron pot warming. Fetch a mug." The boy scurried away, and she sat at his side.

"You're stronger than you look. You must be to beat back that fever. I wasn't hopeful," she said.

"For a greenhorn?" he asked.

"Your humor is back, too. Good." The broad smile that filled her eyes lit the entire room and warmed Phillip's heart. *A man could lose himself in this woman's smile.*

He sighed and his eyes closed. He forced them to open so he could fill his senses with her face, though the effort felt immense.

"Who is Gideon?" she asked. "You called out that name several times."

"My brother." To his chagrin, his eyes prickled with incipient tears.

"Has he died?"

"No, praise God. We found him alive after all those years," he said. The effort to talk exhausted him.

"Nate is here with your broth. Let's see how much you can take. Perhaps you can tell me about your brother some time."

Perhaps. It's complicated. And not pretty. He could only nod.

He slept again. There were bandage changes, and later, they

bathed him. All of it was awkward at best, painful at worst. He felt as useless as a babe.

Still, he thought ruefully as he drifted off one more time, there were worse things than to be at the tender mercy of Nan Archer, the woman who thought him worth saving.

⇛⇚

TWO DAYS LATER, Nan went up after the lunchtime rush and found her patient dressed in trousers and a shirt one of her brothers had left behind sitting on the edge of the bed. The smile he gave her in greeting had more welcome than energy behind it. "Did you dress yourself?"

"I did," he said, as proud as any toddler who put on his own shoes.

Shoes. Damn. He was wearing a pair of Nate's wool socks. They'd have to find him shoes. At the thought of the money, her heart sank. "I hope you didn't open that wound putting on the shirt," she scolded.

"You sound like a governess," he grumbled.

"Four brothers will do that to a woman," she replied tartly, peering under his shirt to check the dressing. All appeared well, so she dropped her hands. Now that he was up, she had no business touching this man. Baptiste could handle the change of dressing from now on.

"Four? Luke, Nate, and…"

"Jamie manages the farm. Does most of it himself. Jake…died."

"I'm sorry."

She shrugged. She didn't want to think of it, much less speak of that horrific nightmare. Her family endured two attacks during Madison's war when many of the Illinoian Indians sided with England. Most of her family survived, all but Jake. He died defending them. Six years older than Nan, he'd been twenty-two.

She didn't blame the Pottawatomies—they had their own problems—but she'd never forgive England for using them thusly. Never.

He started to stand and wobbled a bit.

"What are you doing?"

"Going downstairs."

"Are you a simpleton?"

He sat back down and glared at her. "Miss Archer, I'm deeper in your debt every day, but I expect I'll need your help for a while yet. If I'm downstairs, I can rest in a chair. At least your people won't have to climb the stairs to see to my needs, and you won't have to keep this room so warm all day."

It was more words—and more courtesy—than any man had given Nan in a long time. Perhaps ever. She tilted her head to one side, considering. Her patient seemed to find that amusing.

"It might help. But if you collapse and we have to carry you up, I'll add it to what you owe," she said. "And I'm Nan. Miss Archer sounds like a society lady."

"I can pay you back, believe me. Nan."

"Not likely, and as I said, not soon," she retorted. "If you don't have the coin, you'll have to work it off." She lifted her chin defiantly.

Apparently, he could be stubborn too. He stood and waved off help to walk to the door where he stopped and took a deep breath. She wrapped an arm around his waist. "Put one hand on the wall. We'll go down together."

Goodness. He's bigger than he looks. Nan stood almost six feet high, taller than most men, even her brother Luke, but this one had at least three inches on her. No wonder the trousers he wore didn't quite come to his ankles. The feel of his body against hers sent ripples of heat through her. *This probably is not your best idea, Nan. Baptiste or Nate can do it.*

He made it down, but sank into the wooden arm chair Baptiste had set next to the hearth in the kitchen with a sigh, closing his eyes and tipping back his head. She had decided the kitchen was preferrable to the public room in case he did collapse, and now she was glad. Baptiste, Nate, and Sal all stood watching as if waiting for him to do so.

He rallied, though, and looked around him. "Thank you, Nan."

"What are we to call you then? Nate says you told him to call you Mr. Taversomething. That's as uppity as Miss Archer. Baptiste says your name is Philipe. Phillip, I suppose, but even that is a fancy-sounding mouthful."

He glanced from one to the other for a moment. She couldn't tell if she amused or fretted him. Amusement seemed to win. "Luke called me Artie. Will that do?"

Nate peered at Nan. "I like that." He shrugged, but his mouth quirked as if he fought off a grin.

"Artie it is. Try not to cause trouble. The rest of you—back to work."

She found him four hours later talking with Nate about Julius Caesar. A bowl next to him seemed to indicate they'd set him to shelling peas.

"But this Rubicon. Was it a big river like Big Muddy or a little 'un like the Kaskaskia?" Nate asked.

As much as Nan hated to interrupt his attempt to broaden Nate's horizons, his color had turned pale and he sat a bit slumped. "Enough of this. Can't you see Artie's tiring, Nate Archer? We need to get him to bed before we have to nurse him back again." Now that she studied him closely, his knuckles were white where he gripped the arms of the chair, and gratitude shone in his eyes. "Dimwitted man. Why didn't you say you needed help?"

It took both Baptiste and Nate to keep him upright, but they got him up the stairs without problems.

Nan took the chair he had vacated and pulled out her knitting. *What are we going to do with him?* Luke would have a conniption if she kept him on, a virile, young, single man under her roof. He'd run to Pa with it. *What does my damned fool brother think half my customers are? Single.* She grinned to herself. *Not so attractive, though.*

Luke hadn't come back, however. He said five days; it had been over a week. She didn't worry about him. He knew how to take care of himself, and he'd turn up eventually. Artie was another matter. *If we turn him out, he'll be as helpless as a lamb for slaughter out there.* He seemed to believe he had money somewhere. Maybe first thing when he was able, she'd haul him upriver and across to Kaskaskia to talk to the bankers.

Satisfied with that, she peered down at her work. She'd added five more inches to a sock. With winter coming, they'd need 'em. Once Artie had money, she'd get him on the safest boat she found bound for New Orleans so he could take a ship back east. Why that should cause a pang of disappointment, she couldn't say.

CHAPTER FIVE

STRONGER EVERY DAY, Phillip wandered out the kitchen door one afternoon, and a question that had puzzled him fell into place. The entire upper half story of the Roost had been given over to family rooms, Nan's, Nate's, and the one they generously allowed him to use. Where, he had wondered, were the guest rooms Nan fussed over?

Out the door he found that a row of narrow rooms, each with a door to the outside, had been built onto the Roost. He counted six of them, enough to house a dozen or more tired rivermen. Enough to require hours of sweeping, scrubbing, and laundry.

Looking around, he felt utterly ineffectual, at least as regards the running of Archers' Roost, where a small group of people ran off their feet every day caring for customers and their useless, uninvited patient. He wanted to ease Nan Archer's burdens—he owed her that much and more—but he saw no way to do it.

The kitchen yard had stacks of logs for firewood and facility for splitting it. He also spied a good-sized shed—storage, he presumed—lines for laundry, and a chicken coop. He saw nothing he might help with.

Phillip couldn't chop or even carry wood for fear of reopening his wound. He couldn't carry heavy trays either. When he found Nan scrubbing the floor, he tried to assist, but she had a fit. He became royally sick of hearing about his wounded hide.

The following Sunday, Nan, Nate, and Baptiste closed the place and went to church in Kaskaskia, a process that would, they said, take all day. They left Sal and Phillip to keep a watch on the two travelers who'd stayed the night. Both left by mid-morning. Apparently, locals knew the place closed on Sunday. At first, he welcomed the silence, but it began to grate on his nerves.

Sal, a sturdy woman Phillip guessed to be well past forty, sat polishing pewter utensils, apparently items of great pride to Nan. Sal was, Nate had explained, a widow without children. Nan had taken her in. Phillip had no idea how to begin a conversation with the woman.

"Do they do this every Sunday?" he asked finally when the silence became too much to bear.

Sal's head bobbed up; he'd startled her. "Not in summer." She went back to her work.

He had to ponder that crumb of information. Traffic on the river would be brisk in summer. "More business then?"

"Spring too," Sal said without looking up. "Winter sometimes they can't make it across, but she likes to close up and go when she can."

So, his savior had a religious streak. *Good to know.*

The sun dropped behind the hilltops to the west when the Archers' Roost party returned in the gloaming to catch Phillip sweeping the kitchen. His housekeeper at Woodglen would have had apoplexy if she caught him, but it satisfied his need to make a contribution.

While Nan Archer peeled off scarves and her heavy woolen cloak, he held his breath. He needn't have worried. She seemed pleased by his effort.

"Potatoes are all peeled," Sal said, the most she'd spoken in hours. Nan thanked her, and soon the two of them had a chicken roasting with root vegetables around it. Nate brought in a load of wood and Baptiste went out to collect sheets for the next morning's laundry. Phillip once again felt like he was of no use, especially when Nan shooed him to the public room.

After a while, Nate sat in a corner whittling by candlelight. Baptiste poured himself a bit of rum and offered some to Phillip who took it gladly. The servant pulled out a New Orleans newspaper several weeks old and offered to share it. Phillip took part while Baptiste watched him avidly. Phillip soon realized why. The paper was in French. That it posed no problem to him seemed to please the older man.

"You read French?" Nate sounded impressed.

"Certainly. Gentlemen do," Phillip said.

Nate made a rude nose. "Men have work to do," he said as if that settled some dispute, but moments later, he added, "I'm learning to read English."

Flabbergasted at the idea that a boy of Nate's age was just now learning to read, Phillip thought of Nan and *Gulliver's Travels*. He decided to talk with her about Nate later, if he could get her alone.

They sat in peaceful accord as the women remained in the kitchen and heavenly scents of roasting fowl filled the inn.

A slamming door upended the serenity of the house. Luke Archer stood in the door, a brace of geese in one hand and a long gun in the other. "Nan, I brought provisions," he shouted, dropping the bleeding geese on one table. "Nate, come down to the landing. Help me stow my gear and put Pa's goods some-where safe." He flicked a glance at Phillip. "You lived then?"

Nan came from the kitchen wiping her hands. "Close the wretched door, Luke, you're letting out the heat."

"Going back out. Why is he still here?" He nodded at Phillip.

"Healing. Go wash up. Dinner's almost ready."

Phillip swept up the geese, took them to the kitchen without speaking, hung them in the larder, and saw plates and utensils piled on the table. He lay a pewter fork next to a butter knife at each place and grinned at the thought of his tutor explaining the six kinds of forks used in formal dinners at his father's table.

Nan bustled back into the kitchen. "What is so funny?"

"Dinner with the Archers should be interesting."

Interesting? We'll probably drive him screaming from the room.

Artie had laid out plates, forks, butter knives, and napkins, neatly arranged in front of each chair. Nan knew almost nothing about the man, but one thing was certain. He came from quality. Probably money. He'd been eating on trays in his room or on his own in the kitchen. Sitting down with family would be another thing entirely.

She added a motley collection of sharper knives at each place, confident her brothers wouldn't use them on each other. Among rowdy tavern customers, it might be different.

Luke plunked himself down and shoved the carefully arranged place setting forward to lean on the table. "Smells fine, Nan. Where'd you put the geese?"

"Hanging in the larder," she answered. Artie, she noticed, sat down quietly at the end of the table, watching them all avidly.

"How is Jamie?" she asked, bringing over a crock of boiled beans and a bowl of the roasted potatoes, turnips, and carrots. Luke dug his fork in without a by-your-leave and loaded his plate.

"Fine—worn out a bit, but fine. You probably heard harvest went well. He hired two men to help." Luke stuffed potatoes in his mouth.

Nate shot a glance at Artie and waited with his hands in his lap as Nan had taught him to do. "I helped with harvest, too."

"Thought you couldn't spare the boy," Luke said.

"Harvest is as important as our take here. The mortgage came due the end of September," Nan said. She set the chicken laid out on its platter on the end of the table. For a moment, she was tempted to ask Artie to carve it, but feared it would provoke Luke to derision. She began to do it herself with swift strokes.

She handed Artie a plate with aromatic slices of bird on it. He took some and passed it on to Baptiste, waiting patiently.

"Give me that hunk of leg," Luke demanded. She did as he

asked.

"Mam always said we should pray before we eat. Most days we don't sit down long enough," Nan pointed out.

Nate knew an order when he heard it; he bowed his head. Nan murmured words of thanks to the Almighty while Luke paused, the drumstick halfway to his mouth. "You forgot coffee," he said when she was done.

"I have it," Sal said. She poured coffee for them all before sitting between Nate and Baptiste. Nan sat between Luke and Artie with a sigh.

"Jamie'd have an easier time if we'd sell out and move our stake farther into Missouri. Damned abolitionist bastards running Illinois make it hard to make money," Luke said.

Nan pulled back a sharp retort. It was an old argument. Both Jamie and Nan disagreed with Luke and Pa on the subject of slavery. So far, they'd held their own; they were the ones running the operations. Luke was the worst, and she wasn't about to bandy words with him pointlessly.

Nate glanced from Nan to Luke. "Is Pa coming in before winter?"

"To see you maybe, but I doubt it. Doesn't want another winter in Cape Girardeau. He's preparing to sit out the cold months in the hunting cabin we built."

"I thought you had a camp just past Arrow Rock." Nan said. Far up the Missouri River beyond settlement, Pa's latest abode held little appeal to her.

"Still do, but river traffic has been picking up. Pa wanted to move across the river above Boone's Lick up in the hills. Quiet up there," Luke said.

"Do the Boone brothers still sell their salt through Saint Louis?" Baptiste asked, pronouncing the name in the French manner.

"They sold out to partners a few years back. Still an active salt works, though."

"Who owns the farm?" Artie's unexpected question silenced them all. The siblings spoke at the same time.

"Pa." Luke spoke with absolute confidence.

"We all do," Nate said, less sure of himself.

"Jamie's name is on the mortgage," Nan asserted.

"Pa put up the money," Luke went on, glaring at Nan. Sometimes she thought he bore a grudge against all the rest of them, born as they were to Pa's second wife.

"And the rest of us put up the work. That was our deal with Pa when he dragged us out of Kentucky, sure we'd do better in Illinois Country. Jake insisted on it. Jake…"

Nan swallowed hard at the memory of her older brother. Jake organized the building of the cabin on the farm; he'd even laid foundations for Archers' Roost before he died. He led them when Pa took off. "He left us to clear it, and we all did our share. At least some of us did." She stared right back, letting her resentment of Luke color her common sense. "The tavern paid this year's mortgage. Wheat prices dropped in half, now Napoleon and the rest of Europe are back to growing their own."

She glanced up to see Artie watching avidly and felt her face heat. She stabbed a piece of chicken and focused on her plate.

Luke did the same, grumbling, "No business of an outsider anyhow."

"What news on the river, Archer?" Baptiste neatly turned the subject. "Has that Congress done anything about Illinois Territory?" Baptiste, born under French rule, had lived under many changes—France ceded to Spain. The Spanish governor was still in place, though Spain had ceded the territory back to France, when France sold it to the United States—all without leaving this part of the country. Nan couldn't blame him for not trusting the United States, the latest comers.

"If y'mean did they finish all their nonsense to make it a state? Not yet. Or at least no word of it yet in yonder river towns," Luke answered.

"Maybe they took a close look at that election last summer. Jamie said they were stopping men on roads and having them vote. Setting up in towns and buttonholing them. Jamie says he got asked to vote three times. They badgered till he did it. He thinks there were more votes for statehood than there are men, women, and children in Illinois."

Conversation continued cordially, and Artie kept to himself. At least, he did until the other men went off for a beer, and she rose to clear.

CHAPTER SIX

"Your brothers are a complicated bunch." Phillip carried dishes to the dry sink where Nan had a bucket of water ready to clean them.

"They are that." She put the chicken carcass and leftover meat in a pot, covered it with water, and put it on the hob to boil for the next day's soup.

Questions burned in Phillip's head, but he wasn't sure how to approach them. "Luke is different. Older."

She laughed while she shaved soap into the wash water and swished it around to melt and suds up. For a moment, Phillip was fascinated by the process, one he'd never seen before. Was it done the same way in his kitchens at Woodglen?

But then Nan responded. "Luke's much older. His mother was Pa's first wife. She died in an attack back in Pennsylvania."

"And the two others? Jamie and…Jake, is it?"

"Older also, but not as much. Our mam was Pa's second wife."

"What happened to Jake?"

The conversation died. Phillip, sorry he'd made her uncomfortable, dried dishes, stacking them carefully on the shelf, certain she wouldn't answer. Helping gave him an excuse to talk to her.

Nan finished, dried her hands on a towel, and faced him squarely. "Same as Luke's mam. Only these were Pottawatomie.

Out here. They killed him during Madison's War in 1813. Every time we're at war, the hell-born English stir them up to come after settlers. They don't care about the Pottawatomie or any of the tribes. They don't care how many ordinary folks they murder. The English are evil."

She squeezed her jaw shut and Phillip's heart froze. Did she realize he was English? Had he told her? He didn't think so. Her jabs at his ego had all been about easterners. He turned to put the flatware away.

Her voice behind him startled him. "What about your brother? Older or younger?"

He turned and answered. "Older. Seven years. Also from my father's first marriage." *His first perfectly legitimate marriage. The one he conveniently forgot when he came home. Soldier far from home forgets wife and son in a faraway place when he returns home—it's an old enough story—except this one unexpectedly came into the title Fifth Duke of Glenmoor and took an earl's daughter with a perfect pedigree, my mother, in a bigamous marriage.*

"You said 'not dead.' Something about 'all these years.'"

"Our father announced that he was dead when I was a boy, but he lied. Gideon is very much alive. I'm proud of him. He was sent to the mines as a young man. Now he owns three outright, and he sets an exemplary model of safety and care for his workers. He did it all himself—by his own efforts in spite of the hurdles thrown his way." *And I had everything handed to me. When I set out to try to make something on my own, I made a mess of it.*

Nan studied him carefully. "I would have guessed you came from money. Why was he in the mines?"

What could he say? What could he admit to? "You guessed correctly, I do. Our father rejected Gideon. He denied his first marriage and claimed Gideon was base-born. It wasn't true."

"Ouch. He must resent your father. You too," she said.

"He loathed our father with good reason. But Gideon is content with his life—has every reason to be proud of what he accomplished—and—miraculously—bears me no ill will."

"I wish I was sure Luke felt the same. I suspect he begrudges us. I never saw my mother treat him any different than the rest of us, and yet there was friction," she said.

"What do you mean?"

"Mam wanted to settle, to make a comfortable house. Pa's constant moves were hard on her. Luke sided with Pa, followed him on his wandering whenever he could. He still does. They're both happier in the wilderness."

"So, he doesn't covet that farm you take pride in?" he asked.

"Not the land. Not the work. He may resent the cash it takes for the mortgage and taxes."

Something that had been niggling at Phillip rose to the surface. "Whose name is on the deed for the land?" he asked.

The question startled Nan. "I don't know. I hadn't thought about it. Pa found the place and staked it out years ago."

"What about your mother?"

"She died just before we left the last place in Kentucky, worn out as if she couldn't bear another move. Pa took Jake to the land office to read for him and claim the land."

"Read for him?"

She nodded. "Mam tried to teach all of us, even Luke, but he wouldn't stick with it."

"So, Jake, as next oldest, went with him. Could his name and signature be on the deed?"

"I never thought about it. Why?"

This woman has no idea how grasping relatives can be about inheritance. He let the matter drop. It wasn't his to worry over. "I need to go to upriver to Kaskaskia," he said, changing the subject.

"You aren't going anywhere for at least a week or two. You're still recovering from all that blood loss and fever. Maybe if business keeps slowing, we could go then." She tipped her head and furrowed her brow in thought. "Jamie might come over by then," she said.

"How often does he come?" Phillip asked.

"He used to winter over here, but now we have livestock that need tending. He comes when he can after harvest and before winter, then again before spring planting. I'd have expected him before now." She shrugged.

Luke left the next day, to Phillip's relief, but he came back a mere week later after carrying flour, sugar, bread, and other supplies to their other brother at the farm.

That week passed before Nan quit nagging Phillip to rest and allowed him to contribute to the work. His first effort to chop wood cost him Baptiste's amusement, an ache in his wounded side, and severely blistered hands.

"You may as well continue as soon as these heal," Nan said, applying some foul-smelling ointment. "They'll tough up soon enough if you do real work."

Her gentle touch almost made up for the humiliation. "Take me to Kaskaskia. If I get to the bank, I might be able to pay you back."

She glanced up at him at that. "Tomorrow is laundry day. We'll go on Friday."

CHAPTER SEVEN

FRIDAY CAME SOONER than Nan liked, but Artie remained determined. She would have rather seen to hanging the shutters, but promises are meant to be kept. Shortly after dawn, she left for Kaskaskia with the stranger who had taken up residence in her tavern as she promised she would. He was well enough to go on his own, but he didn't know the way, didn't have coin for the ferry, and didn't have the sense God gave a goose to manage along the territories on his own.

"If I can get to the bank, I can repay your kindnesses," he insisted in that formal way of his when they sat huddled against the cold wind on Watson's ferry. Nan had her doubts about the bank giving money to a stranger in Nate's third best shirt and Baptiste's old jacket, but she didn't say it. She rather hoped he was right. Maybe he had enough for fare to go downriver to New Orleans. The sooner he could get a ship to take him back to Philadelphia, or wherever he came from, the better. *He doesn't belong here.* The fact that she was beginning to enjoy his presence a bit too much added to her determination. She'd learned early there was no point in getting attached to strays.

Artie's anxiety about the counterfeiters drove them to the land office first. As soon as Artie introduced himself as Phillip Tavernash, it became apparent the thieves had succeeded. At least the swindling trash had managed to convince the squirrely clerk with his striped shirt, starched collar, and uppity nose that they were legitimate. He peered at Artie skeptically.

"What proof do you have?" the clerk demanded.

"Proof?" Artie opened and closed his mouth like a Mississippi catfish, as outraged as he was shocked that the man didn't just take his word.

The clerk perused him carefully and sneered "You don't look like a duke."

Duke? Nan had forgotten Luke's words the first day.

Artie glanced at her before he leaned across the counter and hissed, "I am Phillip Tavernash, Duke of Glenmoor!"

The clerk laughed. "And I'm the Prince of Denmark. You sure as hell don't look like one, but then neither did the last one. He at least had the papers."

"What last one?" Artie demanded.

"The one who sauntered in, introduced himself as Phillip Tavernash, Duke of Glenmoor. The one who plunked down the signed application. The one whose signature matches the letter we received from him. The one with the fancy seal on his finger." The clerk glared at Artie who was about to explode like one of her pa's old matchlock guns.

"Thieves and counterfeiters!" he shouted.

"Maybe so, but you have no proof. The bank took the papers they had, they're gone with the deed, and I can't fetch them back. Do you want to put down cash for another?"

Artie heaved a deep sigh and pushed himself back from the counter, lost in thought. The clerk looked past Artie. "Do you want something, Nan Archer, or are you here to keep this one out of trouble?"

"Yes. I want to see the record of my family's land."

"The sale record?"

"Aye. Whose name would be on the deed?"

"It will take me a while to find it. Why don't you look at the deed itself?" the clerk asked.

"It's out at the farm with my brother Jamie. I thought you

might have a record."

"Wait," Artie said, his head bobbing up. "What name will be on the deed the thieves walked out of here with?"

"A grant was made to Phillip Tavernash, Duke of Glenmoor," he said.

"Then it is mine," Artie said.

"It is if you can prove you are Tavernash, locate the other one, and pry the deed out of his hands. Have them arrested in the bargain. Good luck," the clerk said. He peered at Nan. "Come back in an hour."

"Can you give me the exact location of the grant?" Artie asked.

"If you can prove who you are." The clerk's eyes glittered; he obviously enjoyed his tiny crumb of power.

Nan thought for a moment Artie would leap over the counter and throttle the man. She took him by the arm. "We'll be back in an hour."

He insisted they go straight to the bank where, as Nan expected, he had the same problem. He tried to ask for a loan pending funds from his Philadelphia bank, but they weren't having it. At least in that case he managed to be convincing enough for the bank to block the false Phillip Tavernash from loans or setting up an account.

She led him to the more respectable tavern in town. She had her own bone to pick with him.

She sat him down, ordered a pint each, and pinned him with a glare. "You're English."

He blinked back, startled. "Well. Yes."

"I thought you were from back east," she muttered. She realized belatedly why his accent sounded strange. She'd thought him from Boston or Maine.

"Very far east?" He attempted to charm her with a smile.

"It is a good thing I didn't know you were an Englishman when you lay bleeding on my floor. I'd have been tempted to finish you off myself."

He had no answer for that. They eyed each other cautiously. Nan broke contact first. "What's done is done," she murmured.

"Does it help that I had nothing to do with war policy, here or anywhere else?"

She glared at him; resentment hardened her words. She had thought him as helpless as a babe. "Aren't dukes as powerful as princes?"

Artie couldn't meet her eyes. He gazed down at the table. "Not quite, but you aren't far off. I'm afraid I was a bit of a wastrel when I first came into my title. I was just settling into my responsibilities when I found out it wasn't even mine by right."

"Whose is it then?"

Their drinks arrived and Artie concentrated on his for a long time before answering.

"Oh, the title is mine, but it should have been my brother's." He waved a dismissive hand. "I'll explain it sometime. None of it is doing me much good at the moment. Here I'm as helpless as any man and more than most."

She believed what he said, but with no way to prove it, he was just Artie, another stranger washed up with the current, who had only his wits to recommend him. "What will you do next?"

"I have no money. If I work off what I owe you, would you pay me for my labor?" he asked.

"It might take a year for you to earn enough for passage downstream and back to England," she said.

"Why would I do that? I need to stay here and find the miscreants who stole my land, my money, and my identity!"

"How do you propose to do that?" she asked.

"I don't know, but I need the ring."

"What is so special about the ring?"

"It is the duke's signet ring, with the ducal seal. The British envoy in Philadelphia would recognize it if I sent a letter sealed with it. I could send word back east and get both funds and verification. He might even send a witness."

Nan lowered her eyes to avoid his disquieting stare. "It's a good thing Luke hasn't left yet," she declared.

NAN'S WORDS BAFFLED Phillip. Her ruffian of a brother might be a help if they found the thieves and needed to cow them into submission. Other than that…

"Describe the ring," she said.

"It is gold with an amethyst stone. An intaglio with—"

"Amethyst is purple, right? What's 'intaglio?'"

"A carving on the stone. A fox over three trees. Anyone in the upper reaches of English aristocracy would instantly recognize the Glenmoor arms if they saw it."

"We are somewhat lacking in English aristocrats hereabouts," Nan said with an ironic twist of her lips. "But a ring like that would be noticed. Noticed and remembered if your thieves were fool enough to wear it."

"Why Luke?"

"If anyone knows every seedy tavern, questionable landing, or rat's nest town on the rivers, it's Luke. If that ring's been seen, he'll track it down." She polished off her beer and rose. "Now let's go back to the land office."

He had no choice but to follow. They were out the door when she spoke again. "One thing, Artie."

He peered over at her.

"Good for you for staying to fight. You have backbone."

Phillip stood a bit taller under Nan Archer's approval. By the time they got to the office, he was ready to do battle on her behalf. He didn't have to.

"First of all, I found the Archer grant. It is in the name of Amos Archer. Signed with his X witnessed by Jacob Archer—his signature."

Nan glanced over at him. "Satisfied. Pa's name is on it."

And he could sell it out from under you before you know what he's about. That thought sat on the tip of Phillip's tongue, but he didn't say it. "Did you find the location of my grant?"

"The chief said to give it to you. If t'other Phillip Tavernash comes in, I'm to send you word." The clerk appeared shifty-eyed to Phillip, but he got the coordinates for his land.

With the coordinates, Phillip could go have a look as soon as… *What? You have money? Help? You learn how to track?* He could ride. In the English countryside. He could box. According to the Rules of Play learned at Gentleman Jackson's. He could fence. If he had a proper saber. He doubted any of those would do him much good. He missed Nan's next words as they were leaving.

"What did you say?"

"Jamie will know. The land. He can take you there, but perhaps with winter coming on, it will have to wait," she said.

They walked back to the ferry landing in companionable silence.

"Artie?"

His head jerked around to look at her, unexpectedly delighted that she still called him Artie.

"You frowned about Pa's name on the deed. What were you thinking?" Nan said.

He cleared his throat and took a deep breath. "Any chance he might want to sell it?"

"To you?"

"Heavens no! To anyone. Sell it and take the cash," he replied, concern stiffening his stance.

She glanced away, momentarily allowing her vulnerability to surface. "Maybe. I think he'd talk to us first."

Maybe. She's at the mercy of men who could take away everything she values. Phillip wished he could fix that; he hoped she was right for her sake.

CHAPTER EIGHT

ARTIE SWEPT UP after the noon rush, though "rush" might be too strong a word this late in the season. He'd do it again after supper, as had become his habit. Nan respected the effort and the results had improved.

"Are you keeping track of this?" he demanded.

"Am I paying you by the task? Or by the day?" Nan retorted, holding back a grin.

He frowned, the last vestiges of his bruised eye, now livid shades of yellow giving him a piratical appearance. "I'm not giving you a full day."

"I'll credit you a quarter of a day for six days—or one and a half days together—and this week come Saturday at half days for another three altogether. Sunday off."

She could see his mind making calculations. "How many days do I owe you?"

"You were flat in bed for two weeks, and spent the better part of two more on that chair. Twenty-eight, I'd say," she replied, thinking quickly.

"Fair enough."

Nan tipped her head before hitting him with the rest. "Plus, a suit of clothes, the pair of moccasins—we had to buy those, your feet being bigger than Nate's. You also emptied out my herbals and bandage supplies." *And truth be told, we can't afford any of those things. The clothes alone cost me...* "Two months more. Maybe eight-five days in all," she said.

She'd come to stand toe-to-toe where she could gaze directly into his eyes. A treasure, that. She had to peer down at most men. His uninjured eye ticked nervously.

"How much would that be in American dollars?" he demanded, his eyes never leaving hers.

She wondered absently if he realized she couldn't afford to pay him cash money. Not now. Not when and if he worked off his debt. And by January, she might not have enough work to keep him busy. "I pay Baptiste two dollars a week with room and board. Of course, he has skills." She peered directly at him, daring him to respond.

"Pay me one. Write it down. We have to keep track," he said without hesitation.

Their eyes held. They stood so close she could feel his breath. Artie broke contact first, glancing away. "Shall I fetch a bucket from the well?" He grabbed the bucket and headed for the door without waiting, nervous as a tick. Did her closeness make him as agitated as his did her?

Studying his retreating figure, she noticed the way his brown hair came down in waves well past his collar. He'd probably be wanting a haircut soon; she rather liked it as it was. A woman might take pleasure in running her fingers through hair like that. *If he wants it cut, I'll add it to his time owed,* she thought with a grin.

RETURNING TO THE public room, Phillip felt a jolt of irrational jealousy to see Nan hugging a handsome young man.

The newcomer kept an arm thrown carelessly over her shoulder when they turned and saw him.

"Artie! Come and meet my brother Jamie," she said.

Phillip let out the breath he'd held. When the man put out his hand to shake, Phillip took it. "James Phineas Archer at your service."

"Phillip Tavernash. Call me Artie."

Jamie Archer frowned at his sister. "Artie?"

"It's complicated. We'll explain later," she said.

"I hope you're at least earning your keep." The familiar harsh voice came from the door. Phillip had missed Luke standing there.

"Doing my best to make myself useful," Phillip replied.

When Luke snorted, Jamie Archer, still with one arm draped over Nan, frowned. "I hear you had a bad turn of luck."

"Yes! And no. Washing up here was a stroke of good. Your sister saved my life," Phillip said.

"Nan?" Luke growled. "What of me? I dragged you off that sandbank."

"True. And I'm grateful."

Nan sprang into action then, sending bags upstairs and ordering coffee. Soon enough, she had her family around a table and had roped Phillip into joining them.

"Luke asked if you made it to the bank. Do you want to tell them, or should I?" Nan asked.

He did, sparing himself no loss of dignity.

When Phillip described the land office clerk, Jamie chuckled. "That would be Peter Littlefield. Petty little man, petty little power."

"At least the bank put a hold on the accounts by others using my name, but they wouldn't forward me a penny," Phillip said.

Luke glared down the table. "This ring. You think it proves who you are?"

"I know it does, at least it would… Back east." He glanced at Nan uneasily. "I could write for funds and assistance."

"Who are you, exactly?" Jamie asked, a shrewd glint in his expression. "Men come here for two reasons. To work hard and make their fortune or to steal from those who do. You already ran into the second kind, but which one are you?"

Phillip glanced at Nan. She wouldn't meet his eyes. "I came to make my fortune. I had some foolish notions about how I might do that, but I'm not afraid of hard work."

Nan and Luke glanced at each other and at Jamie. "Tell him who you are, Artie," Nan said.

Artie. He took heart from her use of the name, but that wasn't what she meant for him to say. He sighed and studied his hands, folded—white-knuckled—on the table. "I am Phillip Tavernash. Duke of Glenmoor."

He glanced back up to see Luke grinning at him. "Don't be bashful. Tell him all of it."

Phillip raised his eyes to the ceiling. "I am properly His Grace, Phillip Roland George Arthur Tavernash, Sixth Duke of Glenmoor, Earl of Wentworth, Viscount Gradington, Baron Walsh." He glared at Luke. "Happy?"

"Dear God. No wonder no one believes you," Jamie said. "Duke. Like they have in—you're English?"

Phillip nodded. "Do you? Believe me?" He directed the question at Jamie, ignoring the intimidating frown that bloomed on the man's face at the realization Phillip was English, but in his heart, Nan's opinion mattered most.

"I do. You're sure not from around here." Nate piped up without hesitation.

Luke shook his head. "Don't tell Pa you're harboring an Englishman, Nan. He'll strip off his hide and nail it to a barn."

Jamie simply stared, studying him. For a moment, Phillip felt like Gulliver in Brobdingnab again, a curiosity to be gaped at by all and sundry, foreign and exotic.

"I'll take you at your word," Jamie said at last. "What do you plan to do? Get enough cash to go back where you came from?" Phillip feared there was a hopeful note in the question.

"Not until I run the scoundrel who stole from me and left me for dead to ground. Maybe when I see he gets what he deserves, I'll have my good name back." He glanced at the faces around the table. "And then I'm going to see what opportunities this land provides me. I'm not going home until I have something to show for myself. Something I created on my own. For that, I'll need funds to invest."

Nan gave a little nod. He felt shamelessly encouraged by that. "Describe the ring for Luke," she said.

Phillip described it as he had to her.

"Gold?" Jamie asked.

"Amethyst. Purple," Luke mused. "What size?"

Phillip made a shape with his hands. Luke whistled.

"It must be worth a fortune," Nate said.

"If he could sell it. Is there a place in Saint Louis, do you think that might buy it?" Jamie asked Nan.

She shrugged and gazed at Luke. "If he's flashing it along the river, it wouldn't be hard to track down."

Luke shook his head. "From what Artie has told us, this particular snake wouldn't be stupid enough to do that. It's what almost got Artie killed. On the other hand, he might not be able to resist the temptation to show someone. If one person knows, rumors begin. Can you draw it?"

Nan fetched a paper and Phillip sketched the ring from two angles. Then he drew the intaglio carving and handed it to Luke who studied it carefully.

"Fox and trees?" Luke asked.

"Yes. The Glenmoor arms," Artie said.

"I can give it a week. Then I need to be on my way up to Pa's cabin," Luke said.

"Two," Nan objected. "You can leave for the Missouri the day after Christmas."

Luke ignored her. "If I find the ring, I'll bring it to you."

"If he's wearing it, bring his whole hand," Phillip growled. His fingers were still healing.

Luke nodded his approval, but Nan clucked at him with a frown. "Turn him in if he has the ring," she said.

"I'll drag him here so Artie can pound him. Then we'll turn him in," Luke said. "You coming, Jamie?"

"It might be interesting. On the other hand, you'll move faster, and folks're more likely to talk to you without me," Jamie replied. "You check the river rats. Maybe I will head north to Saint Louis and look around."

"I'll come!" Nate's eager reply made both brothers laugh.

"You'd slow me down more'n Jamie," Luke said.

"You aren't going anywhere, Nate Archer. You have studies to do," Nan said.

The boy's disappointment amused Phillip, but he'd just been given an idea, too, one he'd explore with Nan when they had a private moment.

CHAPTER NINE

Nan laid a plate of toasted bread on the battered kitchen table and poured more coffee for Jamie and Artie. Neither paid her a mind, deep as they were in conversation about Artie's land claim. Littlefield at the claim office had described it as fronting the south bank of the Illinois River, and had given him coordinates.

Jamie stabbed the map spread on the table with one finger. "North for sure. I can't place the coordinates precisely, but it would be in this general area. Still pretty wild. Folks are just settling up there. No telling how much is woodland or the quality of the soil." He glanced up. "One other thing."

Artie raised his brows and waited.

"You'll encounter other people, natives. Winnebago for sure, though they're a peaceable lot. Fox and Sac people, too. Some are drifting north, but there are still plenty in the territory. Treat 'em with respect, and you can get on with them."

Artie hadn't considered that, Nan could tell, but she didn't see any sign it worried him. Perhaps he didn't know enough to have fear. Then again, if he didn't plan to work the land, maybe he wouldn't. She went back to cleaning up. Luke had left before breakfast, but the rest of them had feasted on some of the eggs Jamie brought with him.

"Can you take me there?" she heard Artie ask.

Jamie studied him long and hard. "Perhaps if it's mild in January. You may want to wait till spring."

"Would it be difficult to find the outline of the grant? Would we need surveyor tools?"

"That we might. There may be stakes from the original survey. Perhaps." Jamie didn't seem confident.

Jamie rocked his chair back on two legs. "I hear you owe my sister quite a sum. You'll need to work that off first." He shot Artie what she thought of as the Archer grin—wry and full of mischief.

"All too true." Artie looked over his shoulder to where Nan stood at the sink washing the breakfast dishes and eavesdropping. "Which reminds me. What would you pay a school teacher? Or a private tutor for Nate?" he asked.

Her hands stilled. *Damn, why didn't I think of that?*

"They hired a teacher to open a school over in Round Nob. They're paying him $700 for eight months of the year. School closes for planting and harvest," Jamie said.

The sum astonished Nan. "Seven hundred dollars? That would pay off the mortgage. I wouldn't spend it on a teacher!"

"You're willing to pay me a dollar a week to sweep floors and tend the bar. What if I tutored Nate half the time, say five afternoons a week? Would you pay me two-fifty?" Artie asked.

I'd be a fool not to take that. At least until he worked off his debt. The debt would be the other direction after that, because she couldn't afford to pay him. She wiped her hands with a towel. "We can try it. I'll give you two weeks to see if you can help Nate—"

"Help me what?" Nate stood in the door swathed in a red scarf, his cheeks rosy from the cold.

"Read Latin," Artie said. Nan rolled her eyes.

"Are you magic or something?" the boy asked, closing the door behind him.

"Do you want to learn about Caesar? It's best in his own words," Artie said.

Teasing. He must be teasing, Nan thought. Nate looked intrigued.

"Did Luke get off okay?" Jamie asked.

"Yep. We hauled the canoe down to the landing and loaded his supplies," Nate said. "Are there any more of those eggs?" He pulled up a chair. Nan brought the leftover scramble she had warming on the hob.

"When are you leaving for Saint Louis?" Nate asked between mouthfuls.

Jamie gazed at Artie. "Maybe in a few days. Nan needs help with the storm shutters and that's a two-man job. We also need to store up wood for winter; that pile looks pretty skimpy out there. I thought I'd take a wagon to the interior and cut some trees."

Nan poured herself coffee and sat. "It'll be farther to find public land this year. You might best ride south a bit toward the hill country if you plan to do that. A wagon won't work there. Take the horses and the sledge. Borrow the Howards' mule to carry supplies."

Jamie lifted his cup to her. "Practical as always. Are you up for it, Artie?"

Artie assured her brother he was, but Nan had doubts. "Help with the shutters first," she suggested. If that didn't set him back, she'd have a look at his hands to see if they'd toughed up. If not, Nate could go.

PHILLIP STACKED THE rest of their wood after Baptiste split it. Phillip had helped some, and his hands were getting tougher, but he could feel a blister rising. Nan had been right to send Nate with her older brother.

Perhaps next year…

The thought took him off guard. *When did I start thinking I might still be here next year? I won't go home until I make something of myself. It will take longer than that. Probably years.* He turned that around in his mind. It felt oddly right. He smiled.

"You find firewood amusing, Philipe?" Baptiste, leaning the ax on a stump, asked.

"I find my life amusing, mon ami—far better than thinking it a tragedy, don't you agree?" Phillip answered. It certainly took some interesting turns. *Would Gideon laugh?* Phillip hoped he'd approve.

He carried an armload of wood to the hearth in the public room and found it busy. Sal looked run off her feet. He scooted behind the bar and began filling pints of beer. That was one skill he'd learned and took pride in.

I'll be here next year, he thought again. *But not as a barkeep.* At least he would if he could prove his identity, contact those who could help, and use his riches for a stake in an enterprise of some sort. But what?

Nan's harsh criticism had taken land speculation off the table. After he secured his claim, he'd leave the land be. Maybe for a generation or so. One thing an Englishman knew was that land is finite. They don't make more of it. The other thing an aristocrat understood is that generations matter. His grandchildren might need that land.

He gazed over at Nan, charming a river boat captain. *Grandchildren! You are getting sentimental, Glenmoor.* He shook his head at reverting to Glenmoor even in his thoughts. Still, something about this woman drew him.

The rush over, he wandered into the kitchen. The Archers' meager supply of books had been stacked on the table so that he could plan some lessons. A much-creased paper with the words *Union Battledore* down the side, a pamphlet-sized work with alphabet and illustrations for phonetics, lay on top of a simple wooden hornbook covered with the alphabet, the vowels and some pairs of letters for sounding. *The Lord's Prayer* covered half of the hornbook, intended for reading practice, no doubt.

Those two and the third item, a book entitled *The New England Primer,* had no doubt been used to teach the older Archers to read. The book was also heavy on religion. It illustrated the letters from A, "In Adam's fall we sinned all," to Z, "Zaccheus he did climb a tree Our Lord to see." He shook his head. If he was going to interest a boy in reading, he'd need something less childish and filled with less sin and damnation. Leafing through the book, Phillip was struck by the fact that no Archer family Bible had been forthcoming. Nan did promise he could read to the boy from Gulliver. Eventually.

"You told me this village has a lending library," Phillip said when Nan carried in a tray of dirty dishes.

"Aye. On past the tailor, in the rear of the general sundries store," she replied. "Why?"

"I want to look for something I can use to entice your brother to read."

"Maybe you can do better than I do. All we do is argue. It was the same with Luke and Mam. It's why he still can't read."

Phillip picked up the primer. "If this is what she used, I can see why. 'While youth do cheer, death be near?'"

"The letter Y." Nan smiled. "See. I remember it still."

He rolled his eyes. "Is that library open this afternoon?"

"Should be. It's open whenever the store is."

Phillip had walked to Cape Girardeau's market street with Baptiste once, but wasn't paying attention. Today, he walked the length and counted twenty-two stores, just a bit more than a typical English village, but their appearance differed sharply. Most of them looked similar to Archers' Roost—log buildings, built the French way with upright logs filled with mud in between. It gave them a vertical striped appearance. Baptiste called it poteaux-en-terre, posts in the earth or poteaux-on-sole if the building had a stone foundation.

For now, he found the general store easily enough and was waved to the back. It was not what he envisioned when he heard the word "library." Floor-to-ceiling shelves lined a twelve-by-twelve-foot alcove built out the back of the store. Someone had sorted the collection, a motley assemblage of books clearly gleaned from works hoarded by local families by subject. He thought of Woodglen's magnificent two-story library with its dark wood paneling and thousands of carefully curated volumes and shook his head.

You aren't at Woodglen any longer... Scanning the shelves, he spotted a copy of Shakespeare's *Julius Caesar*, delighted to discover it had illustrations. Further on, he found two volumes of Edgeworth's *Popular Tales*. They would have to do. Maybe when he returned home, he'd send books to Cape Girardeau. Maybe he'd fund a real library.

Returning the way he came, he decided that at least a third of the businesses had some relationship to outfitting, repairing, or stocking boats. He ought to have anticipated that. Even Archers' Roost depended on river traffic for most of its trade. Commerce, if it was to be had, was river commerce. Saint Louis would have more. He made up his mind that if Jamie Archer went there, he would go along. He had much to learn if he was to found an enterprise.

He got back to find Nate and Jamie pulling in. One horse pulled a flat sledge piled chest high with what looked like tree trunks. The borrowed mule pulled what Baptiste called a travois, a device they'd rigged in the woods and strapped to both sides of the mule. It dragged a mass of wood with narrower diameter.

"Welcome back. That is quite a load in three days!" Indeed. There would be a great amount of chopping and splitting in coming weeks. *You'll have tough hands for certain, Tavernash.* "Let me take these books in and come out to help."

Jamie unhitched the travois from the mule. "Bring Baptiste, too. We'll stow this out of the way."

It was over an hour before the four of them, working together, cared for the horses and piled the logs out of the way, yet near enough to easily work. Nan came out to hug her brothers and express her gratitude. "I'm afraid it's rabbit stew for supper."

Nate groaned. "Jamie roasted rabbit the past two days."

"Will apple pie for dessert help?"

Nate's eyes lit up. Watching the sibling byplay filled Phillip with longing to be part of something like that. He'd had a bit with Gideon before their vile father sent him away. He'd come to a place where a man could make his own way, determined upon business success like his brother. He wasn't sure how to create family bonds, but he was determined to do that someday as well, as Gideon had done. His brother had built a home for his wife, alas now deceased, and children. Memory of the warmth and affection he found there haunted him.

"If you want some, all of you will have to go wash up before you come in my kitchen." She pointed to the water trough next to the door. The brothers went to it and, with much splashing and laughter, did as they were told.

Phillip stood on the outside and waited. He thought of the massive opulence of Woodglen and the women in London eager to be his duchess and shuddered. He wanted what his brother had. What the Archers had. *Can the Duke of Glenmoor manage it?*

"You coming, Artie?" Jamie called from the door.

Phillip rinsed his hands. "Be right there. I want to talk to you about Saint Louis."

⁕

CHAPTER TEN

"YOU'RE DAFT. THE man is still recovering and Saint Louis is at least three days away by horse." Nan frowned at her brother rocking back on his chair in the empty public room. Artie and Nate had taken over cleaning up after supper to Jamie's horror.

"Why would we go overland? The river is faster even paddling north against the stream, and we'll come back with the current," Jamie said, his calm assurance infuriating her.

"Artie will be no help paddling. Especially against the stream!"

"He'll learn." Jamie shrugged.

"Where will you get a canoe?"

"Baptiste has a friend."

"Baptiste always has a friend. It will probably leak."

That set Jamie off laughing. "I see your point, but I think I'm capable of checking the thing out. I already did."

"Why did you volunteer to look for the twice damned ring anyway?" Nan demanded.

"It is obviously valuable and important to your newest stray. Besides, I'm curious."

Curious. That's how the farm acquired a dairy herd. Jamie wanted to learn cheesemaking. As if he didn't have enough to do. "Mam always said it killed the cat, and it would get you too if you didn't watch out. What's so interesting about a ring, valuable though it is?"

"Not the ring. I'm curious about Artie. He isn't the puny thing I thought he was, even if he does volunteer for women's work. He wants to go."

"He owes me work," Nan insisted.

"So, extend his time," Jamie said. "Think what might happen if he gets a bank in Kaskaskia or Saint Louis to accept him. You could charge him—"

Nan raised a hand to stop the flow of words. "I'm charging him what he cost us. No more, no less."

"Then stop worrying about your latest pet. He says he's up for it. He's a grown man. We're going to Saint Louis."

"Pet?" Nan jumped at the sound of Artie's voice.

"Ignore Jamie. He likes to tease me."

Their new friend ignored her. He gazed at Jamie. "Thank you for defending my manhood."

"We have to stick together where Nan is concerned," Jamie replied with a grin.

"When do we leave?"

"First light," Jamie replied.

"You're both daft," Nan said, examining Artie closely. "At least the bruises on your face are fading, and you don't look like you've been in a tavern brawl."

"Darn. I had such high hopes," Artie said, winking at her brother.

He's gotten full of himself lately; my brothers' influence, no doubt. Nan stomped out into the kitchen to find the dishes neatly put away and Nate staring at the illustrations in *Julius Caesar*.

"Romans wore skirts," he said. "Only they called them togas and tunics."

"That doesn't sound useful," Nan said irritably, peering into the stew pot. The leftovers needed to be removed so she could do a fresh pot for customers the next day. She'd store today's leavings in the cold room. Family could finish them up tomorrow—at least those who weren't off on pointless jaunts.

"Look at the swords they carried, Nan. Not much longer than a hunting knife, but Artie says they were effective."

"Is that what he's teaching you? How is the reading coming?"

"Better. Artie has much better words for remembering the letter sounds." He waved a paper with small drawings on it. "But I still don't understand how C can be for both cat and Caesar. Reading is hard."

"He's leaving in the morning with Jamie," she said.

"He'll be back. I'll practice while he's gone."

"He's supposed to be teaching you," she said. The sound of petulance in her voice embarrassed her. Why should she care? All men were unreliable. Hadn't life taught her that?

"What's your problem, Nan? He'll be back soon enough, pounding learning in my head."

"I have no problem," she snapped. "Phillip Tavernash can do as he pleases once he works off his debt. You get yourself to bed now. We'll be shorthanded tomorrow."

Nate shut the book reluctantly and shuffled to the door.

Artie—Tavernash—stood there watching. How long had he been there?

"I'll be back, Nan. I'll work off what I owe you. You have my word of honor."

Honor. What does he mean by that? Nothing that concerns me.

She went past him and on up to bed.

✦✦✦

AFTER TWO HOURS of fruitless effort, Phillip threw off the covers. He'd be a sleepy mess when he met Jamie at dawn, but he could do nothing about it. Sleep would not come.

The shaft of moonlight shooting through the tiny window at the top of the eaves above him didn't help. If moonlight meant to keep him up, he may as well go out to meet it. He passed by the candle, unlit in its holder. He had gotten used to the smell of burning tallow, but hadn't learned to like it. He felt his way down the stairs into the public room and out the door.

Archers' Roost stood on a gentle rise with a sloping lawn, facing the river. The boat landing lay less than a quarter mile away. The stone-paved path to Cape Girardeau proper branched to the tavern at the landing, bringing business. The front of the tavern, however, was grassy and pleasant. A bench placed in an opening in the trees gave a view of the river making its unrelenting journey south. Mornings they had a view of sunrise unlike any he'd ever experienced—not that he rose at dawn during his days as a man-about-town in London or Paris.

Tonight, however, the land across the river was shrouded in darkness. Moonlight glowed on the water, bright down the central channel, soft through the wisps of mist along the shores, but he couldn't make out the moon itself through the big elm to his right. Moonglow drew him closer to the water where he stood behind the bench and turned his head south in search of it.

Lopsided, and just less than full, the moon shone over the big bend in the river.

"Beautiful, isn't it?" Nan's voice, soft and deep, washed through him, stirring up a physical reaction, as tender as it was powerful, to savor. It wasn't the first time her voice had impacted him thus. He closed his eyes and breathed deeply. He suspected she stood in the tree-shadowed spot behind and to his left. He didn't turn; he waited for her to speak again.

"The moon," she said, nearing him. "Beautiful."

"Yes," he murmured, heart pounding.

"You couldn't sleep either," she said, next to him now.

He opened his eyes to find hers, level with his in the dark, lit by the moon that caressed her honey-colored hair. So close that he could kiss her. He realized with an electric jolt that he wanted to, fiercely. What she wanted he couldn't say.

To kiss her would be a breach of trust. It might destroy his growing friendship with the Archers. With Nan. For one insane moment, he didn't care. The feeling shamed him; Nan Archer deserved his protection.

She moved away and the moment passed. "You ought to be sleeping. You're leaving at first light, Jamie told me."

"Yes." He wrenched his eyes from Nan and stared at the moon.

Neither spoke for a long time.

"Some folks think a waxing moon can bewitch you," she murmured.

Her voice, not the moon, held Phillip in thrall. "No, I don't think so. In a telescope, it appears to be rock. There's nothing fey about it."

"A telescope," she sighed. "I saw one once or twice. Ship's captains carry them."

Telescope. The word broke Phillip's spell, outlining the differences in their world as it did. *Probably not like the large ones at Oxford.* He wished he could show her, to open a wider world to this bright, inquisitive woman.

He opened his mouth to describe the observatory and closed it again. It would sound like bragging and denigrate her pleasure in boat captains' scopes. Besides, nothing was as glorious as what could be seen with the naked eye on a night like this.

He turned to see her examining him carefully. "Still worried I'll collapse on the way to Saint Louis? I may be a greenhorn, but I'm stronger than I look." *Stronger than I knew before I came here.*

"If you do, it's your own fault. You still owe me for your care." The tart landlady had returned, the mood gone.

"I haven't forgotten. You will get your pound of flesh."

"Flesh? What on earth do you mean by that?" she demanded.

"The expression is from Shakespeare. It means everything I owe and then some with no mercy."

"But I—"

"That sounded worse than I meant it to. It is merely an expression about debt owed. I pay my debts. Are you afraid I was going to run out on you?"

"No, I…"

"You were, weren't you?"

"I've had good reason to know the word of a man cannot always be trusted," she said. She clamped her jaw so tight the muscles quivered.

Who had hurt her? Her father? Some unknown man? Phillip leaned toward her, suddenly protective. "I am not that sort of man. I keep my word."

Temptation warred with honor. Honor won. He took a few steps toward the tavern.

She scurried after him. "I'll take your word, Artie. Don't let Jamie get you distracted by Saint Louis. The city has… That is, it isn't always a decent place."

He bit back a chuckle. It had what cities had. What would she make of London, the ruin of many young men? Gambling, gin, and degenerate pursuits. "Is it Jamie who worries you or me?" he asked.

She raised her chin and clutched the side of her skirts. "Both of you," she said, parading past him.

He let himself enjoy the sway of her hips as he watched her walk away. She worried about him? He rather liked that.

"Nan Archer," he called, bringing her to a halt.

She paused but didn't turn.

"*The Merchant of Venice,*" he said.

She peered over her shoulder, delightfully befuddled.

"'Pound of flesh' comes from that play. Try the library. It may be there," he said.

She continued on her way without answering.

He turned back, whistled by the river bank for a few moments, and let the night air cool him so he could go in to sleep.

CHAPTER ELEVEN

PHILLIP ROWED IN an eight-man crew at Oxford. He assumed paddling a canoe could not be any harder. He was wrong. For one thing, the Mississippi current was significantly stronger than the placid Thames at Christchurch Meadows. For another, paddling one side of the boat required coordination with a partner paddling on the other to keep the vessel straight.

"The last thing we want is the flow of the river to hit us broadside," Jamie explained. "Your job is to keep us pointed directly into the current."

After a fraught hour of trial and error, including one close call when the river threatened to topple them sideways, Phillip managed the thing reasonably well. They kept to one side or the other, seeking the slower current.

They stopped to camp near Sainte Genevieve the first night. Shoulder and arm muscles complained forcefully that they had been long disused. Phillip collapsed onto the ground when he got out of the canoe, but quickly noted Jamie had not. He rose to help gather the leaves and pine boughs that Jamie assured him would be more comfortable than sleeping on the hard ground. Nan's brother was right about that, as he had been about many things.

Jamie grumbled that a clear night would be colder before he rolled over and went to sleep. Was it? Phillip had no idea, but he had to trust his new friend's knowledge. As it was, Phillip watched the moon until it set, thinking of Nan in spite of his efforts to remind himself of his honor and the debt he owed the Archers. He would return home in due time, and they were from different worlds. Nothing honorable could happen between them.

When the moon set, he blinked his eyes shut, knowing he should sleep, but he opened them again. A glorious canopy of stars from one edge of the sky to the other left him in awe.

The sky must certainly have been visible at Woodglen, his country estate, all his life, but he'd never experienced it. Not like this. He'd wasted too much of his life in the smoke-filled world of London or Paris salons and ballrooms, never feeling as fully alive as he did lying on the ground wrapped in a blanket. He stared at the sky lost in wonder until he nodded off to the sound of the river passing.

Phillip groaned the next morning when he reached down to pick up his blanket.

"Shoulders paining you?" Jamie asked.

Phillip nodded. "Haven't rowed in several years." He moved his stiff shoulders in a circular motion to loosen them up. "Hurts like the devil. Sleeping on cold ground didn't help."

Jamie grunted. "It'll loosen up after a bit on the river." He passed Phillip an oatcake. "No coffee. Sorry. With luck and hard rowing, we'll reach Saint Louis tonight. Think about a warm bed and hot meal while we travel."

Traffic and commerce motivated Phillip more. The day before, he had counted four flatboats and three keelboats going south. They had passed another keelboat poling its way north. This morning, a raft floating south with the current caught his eye as they pushed off.

"Latecomer," Jamie muttered as he maneuvered their canoe out of a back channel along one of the river's many islands.

"What do you mean, 'latecomer'?"

"Rafters are usually farmers. The peak time for them is early

October, just after harvest. They build a raft to haul their goods to New Orleans, floating with the current, sell the lumber along with the goods, and walk back north."

"What are the flatboats carrying?" Phillip asked. He had to shout over his shoulder.

"The same, and also commercial cargo. Farmers and small holders band together to buy one and then they dismantle them and sell the lumber in New Orleans just like the rafters do.

It occurred to Phillip there might be money in the manufacture of flatboats, and yet… "What about keelboats? They're bigger and go both ways."

"That they do. They haul both passengers and cargo," Jamie said. "If you had money, you could pay for a ride back to Archers' Roost."

"Commercial cargo?" Phillip asked.

"The serious commerce on the river goes by keelboat. Still mostly furs. The big dealers have trading posts out in the territory and warehouses in Saint Louis. Lumber. Some agricultural goods. Some farmers prefer to pay a fee to ride their goods down and come back up. Or they take a lower price from middlemen in Saint Louis rather than raft their own goods down. And salt, of course. It's outpacing furs."

"Salt?"

"Missouri country has salt springs. Lucrative business, that," Jamie said.

"I remember Nan saying something about the Boone brothers and salt," Phillip said.

"Boone's Lick. Old Daniel's sons. They got in early and staked out a claim. I think our pa resents them." Jamie called to Phillip to raise his paddle while he neatly navigated them around a sweep of low-hanging tree branches that threatened to entangle them.

"Your father wants to build a salt works?" Phillip asked. He filed the idea away in his mind. Perhaps salt was a commodity he could make into business.

"I doubt he has the patience to extract and ship. Or anything. He just hopes the earth's blessings will fall into his lap," Jamie muttered.

"If you were looking for a commodity to make money, what would it be?" Phillip asked.

"Cheese. I sell it in Kaskaskia, Round Nob, and Cape Girardeau," Jamie said with a grin.

"I meant selling. Dealing. Shipping. Furs or salt?"

"Furs are on their way out," Jamie said.

Phillip continued to mull over what he saw and heard. *Not furs then. Timber or salt…*

When they passed Sainte Genevieve, all he had seen was a line of log buildings strung along the shore. At Kaskaskia, he'd seen even less from the river, however, the bulk of it being behind a rise. Perhaps Sainte Genevieve had more than met his eyes, but he doubted it.

They hadn't gone far when they turned into a bend and a horrific noise ruined the peace of the morning. Further around the bend, an impressive sight met Phillip's eyes. A boat the size of a large keelboat approached, pushed by a turning wheel, with a stack in its center belching clouds of smoke.

A steamboat! He heard they were being tried but had never seen one until he came here. It was only the second time he'd caught sight of one since he arrived. The first had been up the Ohio near Cincinnati. He wondered how long this one took to travel the length of the river.

As they moved close to shore to let the great billowing boat pass them, Jamie cursed and complained. "Damned filthy beast. It's enough to make a man deaf. I don't see how they avoid burning down the towns they dock in—or blowing up."

"I expect sometimes they do," Phillip replied. "They're the way of the future, though." He craned his head around to watch the boat go by. "How long do you think it takes them?"

"To New Orleans? Less than a week, I think. They dock down there awhile then take maybe ten days or a few more upriver to disturb the peace of honest citizens."

They continued on in silence. Phillip vowed to pay more attention to the river traffic that stopped at Cape Girardeau.

Shadows covered the river when they came alongside the landing in Saint Louis, cast by the multi-story brick buildings fronting the river. The facilities and vessels had little to commend themselves when compared to the Port of London or even Philadelphia. Yet, the place had a palpable sense of energy, life springing from the earth, even at twilight. A cacophony of accents met his ears, and French outpaced English in much of it.

Jamie led him to a plain but respectable inn. He was too hungry and tired to talk or even think straight, but another day lay ahead of him, one that promised information and adventure.

NAN, IRRITABLE AFTER a sleepless night and fretful about the Saint Louis-bound men, went about her tasks with grim determination. With only two guest rooms in use, she attacked the other four with a vengeance. She went after Artie's room as well. Coverlets frequently reused without washing went into the laundry along with the linens. Curtains came down too while Nate was assigned to wash windows. She hauled worn rugs and set Baptiste to beating them. Once floors were scrubbed, she set to waxing them.

By noon, Nate, Baptiste, and Sal looked for ways to avoid her, grateful when customers filtered in for lunch. Sal being occupied with cooking, Nan sent Nate to hang their laundry on lines strung between trees, ordering him to make more lines if needed.

The public room traffic slowed by late afternoon; everything that could be laundered had been washed and hung, and Sal had dinner underway. Nan sat in the rocker by the hearth with a restorative cup of tea, but her peace was short-lived. Memories of moonlight and Artie, no longer held off by work, flooded in.

He meant to kiss me. If we'd stood there much longer, he would have. Nan wasn't a complete innocent. She hadn't gotten to four and twenty years without experiencing the advances of a man. Several men, if she were honest, willing to overlook her great height and forceful manner, there being a dearth of single women on the frontier.

When she was younger and much more foolish, she'd allowed a few more liberties than she ought. One promised marriage and she almost succumbed until she caught him half-dressed with Sadie Parker. She held on to her virginity by luck, but she knew what pleasure and desire felt like. She also knew not to trust men who professed more.

Artie meant to kiss me. I could have allowed it. Why didn't I? She knew the answer. Men were unreliable as general rule, and river travelers more so. Only catastrophe had held Artie in place so far. Sooner or later, some shiny thing, some chance at riches, some new fascination would call to him. Sooner or later, he would go home and do whatever it was dukes did. She would be only a misty memory of his great adventure, when he shed his fancy life to rough it. Briefly.

The teacup shook under the force with which she set it on the table. "Nathan Archer, are you about your lessons? It is time." With luck, literacy for Nate would be one gift Artie could leave behind.

She drilled his letters using the pictures and words Artie created to teach sound. A is for arrow. B is for bear. C is for Caesar. And Cat. That one made her smile. When they got to Z, there was no picture.

"Zebulon Pike," Nate said without prodding.

"The man or the steamship?" she asked.

"I didn't think of the steamship. Same sound though," Nate replied.

"Does Artie know about Pike or did you tell him?" The great explorer was a popular figure in Missouri, as much as Meriweather Lewis and William Clark, who was now the territorial governor. They all had passed through the Archers' way, but the latter two settled in Saint Louis while Pike died a hero in Mr. Madison's war.

"He knew all about him. He has his own copy of Pike's book about his expeditions. Or had. The thieves stole that and his copy of Pike's map of the Mississippi along with everything else. Pity. That's a book I'd like to read," Nate sighed.

"You have to work at the reading first," she said. She thumbed through the primer and found a story that wasn't terribly childish for him to work on, sounding words one by one. He surprised her. Artie had already helped the boy make great progress.

She kept him at it as long as she could. By that time, there were dinner guests, evening chores, and their own supper to see to. Nate happily agreed to an early night when she offered to read to him. He wanted *Julius Caesar*, but she insisted on reading *The Merchant of Venice* first. He nodded off, and she blew out the candle. She sought her own bed with the book and memories of moonlight for company.

CHAPTER TWELVE

"WELL, THIS WAS a waste. At least I can tell Luke I did my part." Jamie sighed into his beer. They sat in a public house around the corner from what turned out to be the only jewelry store in the city, and not much of one, being part of a dealer in leather goods. Taverns were much more abundant, that much was certain.

"We got his attention. Did you see his eyes when I described the ring? He'll be alert to any sign of it," Phillip said with a shrug. "Of course, that doesn't mean he'll send me word if he does."

"We can leave for Archers' Roost in the morning," Jamie muttered.

Phillip groaned. "Give my shoulders a day to recuperate. Besides, there are some other things I'd like to do here."

Jamie grinned wickedly. "I wouldn't mind exploring the entertainments the city has to offer."

"Gambling or women?" Phillip asked with a raised brow.

"I know better than to gamble. Besides, I have too little cash to start with."

"You should know better than to visit brothels, too."

Jamie forced his eyes wide in faux innocence. "I don't know what you mean."

Phillip chuckled and sipped his beer.

"And how would you know? Do dukes chase light-skirts?"

"I was as foolish as any young man, and there are plenty of high-class establishments in London and Paris. I found it distasteful soon enough."

"High-class?" Jamie, obviously intrigued, asked.

Phillip shrugged. "Safer. Cleaner. Less likely to give you an unpleasant disease. Still, the women deserve better than to be used like that. After a while, I couldn't stomach it."

Keeping a mistress had been mildly better, but he'd ended up pitying the girl and sent her back to her home village with money to open a small shop. He'd moved on to willing widows, but even when he didn't find some of the demands distasteful, the sense of being used himself didn't sit well either. His peers would laugh; he'd been celibate for four years.

"Spoilsport. Can't gamble either. That leaves drink." Jamie gestured to the keeper for another pint. "What do you plan to do?"

"I thought I'd visit the post office on the chance there is mail, though the letter I sent from Philadelphia probably hasn't reached my brother. Then the bank."

"All business. You're a dull stick, Artie Tavernash, Duke of Somewhere."

Jamie's teasing slipped off without hitting its mark. Phillip stopped thinking of himself as dull the moment he embarked on this journey. That it didn't go as planned didn't change that. He would yet succeed. His determination increased daily.

"You should talk! What do you plan to do besides drink?"

Jamie rolled his eyes. "I promised Nan I'd visit the bookstore and see what they have on the used shelves."

Phillip wished he'd thought of that, but with empty pockets, such a visit would be pointless. "What does she want?"

"My sister will read almost anything. She wants something about Caesar for Nate, and whatever I can find for her."

"I'll leave you to it. I'll see you tonight." Phillip rose, realizing with a pang that Jamie would pay for his drink. More debt to the Archers.

"Maybe," Jamie said with a wink.

The post office visit proved as fruitless as Phillip expected. He'd gone there more in hope than faith. He had mentioned Saint Louis in his letter to Gideon, but it was far too early for anyone who knew his destination to write to him; it would take at least three months for a message from England. Probably longer. Mail, he was told, came in and went out weekly. He longed to write to Gideon about his situation, but he had no money. The cost of posting a letter to Philadelphia, much less Dorset, was high. Even if it had been a penny, he couldn't afford it.

Convinced queries at a bank would be equally foolish, he circled back to the tavern where he left Jamie, and found him there staring morosely into an empty glass. He perked up at the sight of Phillip.

"Back so soon?"

"Wild goose chase. Buy me another and add it to Nan's tab," Phillip said.

Jamie obliged. When the waiter came to the table, Phillip asked if there was a bank in "this fine city."

"Was two. Rumor is the Bank of Saint Louis is going under. I wouldn't put my money there," he said, wiping his hands on a towel fastened to his waist. It turned out their "waiter" was the proprietor. It took little to persuade him to sit down and chat.

"The other bank?" Phillip asked.

"New one. Bank of Missouri. Banking is a growing thing. They say there are two new banks at Kaskaskia, and even some coming to towns further south."

"How big is this city anyway?" Jamie asked. "When we came to this country, it was a fur trading post."

The man chuckled. "Still is, only we aren't talking small potatoes. The Chouteau family got fat and rich on it. Auguste and Pierre built those big stone places up on Main Street. Bigger than Governor Clark's, so you know who has the real power in Missouri. Look like castles, don't they? I heard they were built to fight off Indian attacks." He shook his head.

Phillip wasn't interested in houses. "One family dominates the fur trade?"

"Mostly. They call it the American Fur Company now. They have partners in New York if you can believe it. Some swell named Astor. But there is talk of competition."

"I thought fur was fading away," Phillip said.

"Who told you that? Beaver may be dropping some, but buffalo hides are big business." Their companion rose to wait on some incomers.

"Wait, you didn't answer my question. How big is this city?" Jamie demanded.

The man scratched his sparsely-covered head. "Dunno. Last I heard, three thousand, but I suspect closer to four. There are over twenty good-sized houses inside town itself. Three times as many businesses. We have a newspaper, pottery works, and they're building a sawmill and foundry."

Sawmill and foundry. In service to shipping, no doubt. Phillip peered at Jamie. "Did you ever find that bookstore?"

"Our friend there gave me directions, but I didn't go yet."

"Want help?"

They polished off their beers and left.

NAN LET ARTIE and her brother regale Nate with their tales of brick buildings, cobbled roads, and steamships for two days. Their description of the mechanical ship enthralled him, though the boy could catch sight of that steamship every month or so when it passed. Their trip had actually amounted to nothing, a big waste of time, but the books they brought inclined her to forgive them.

Nate had been sleeping with his copy of *The Iliad* by Homer. Nan hoped to read it eventually. She kept the one Jamie brought her on the kitchen table and refused to stoop to any such dramatic gesture, even if she was sure Artie directed Jamie's choices. Pike's *Expedition* wasn't exactly a romantic piece in any case. It was merely useful, with its detail about the big empty places to the west. *Not that I care about such things; useful is good.*

"Enough sitting around, you three," she said on the second day. "That wood won't split itself. Now that Artie has paddled the river, maybe his hands are tough enough to be useful." They were. She'd noticed. She noticed everything about him, but she needn't give him the satisfaction of knowing.

The men grumbled, but they went. Nate, though pleased to be included as one of the men, imitated their complaining. Soon her workday was punctuated by the rhythm of axes on wood. In between customers, she kept at her knitting. Socks and scarves for Christmas, something good and practical—unlike *The Iliad*—were to be her gift.

The echo of pounding axes had silenced and the sun was sinking when the thud of a body thrown through the front door upended her peace. Two boatmen, her only customers, leaning on the bar, turned and gaped.

"Where's Artie?" Luke bellowed.

Nan studied at the man on the floor. Someone's fist had rearranged his face something bad. She glanced back at her brother and began to chastise his crude behavior, but something in his face stopped her. "He's out back stacking. I'll fetch him."

There was no need. Artie stood in the kitchen door with Jamie and Nate on his heels.

"Is this one of the bully-boys that robbed you?" Luke demanded.

Artie came close to peer at the man struggling to rise. "I can't tell. Lift him up."

Luke grabbed an elbow and yanked the man to his feet. He swayed but stayed upright. Nan held her breath.

Artie shook his head. "Something seems to have happened to his face," he said, throwing a sardonic glance at Luke before examining the man more closely. "Doesn't look like Carpenter, especially not in those clothes. I don't recognize that straight black hair either, and he isn't quite big enough to be one of the ones that beat me."

"I never beat no one," the man whined.

"He had this around his neck," Luke said, reaching inside his buckskin shirt and pulling out an object dangling on a strip of rawhide.

Nan gasped. A ring glinted in the light from the window. Gold. With a big purple stone.

CHAPTER THIRTEEN

PHILLIP GRABBED HIS signet ring, pathetically glad to see it. After weeks of confusion, sometimes feeling as if he was living as an alien in a strange land, it was a tangible piece of himself.

"Thought so," Luke said, still holding the man's arm. He gave him a shake and let him fall.

Phillip untied the filthy leather string and raised the ring to his left hand. The broken fingers had healed to the point he could use them, but the knuckle of the ring finger bulged and the new calluses he took pride in an hour before didn't help. The ring would never fit. He clutched it in his hand, glared at the disgusting specimen of humanity at his feet, and felt a blinding rage take hold.

He dropped to his knees on the tavern floor and grabbed the neck of the man's filthy shirt with his free hand, pulling it tight enough to choke him. "Where did you get this?" he demanded, shaking the fist that still held the ring.

All that came out were gurgling sounds. Phillip could hear only Nan's voice through the red haze that had engulfed him. "Don't kill him, Artie. You'll never get information that way and the law frowns on it."

He loosened his hold. "Tell me, dammit. Where did you get this?"

"Told 'im," the man gasped, weaving his head toward Luke who leaned on his long gun, watching them closely. "Found it."

"I attempted to persuade him to give me more information, with no success. I thought you'd like to give it a try."

Phillip banged the man's head on the floor, let go, and stood, noticing the avid watchers at the bar for the first time. It was Nan's anxious expression that gave him pause, however. "Get him in a chair," he growled.

Nate and Jamie grabbed each arm and pulled the man up under Luke and Phillip's watchful gaze. "Here or the kitchen?" Jamie asked.

"Here." Phillip spoke through clenched teeth.

They shoved him in a chair. "Nate, get that length of rope from out back," Jamie said, holding the ruffian down with a hand on each shoulder.

"And fetch a beer," Phillip added.

Nate shot him a puzzled glance, but did as he was told.

"What you gonna do to me?" their prisoner whined.

Phillip waited in silence, glaring down on him until the man squirmed in the chair. "You can't kill me. There are witnesses."

Phillip never took his eyes off the man. "What's the penalty in this territory for kidnap, robbery, and theft?"

"Hanging," Luke replied, calmly rising to his full height and stowing his musket behind the bar.

"Maybe I'm mistaken. Maybe this piece of offal was one of them. He had the evidence on him."

The prisoner's eyes went wide with panic. His mouth worked, but no words came out.

Nate ran back and Jamie set to work securing the man to the chair. Phillip pulled up a chair close to him. Nate brought the beer and Phillip slammed it down just out of the prisoner's reach. "Thirsty business, traveling on the river," he drawled. He peered directly at the man's eyes. "Best fetch one for Luke too."

Jamie fetched himself a beer as well. He and Luke took a table across from the inquisition. Nate drifted over to stand behind them.

"Let's try this again. Who gave you this ring?" Phillip asked.

The lowlife refused to meet Phillip's eyes. His gaze darted around the room, settling on Nan as the likeliest source of mercy. "I done nothing wrong."

Nan moved behind Phillip's chair. She pointed to his clenched fist. "Are you the one who broke his fingers getting it off?"

Phillip took a long, slow drink of beer. He spoke without taking his eyes from the prisoner, who transferred his stare to the mug of beer. "Luke, do you remember seeing a man when you picked me up off the river?"

"Mighta."

"Would you swear to that to the magistrate?" Phillip went on.

"Probly. If I have to."

"It wasn't me. I wasn't there!" the scoundrel shouted.

"You weren't where?" Phillip asked.

"At—The—That is, wherever whatever they did to you," the man babbled.

"Who do you mean by 'they?'" Phillip asked through clenched teeth. He wasn't getting anywhere and he could feel his anger rising again.

"I—I can't."

"Can't what?" Phillip kept up the pressure.

"They'll kill me."

Phillip sat back, glanced at Luke, and then at Nan. "Is there a magistrate in Cape Girardeau, or do we take him to the capital for trial?"

"You can't do that! You'd be lying."

Phillip shook his clenched fist in the man's face. "This ring doesn't lie. Someone beat me, broke my hand, left me for dead, and took it. You have it. That makes you guilty." He rose abruptly. "Well, is there a local magistrate?"

Nan and Jamie exchanged glances. "There's a constable. He can take our statements and bind this pile of garbage to Saint

Louis for trial," Jamie suggested.

"Wait. No." The man looked from one merciless face to another. Nan took Phillip's place in the chair. She shoved the beer closer. "Maybe a sip will loosen your tongue and improve your memory." She yanked it away after he took a swallow, sloshing it on the table.

"Now that I think of it," Luke said, "The crime happened on the Illinois side. Kaskaskia is much closer. They're building a genuine courthouse, though I hear they may just make it a statehouse."

Nan studied the prisoner. "What's your name?"

"Gordy."

"Well, Gordy, did the beer help? If it improved your memory, there could be more," she said. "I don't think you found that ring. Someone gave it to you. I wonder why. Perhaps you earned it fair and square."

Phillip watched in astonishment as the man relaxed. "That's it. I earned it. Did a big favor for, for someone."

"Who was it, Gordy?" Nan spoke softly, but there was steel in her voice.

"They'll kill me. I'll have to go west. I can't—"

"We can arrange that," Luke said. "Or we can take you back to Smithland and publicly thank you for everything you told us about the ring. That might be faster than going through the law."

"No! No! Hanging would be easier."

Considering how the men who took his ring had treated him, Phillip didn't doubt they were capable of far worse than hanging. He almost felt sorry for the worm on the chair. Almost.

Nan spoke up next. "It'll be one or the other if you don't talk. If you do, we may find a way to send you downriver to New Orleans."

"Or up the Missouri to the open country beyond Arrow Rock, though I'd hate to inflict you on folks up there," Luke put in.

He began to shake. "More beer, please."

Nan gave him the mug and he drank deep. She took it back and waited.

"They were working the area north of Post Creek and they needed an errand boy. I was taking messages to farms and—"

"Wait. What do you mean 'working?'" Nan asked. Phillip looked at Jamie and mouthed "Post Creek?" Jamie shook his head, so Phillip took it the Archer farm was not near there.

The prisoner swallowed. "The usual stuff. They come up with paper they claim the dirt diggers signed. You know—loans and such. Sometimes deeds claiming they sold the property to the Sullivans." He blinked at that.

Phillip suspected the name slipped out. "Describe the Sullivan men," Phillip demanded through clenched teeth.

The man sank back. Phillip couldn't tell if he saw resignation or despair in his face. Perhaps both. "Clean. Gentry-like in speech. Come from Ohio and Virginia beyond. Not mountain folk. Taller'n me."

"Eyes?" Phillip asked.

"Grey. Stone cold, both of them. No heart. They'll kill me same as look at me after this."

"That's Carpenter," Phillip growled. "There are two?"

"Brothers."

"So, your job was to carry their threats and demands to un-suspecting farmers," Nan said sweetly, though Phillip doubted butter would melt in her mouth.

The man nodded vigorously, committed now. "Not unsus-pecting, though. They'd already been showed the papers. They're given time to pay up. I was just carrying reminders."

"Reminders with teeth," Jamie muttered.

"Now, Gordy, you can't expect us to believe you were given that fine gold ring for carrying messages. What other services did you perform for the Sullivan brothers?" Nan asked.

Gordy seemed to collapse in on himself, eyes closed, shoul-ders slumped.

Phillip thought he wouldn't answer. "They use crews of

bully-boys to beat innocent folk," he said.

Gordy jerked upright. "No! I—" He glanced from Phillip to Nan to her brothers and sat back. "I seen Mike Sullivan kill a man. It was by McFarlan's Tavern, just below Cave-in-Rock. Man owed money and lied. Mike, he…" Gordy shuddered. "He used a knife. Killed him slow-like. I thought he was going to do me, to keep me quiet. Pat told him I'd been loyal and useful. Mike handed me the ring to keep quiet. Said they couldn't hardly sell it, and I best keep it hid. Said if he found out I talked, he'd gut me. Slowly."

Nan glanced up at Phillip. "That sounds plausible."

"It's true. I swear," Gordy whined.

Phillip nodded. "The magistrate will want to talk to him, though."

"I can't. If I testify, they'll have me killed. I won't. I can't. I—"

"Shut your mouth," Luke broke in. "What do you want to do, Artie?"

Good question. They could still hang this slime or put him in prison, but it wouldn't get to the Sullivan brothers, the real culprits. "Lock him up while we think about it."

CHAPTER FOURTEEN

JAMIE AND LUKE tied their prisoner's hands and moved him off with a rope lead after Nan suggested that they ask Pierre Jolie, the blacksmith, to lock him in the smithy's storage shed. Artie started to follow, but she pulled on his arm to stop him.

"They'll manage him. You take a breath and finish that beer." She gave Nate the eye, and he went to pour another.

The two boatmen shoved their empty mugs across the bar. "I'll give you this, Nan, you provide good entertainment with your drinks." The speaker, a large man who obviously enjoyed his victuals, laughed heartily. His quiet companion who, by contrast, had the lean frame of a man used to hard work, frowned at him. The laughing boatman tipped his hat and the two of them left.

The first man's sharp eyes and knowing expression gave Nan pause. "That'll be all over the river in a week. Our Gordy is a dead man," she said.

Artie didn't answer. He opened his fist and stared at the ring he had held so hard it left an indentation in his hand.

"What do you want to do now?" Nan asked.

He picked up the ring. "When I saw this, I wanted to do murder," he said, turning it around and studying it. "Fox over trees. My family crest. Tainted though it is, it's mine."

Nan took his injured hand in hers. She gently rubbed the ring and middle fingers. "Still swollen." At her touch, he closed his eyes and moaned with pleasure. She dropped his hand as if scalded, causing his eyes to fly open. He gazed at her with a peculiar expression.

Sudden noise at the door broke the tension between them.

"Nan, be careful!" The leaner, quieter one of the two rivermen had returned. He glanced back over his shoulder. "I'll try to keep Paul quiet, but he loves to spread a good yarn. The Sullivans aren't people you want to mess with. They hear what happened here, and they'll come for that man and put you in their sights too." He spun on his heels and left like the devil was chasing him.

Artie grasped the ring in his fist again, rose, and went to the door to watch the man all the way to the landing path. He turned and met Nan's gaze. "Does that alarm you?" he asked.

"It's a caution for certain," she said. "They may come after you to finish what they started."

"It's you he came to warn. My situation may have put you and your family in danger." He stared at her fiercely, fighting a sudden desire to take her somewhere safe. England, if he could.

She brushed his comment away with a dismissive gesture. "You didn't answer my original question. What do you want to do now?"

Artie sat back down. "I want to rid the territory of the Sullivans and their gang. They're a threat to more than just you—from the sounds of it, they're a danger to a lot of innocent people. I will get as much detail as I can out of our friend Gordy and then send him as far from here as possible." He frowned down into his beer.

Nan's temper rose. *Who put him in charge like some God ordained hero?* She glared at him, irritation sharpening her words. "You aren't in this alone, Phillip—Artie—Tavernash. Don't even think you're making all the decisions."

Artie blinked, but he didn't argue. "If I take what we know to authorities in Kaskaskia, will they help?"

"Maybe. We won't know until we try. *We.* Anyway, you're

getting ahead of things. What I was actually asking was, what are you planning to do with that ring?" She glanced at the dirty leather string he had tossed on the floor. "Does it fit a different finger? I could find something to hang it around your neck," she said.

He glanced at his signet ring, now lying in the palm of his hand, and peered back at her so intently her insides quivered. A slow smile transformed his face, heat began to pool deep in her belly, and her heart raced. "Why don't you wear it for me? Take it as security on my debt. Proof I can be trusted." He held it out to her.

She took it warily, suddenly reluctant to touch him. "Are you sure?"

"I trust you to keep it safe. I'll tell you when I need it back."

CLEANED AND RESTED, Luke Archer could be pleasant enough company, and Phillip needed his thoughts on the Sullivan gang. Sitting among family, he seemed happy to give it. So did the rest of the family.

Two days of unrelenting questioning of Gordy had resulted in a list of names and places, but no clear direction to any one place they might find the Sullivans, or how they might bring them in.

From his seat in the little circle around the kitchen hearth, Phillip's eyes continually strayed to Nan while her brothers reviewed what they'd discovered from the weasel who'd been found with Phillip's ring. When she spoke, which was less often than the others, her thoughts were cogent and her logic sharp, but her concern always was the safety of every man around the fire.

"Perhaps they'll move on since they know we have evidence against them," she said.

Luke shook his head. "The Sullivans will keep at it until the country grows too hot for them or they've gotten all they can from the locals. They won't move on till one of those things happen," he drawled. "That kind of vulture always does. I doubt they've squeezed all they can get yet."

"We're going to need more proof to bring them to trial. Do you think we can get their victims to testify? I will, of course, but we may need more," Phillip said.

"You're assuming we can trap them," Nan said, drawing frowns from the men about her assumption she would have any part in capturing dangerous men. Phillip was relieved to have her brothers' support in that.

"She's right. First, we have to get them in cells," Jamie said.

"We'll need help with that. I'm assuming we'll take what we know to the authorities in Kaskaskia and…" Phillip sputtered to a stop.

"Exactly—and what? We can't assume they'll help. Law and order comes slowly out here," Jamie said.

Luke stretched his long legs toward the fire. "There's no guarantee that they would even bring them to trial. The other thing is folks across the river are in a fever over statehood. Word is the Congress declared Illinois a state December third, and the river towns were buzzing with it," Luke said. "It may be hard to get attention in Kaskaskia for much of anything else."

Phillip rose up in his chair, bile in his throat. "Are you suggesting we send Gordy on his way west and forget it?"

"Hell no!" Luke leaned over toward him, elbows on knees. "I'm suggesting we may need to deal with the Sullivans ourselves before they come to deal with us."

Silence greeted that pronouncement.

"What are you proposing, Luke?" Nan asked, studying her older brother.

"Jamie and Artie here can carry the complaint to Kaskaskia. I'll drag Gordy's filthy carcass upriver to Pa and come back. If the good people in suits haven't done anything by then, we'll start baiting traps." Luke peered around the circle, meeting every eye.

Nan nodded. "Good plan. Artie, what do you think?"

"It makes sense. We'll go through legal channels and give the law a chance, but we have to clean that particular nest of river rats from the territory one way or another. I like it." Phillip crossed his arms and nodded at Luke.

"One thing, though," Luke said. He had all eyes now.

"Nan goes to stay with Pa until we deal with the Sullivans. They'll come after this tavern as sure's my name is Archer.

Luke just saved me the trouble of suggesting it. I'll be damned if she's going to be in danger because of me. Phillip watched the color rise up Nan's neck.

Convincing her to go was another matter entirely.

CHAPTER FIFTEEN

THERE WAS NO point in arguing with Luke about dragging her to Pa. Yet. Nan stood and crossed her arms over her middle.

"Before we can do any of those things, we have Christmas to celebrate." Nan didn't make demands often, but she was determined they would do the holiday right. She pinned each of her brothers sitting around the fire with a glance. Artie too for good measure. "I am going to celebrate Christmas with all three of my brothers, and I won't tolerate any disagreement. Do you hear me, Luke Archer?"

Nate grinned at Luke, happy to see someone else on the pointed end of Nan's determination.

When Luke agreed to stay five more days until Christmas passed, she eyed him skeptically. *If he thinks he can pacify me until he can force me to go to Pa's with him, he's in for a surprise.*

"Not only that. We're going to church on Christmas Eve!" she added, bracing for disagreement.

"Did Cape Girardeau erect one this year?" Jamie asked, sarcasm thick in his tone.

"You know we have not. Kaskaskia is where we go," she said.

"Nan's right. Pa would do it if he was here," Luke murmured staring into the fire.

"Well, he's not, and it's foolishness. It's too long to get there; it'll be too dark to come home after. We'll have to stay over at

Miller's rooming house and spend the next day coming home so you can stuff us with goose and fixings." Jamie glared at her.

"Since I'm doing all the work to feed you, why do you care?" she shot back. "We're going. Nate needs to be taught properly."

"Your Mam would have insisted," Luke agreed. "Nan looks like her when she gets all het up like that."

Jamie shot a sheepish glance at their oldest brother.

"We'll just have to turn around a couple of days later and go back to see the magistrate," Jamie grumbled, peering over at Artie.

"We can't go to the authorities until after Christmas anyway," Artie said.

"Who'll look after the Roost?" Nate asked. Baptiste had gone to visit his niece. Sal left with him, but didn't plan to return, Baptiste's niece having offered her a place as nursemaid. Nan had deemed her loss a problem to be solved on another day. For now, it meant more work for Artie.

"I gather Baptiste won't be back until Boxing Day. I can look after the place while you're gone," Artie said.

"You'll do nothing of the sort. We're just closing it up," Nan said.

"What is 'Boxing Day?'" Nate asked.

"You're going to Mass with us," Nan added, giving him her sternest look.

Artie looked as if he'd been bludgeoned with a log. His voice came out a squeak. "Mass?"

"Holy Mass. Church," she replied.

"The man's Protestant!" Jamie grinned.

Nan didn't see the humor. She wasn't about to tolerate any anti-Catholic troll in her house. She glared at Artie.

"You're papist?" he asked, as if he hadn't already figured that out.

"Pa's parents brought the faith from Ireland," Luke said, studying him carefully. One wrong word and he'd have Artie on the floor.

"Irish and papist. My father is rolling over in his grave." Artie's sudden grin filled the room with joy just like the sun coming up in the morning.

"From what you said, it will serve the old sinner right." Nan gave a pert nod.

Artie laughed out loud until she spun and began fussing around the kitchen, making as much satisfying noise as possible.

Luke heaved a sigh behind her back. "Read back to me what we have from Gordy," he said.

Artie quietly answered Nate's question about Boxing Day first, so Jamie picked up the notes. "There are only four farmers on this list. I'd bet my best boots—if I had them—there are more, and his dates are pretty vague."

"Sounds like we need to pay him another visit," Luke said. "Coming, Artie?"

Nan grabbed Nate's arm so he couldn't follow. "Oh, no you don't. See to your reading."

"But Nan, Artie's going with Luke."

Artie's hazel eyes, green in the firelight, bore into her. "He can practice without me. I'll test him later. I'll be back."

He'll be back. Whatever else she knew about their unexpected guest, he was a man of his word. If he said he would do something, he would do it. And he didn't hate her faith. She hummed a little to herself and set about preparing dinner.

⸎

CHRISTMAS DAWNED CLEAR and bright, the sun painting the horizon above the east bank of the Mississippi pink and purple, then orange in turn. Phillip, the collar of his borrowed jacket turned up against the sharp cold, leaned against the big elm tree, letting the promised peace of the day fill him.

Jamie had managed to convince Luke and Nan to compromise. They would spend this day quietly. Here in the serenity of morning, Phillip gave thanks for that. In two days, they could travel to Kaskaskia for Sunday Mass in lieu of Christmas. Baptiste would return by then to keep an eye on the place so they could stay over, and see the magistrate Monday morning, thus managing a single trip. Sensible. Nan was nothing if not sensible.

"Artie?"

He turned to see Nate on the porch calling and waving him over.

Nate glanced at the sunrise with the disinterest of a young person who still believed he'd have unlimited opportunity for such a sight. Phillip knew it for the rare joy it was.

"Nan made coffee and cake. We're going to do presents," Nate said impatiently.

Presents? "I don't need to intrude on your family time," Phillip said, standing up straight.

"Don't be daft. You're expected." Nate turned on his heels back inside, and Phillip followed.

They'd pulled up chairs around the fire. Jamie handed Phillip a mug of coffee that he quickly discovered had been laced with spirits. Luke winked at him.

A small pile of gifts lay on a table between Nan and Nate. Nate was given the job of distributing them. To Phillip's horror, some were laid in his lap.

"But I have nothing…" he began, drawing a stern glare from Nan.

"Of course not! We know your situation. Part of Christmas is accepting the kindness of others as it is intended," she said.

That put Phillip firmly in his place, but his empty pockets weighed on him. *You have everything, and yet here you have nothing, Glenmoor. What good are you?* He shook the thought away. He opened the first one. A note on the brown paper wrapping said it was from Nate. A tiny wood carving lay in his hand, a decent rendition of a man in a toga. "Caesar!" he said.

"I thought it would help you remember our reading lessons," Nate told him, bowing his head shyly. "After you're gone, that is." The words touched Phillip's heart deeply. He would most certainly leave them, but he wasn't ready to think about it just then.

A soft package wrapped in muslin had to be from Nan. The reason for her ever-present knitting had already become obvious: a scarf for Luke, a bright red hat for Jamie, socks for Nate. Phillip brushed the wrapping aside to find a blue scarf and matching hat. He thought of the fine Indian wool and silk scarves in his suite at Woodglen, of the beaver hat lost to thieves, and of the ornate clothing in the trunk in Philadelphia. He doubted he would ever treasure any of them as he knew with perfect assurance that he would treasure these simple knit gifts. He caught Nan's intense gaze. "Thank you," he whispered.

She ducked her head. "Did you see the owl Nate carved for me? He knows they fascinate me." She stood and put her little owl on the rugged mantle.

A perfect gift from a brother that pays attention. All the gifts were thoughtful, representing an expenditure of thought and time rather than money. *You could have done as well, Phillip, had you but considered it.* In London, he'd have ordered his secretary to buy gifts for the servants on Boxing Day. If he had a family, he probably would have had the man purchase gifts also. None would be as meaningful as the ones the Archers gave each other.

He picked up the last, a suspiciously-shaped package.

"It's from both of us," Jamie said. "Luke had a spare, and I cleaned and sharpened it."

Phillip unwrapped a long knife with a wide blade. A very sharp blade.

"No man should be unarmed in this country," Luke said, his gravel voice deeper than usual.

A leather sheath lay under the knife.

"Baptiste helped me with the sheath," Jamie mumbled.

There was nothing for it but to teach the greenhorn how to use the thing. Soon, wrapped in his new scarf and crowned with a blue knit cap pulled over his ears, Phillip followed Luke and Jamie out back so they could show him the fine art of knife throwing. His first efforts were less than stellar, but when a toss finally hit the target dead on with a satisfying whack, Nate let out a whoop of applause. A burst of pride flooded Phillip and almost knocked him over. He threw it again. And again, hitting the target both times.

"You may survive out here, after all," Luke drawled.

The brothers set up a target for Nate to practice shooting. The pistol was new, a gift from their father. "And about time too," Luke had said. "Fourteen is getting on to be learning." He looked over his shoulder from where he set up slabs of wood along a fence rail facing the empty country. "How about you, Artie? Do you shoot."

"That I do. I have several pistols and hunting muskets," he said. "In England." He rubbed the back of his neck. "I brought one with me; it didn't do me much good. The Sullivans got it."

"How old were you when you got your first one?" Nate asked.

"Of my own? Eighteen," Phillip said.

Luke's astonished face sped him to continue. "My father took me out to shoot as a boy. Ten or so, I think. Blasting birds with one of his great hunting muskets. It about knocked me down. But I went off to boarding school soon after and hunting wasn't much part of my life. I bought a pair of fine dueling pistols on my own when I went to university."

"Dueling pistols?" Jamie laughed.

"And learned to be a dead shot. Just in case." He didn't admit he'd never actually used them with intent to hit a human. Targets were another matter.

Phillip went to his cot upstairs that night, goose and pie filling his stomach, comradery filling his soul, and celebratory joy such as no society ball or formal event had ever provided filling his whole being. He slept with a smile on his face.

Two days later, Baptiste returned as scheduled. They bid him goodbye at dawn and set out for the ferry landing.

Phillip wore his gifts, grateful for protection from the cold wind. Two flannel shirts augmented the warmth of Baptiste's old jacket, and the sheathed knife strapped to his hip added a swagger to his step when he followed the Archers to Kaskaskia's French church, another log building. He wondered what the Almack's patronesses would think if they could see him now, and bit the inside of his cheek to hide his amusement.

Lightning didn't strike his Church of England soul when the priest approached the altar and began to pray in Latin. Nor did it when he realized he found the air of worship comforting. He glanced at Nan, who prayed piously, head bowed.

A wave of longing came over him for this strange being—Irish, papist, frontier farmer, tavern keeper, strong, simple—Nan appealed to his deepest heart as no woman had. He turned his gaze away. How could there be anything between them? They were denizens of different worlds. She belonged to this place, root and branch. He belonged…

Where? He'd begun to wonder.

CHAPTER SIXTEEN

"WHERE IS THIS witness now?" The magistrate, Josiah Welling, puffed out his cheeks and waved the list of names and places they'd gleaned from Gordy.

"He escaped," Jamie said—rather too quickly, in Nan's opinion. Gordy had, in fact, left with Luke the day after Christmas, heading up the Missouri to Pa's hunting cabin. There'd been a row over whether Nan ought to come too, but Jamie gave in when he realized that Luke would never convince her, swearing he could protect her. Artie argued longest, but in the end, he gave in. It amused her to watch her wounded duck, who'd come to her helpless as a puppy, turn protective.

"Pity. We've only his word. We'd like to nail those Sullivans to a barn door. Or run them out of the state." Welling swelled with pride. "We're no lawless territory here. Not like you folk in Missouri."

Nan decided not to take offense. She pulled Artie's ring from her bodice. Her cheeks heated when she noticed Artie watching intently. "This is his lordship's ring. Our most important evidence." She lifted the ribbon over her head and handed the ring to Artie.

Welling glanced from Nan to Artie and back. "Lordship?"

Artie spat out his long fancy name and title with a dip of his head. "They set upon me near Smithland, Kentucky and took everything I had, including this signet ring with my family crest. I would be dead but for these good people. Luke Archer found the ring on our witness and hauled him back for questioning. Unfortunately…"

"He escaped." Welling's skepticism was obvious. "His life won't be worth spit if the Sullivans know he's talking."

Welling studied the ring in Artie's hand. "Distinctive. That might turn it, especially if you can identify them." He didn't try to take the ring. "You keep that safe," he said.

"If you know the Sullivan gang so well, why haven't you done them in before?" Nan demanded.

Welling shifted uneasily. "Slippery devils, ain't they? Arrested them once and set up a trial in Elizabethtown, but no one would testify. Had to let them go." He eyed Artie slyly. "How about you, yer lordship? If we haul their carcasses up here, will you come in to testify?"

Artie stood tall and, for once, Nan could see the powerful man he claimed to be. It took her breath away. "Without question, Mr. Welling. You have my word. And it is Your Grace, if you please."

"Grace?" Welling scratched his chin.

"A duke is addressed as 'Your Grace.' Lesser peers are 'my lord.'" Artie stared the man down. It tickled Nan.

Welling's eyes skittered away. "We'll send some men to find them and drag them in. We'll send word when we do—yer honor."

"The British envoy to Washington will be most grateful to you," Artie said, inclining his head.

Nan hadn't thought of that. A man as important as a duke ought to have folks looking for him. She studied Artie more closely.

"What about the list of names we gave you?" Jamie asked. "Some of them can testify too."

Welling shrugged. "Mebbe they will, mebbe they won't. Mebbe we'll get lucky and the Sullivans'll try to resist so we can shoot them. It's worth arresting them if we can count on the duke here, though."

"Fair enough," Artie said, and they all turned to leave, Jamie and Nan leading, Artie with an arm around Nate's shoulders.

"You best watch yourself," Welling called after them. All four stopped in their tracks. "All of you. If the Sullivans get wind you plan to testify, they'll come after you."

None of them turned around. "We're aware of it, Welling," Artie said.

⫸✦⫷

"Well, yer grace, now what?" Jamie drawled.

"Stubble it with 'Your Grace.' That was for Welling. I need to think. Is there a…"

"Tavern, yes." Jamie said hopefully.

"Coffee shop," Nan countered. "We need clear heads." Phillip agreed.

Hot coffee and biscuits did little to improve the obviously grim mood around the table.

"Welling will lay your life on the line to get rid of the Sullivans," Nan said.

"I got that. He offered no protection whatsoever," Phillip said.

Jamie rubbed his chin. "His authority stops at the Mississippi River—not that I think he'd be much help on the Illinois side."

Phillip grunted. "I forgot that detail. You're right. He'll handle the legalities, but we're on our own at Archers' Roost."

"What did you mean about this envoy in Washington?" Nan asked.

Phillip sighed grimly. Perceptive as always, she didn't miss much. "If I got word to him, he might send help, but it would be a month or more. If I had the money, I could go myself to fetch help and not rely on the mails, but I don't have money for

97

passage."

"If you leave, Welling will do nothing and the Sullivans will come after us anyway," Jamie pointed out. "Don't do it."

"You're probably right. He probably couldn't send troops in any case." Uglier thoughts struck Phillip and he leaned toward Jamie. "Once they know Welling has a witness, they'll come after me—or their bully-boys will. It puts all of you in danger. We should have sided with Luke and sent Nan to your father."

"Don't talk about me like I'm not here. My life isn't yours to decide!" Nan said. "But we should have sent Nate."

"Hey!" Nate growled.

Jamie waved a hand for quiet. "None of that matters now. First of all, even if Artie disappears, they'll still come after us. They'll know we had Gordy. Blame Luke. He grabbed the weasel, and the Sullivans will know he talked."

Nan sank back in her seat frowning.

"Archers don't run," Nate murmured under his breath, obviously reciting a family motto.

If they had a coat of arms, that would be on it. "It's me they'll want," Phillip insisted.

"Maybe you should go then. To hell with the Sullivans," Nan said. "But where would you go? There is no hiding place along the river where they can't find you. If you can get to Philadelphia or Washington, it might be far enough."

"Did you hear what your brother said? I can't leave the territory until the Sullivans are dead or in jail. I promised to testify and I plan to—"

"You can't do it if you're dead," Nan muttered.

"And they'd still come after us," Jamie reiterated.

"What do you suggest?" Phillip asked.

"Wait, and take care of them when they come," Nan said.

"Exactly. We have to decide where we make our stand," Jamie said.

"Sit and make a target out of me? Out of all of us, even Nan?" Phillip sputtered.

Jamie went on as if he hadn't spoken. "The tavern is more visible and exposed. What about the farm?" Jamie asked.

"What about Artie's land up north?" Nate asked.

"No buildings to barricade," Nan responded.

Phillip glanced between them while they discussed the benefits of each like generals preparing for war. In a way, he suspected, they were. They settled on the tavern as easiest to defend. Phillip couldn't argue, though he still believed he should leave them.

"We may have a bit of time before word riles them up. I can get to the farm and ask neighbors to take care of the livestock. Closed up, the place will be good until spring," Jamie said.

"If you leave from here, you can be to The Roost in three or four days. We'll ready Archers' Roost," Nan agreed. "What do you think, Phillip?"

"I think you're both crazy. What about all of you going up river after Luke? Leave me at Archers' Roost," he countered.

"We may be making too much of this. If Welling arrests the Sullivans, they may not be such a big threat," Jamie said with a shrug.

Phillip rubbed the back of his neck. "Maybe. It's impossible to judge. So, you're saying wait and see?"

Jamie nodded. "I'll close up the farm for winter and join you at Archers' Roost. If Welling's men get them and nothing happens, we'll be nearby for the trial. If they come after us in the open, we'll handle it."

"'The open?' What else?" Phillip asked.

Nan and Jamie exchanged glances, shifting in their seats.

"Spill it."

"They may try to pick us off one by one," Nan said. "They're not known for fighting fair."

"I can testify to that," Phillip said.

"They could try to burn us out," Nate put in, sending chills down Phillip's spine. *What did this lad endure during the war?*

"We can go up the Missouri later if we need to," Jamie said. "I say we sit tight until we know more."

Phillip studied Nan. He saw more calculation than fear, and probably for her younger brother. Determination quickly wiped that away. "If giving a ring that distinctive to Gordy is any indication, they're not as smart as Welling thinks. I agree. We sit tight."

Phillip pulled the ring from his pocket. His tongue had almost fallen from his mouth when she pulled it from between her breasts. It had been warm from her body when he took it, scrambling his brain. "One more thing," he said.

"Do you want to try the land office again?" Jamie asked.

Phillip shook his head. "The Sullivans still have a title, and there's no way to defend a patch of empty ground, as you said. No. I want to try the bank again," he said, holding up the ring.

The bank clerk seemed nervous, a change since Phillip's last visit. He found the bank president's smile unconvincing when he demanded to see him. While impressed with his ring and the tale of the Sullivan gang, they still refused a loan unless he left his ring as collateral. Phillip refused; he gritted his teeth and rejoined the Archers on the street.

"No luck?" Nan asked.

He shook his head. "I left funds in my bank in Philadelphia. By now there may be considerably more as I requested from my business office in London. It doesn't do us any good here."

They walked toward the ferry landing without discussion until Phillip asked them to wait.

"Can you spare me the cost of postage to Philadelphia?" he asked.

"That far? It'll be twenty-five cents a sheet! That's a day's pay," Nan said.

"I'll need at least two," he replied. "With the ring, I can identify myself by mail."

She rooted in a slit in her skirt for the little purse in the pocket of her petticoat. "I've enough for three," she said. "I'm beginning to wonder if you're worth what you cost us," she grumbled.

I'm probably not, and it is likely to get worse. It took him the better part of twenty minutes to write to his bank in Philadelphia, write to the British envoy, and talk the clerk into ink for his seal to stamp the letters. Wax cost him—or Nan—an additional ten cents. Given the hazards of travel, he added his seal to the inside of the letters as well as out and signed them with his usual flourish. Glenmoor.

"They'll go out Monday, most likely," the clerk said.

Phillip groaned. A reply would take weeks. Maybe months. It was the best he could do. *What did Jamie say? Now we wait.*

Jamie led them to a gunsmith. While they waited for him to package up what Phillip thought was an enormous purchase of gun powder and shot, he and Jamie surveyed firearms. Phillip, weighed by his lack of funds, could only watch.

"Luke left a long flintlock at Archers' Roost. Nan keeps two others. And you have Nate's pistol. I'll bring what I have at the farm. We'll manage," Jamie said grimly.

Dear God, they—we—are preparing for a siege. "Do you really expect a frontal attack?" Phillip asked.

"Can't be sure," Jamie muttered. "One by one is more likely."

Jamie walked with them to the Kaskaskia ferry landing. As they approached, Jamie rapped his knuckles on the sheath at Phillip's waist before waving them off. "You best practice when we get back. You're going to need it."

Phillip held out a hand to help Nan aboard. She glanced at his hand and took it gingerly, as if unused to a gentleman's courtesy. And yet, this woman was prepared for war; it would not be her first siege. The Archers had survived Indian attacks in Pennsylvania and Illinois—or most of them had survived. "Tell me about the attack on the farm," he said.

Nan, still staring at the hand he'd touched, blinked up at him and nodded.

CHAPTER SEVENTEEN

THEY MADE THEIR way across the river to the ferry landing and on to Cape Girardeau via the cart road along the river. Dark comes early at the end of December and shadows stretched across the lawn in front of Archers' Roost. Nan paused in the shelter of the trees and shivered a little. Something felt off.

"Baptiste let the fire go out. Business must be slow," Nate murmured staring up at the chimney.

Artie followed his gaze upward. It was plain to all of them no smoke rose from the dark building.

"The door's hanging open. Something isn't right!" Nan started to run, but Artie grabbed her arm.

"Easy. We can't just rush in there," he said, holding her waist in an iron grip. Had she really once thought this man a weakling?

Nate huddled close. "I could sneak in the back and take a look."

"No!" Nan and Artie shouted simultaneously.

"I'm not a baby," Nate complained.

"We should survey the outside first," Nan said.

"Good idea—except it puts us out in the open," Artie said, glancing to his left, studying the tree line. "Nate, go back a ways and come up to the town farther down. See what Pierre Jolie knows. Be cautious. For all we know the Sullivans have taken Cape Girardeau."

Nan resented his assumption of command, but she had to admit it was a good plan. *So far.*

She watched her brother trot down the cart trail, fearful for his sake. "I'm going up," she said, not even looking at Artie.

"We," he replied. "If we keep to the woods, we can make a dash for the shed."

"I see no sign of life in there," she said, turning to study her tavern again.

"Nor do I, but let's go slowly."

She nodded. They made their way through the underbrush as quietly as possible. The edge brought them within ten feet of the corner of the building.

"No movement in the windows," he whispered.

"It feels empty," Nan said quietly.

Artie glanced down at her quizzically. "Are you fey?"

No more than any Irishwoman. She'd learned young to trust her hunches. She didn't answer him. "The shed is no closer to the building than here. We should approach directly and duck below the windows."

Artie studied the situation. She could almost see the wheels in his mind making calculations.

When he nodded, she found it more gratifying than she should.

"What are you doing?" His whisper had a desperate edge to it.

"Hiding our ammunition," she said, covering the bundles they had carried with brush. "And looking for a weapon. I wish I'd brought one."

She gathered four good-sized rocks and put them in her pockets. "I'm ready." She darted out before he could respond, one rock in hand, head low. He followed immediately and leaned against the wall beneath the window. The front end of the tavern was on the downhill slope and held up on piles of stones, putting the windows out of reach.

"No sounds," she breathed, turning her head toward the back

of the tavern. She ducked again and led the way, crawling in that direction.

Nan bobbed up to look in the kitchen window; Artie pulled her down, earning a glare. "I see no one. Look yourself," she whispered.

He did and nodded to her. His knife, she noticed, was in his hand. They held eyes for several moments, coming to a silent agreement.

"Quietly," he murmured. "No bursting through the door."

Mr. High-and-mighty is right again. She opened the door softly before he could issue any more orders and stepped into the kitchen.

Dark and empty, the kitchen had none of its welcoming warmth; an ominous chill crept through her. Artie opened the larder, knife at the ready, and a rat ran out, scuttling toward the open door to the public room. Artie met her eyes, his nose pinched as if he had recognized what she had; something more disquieting than the smell of stew left to rot assaulted them. Nan knew the smell of death. Knew it better than she wished to.

He moved before she could and stopped short in the doorway, blocking her way; the fool man meant to shield her from something unpleasant.

"I'll not be treated like some frail flower, yer grace," she spat, giving him a shove. He resisted and his arm came out to protect her. She ducked under, but quickly jerked to a stop.

Baptiste, dead and almost unrecognizable from wounds and rat bites, lay sprawled across the floor. The sight of rodents continuing their attack filled her with blinding rage so strong it drove out both grief and caution. She grabbed her broom from behind the bar and set on the vermin in a frenzy, beating them and tossing them in the air before beating again, as if they were the Sullivan brothers themselves. A few escaped through the front door, but Nan continued to attack the tiny gray corpses that littered her tavern's floor, shouting curses until she was hoarse.

"Enough." Artie's voice came from far away. "Enough!" He

shouted the second time. "They are all dead." She tried to fight him when he yanked the broom from her hands and swatted at him when he pulled her into his arms. His grip, so iron-hard she couldn't escape, yet so tender she couldn't resist, held her in place while she fought him. He rubbed gentle circles on her back until her struggle weakened and she sank against his shoulder, rage and curses giving way to grief and weeping.

She didn't know how long she cried while the world outside faded to full dark. She glanced over at the body. Artie had covered it with one of the tablecloths she kept for special occasions. Her throat was sore and her voice weak when she finally managed one word wrenched from her broken heart. "Baptiste."

He didn't respond. One gentle hand wiped her hair back; his long fingers cupped her cheek and raised her chin while he murmured soothing words. Before her eyes could even focus on his face, his mouth came down on hers, gentle at first, his kiss meant to comfort.

The fury of feelings that had consumed her swirled into one single blaze of fire, one need. She gripped his shoulders and kissed him back with blind passion.

WEEKS OF PENT-UP longing enflamed by Nan's sudden passion almost knocked Phillip's self-control and honor to the rubbish heap. Almost. He eased his responses to Nan's enthusiastic onslaught. He kissed her check, her ear, her hair, pulling her head down as he did. Her wide-eyed confusion came even closer to undermining his good behavior. He kissed her nose and gently moved her a few inches away from where she clung like a limpet.

"This horror has left us both shaken," he murmured, urging her to regain control with the force of his gaze.

She blinked twice and dropped her head. "I, I'm sorry. I—"

He raised her chin with the knuckle of his index finger. "Don't. There's no time for foolish regrets. We may be in danger, and we have to deal with this catastrophe."

She glanced at the remains of their friend, eyes swimming with moisture that threatened to overflow. "You covered him."

A sound from the rear of the house, and another from the front, put every sense on alert. "Where are those guns you told Jamie you had?"

"Under my bed," she replied.

He didn't dare send her upstairs alone. The miscreants may yet lurk above stairs, though Phillip thought it unlikely. He didn't dare leave her alone downstairs either. He went to survey the situation outside, parting the front curtains. A shaft of moonlight showed him a familiar form skulking toward the door. "It's Nate. He's not alone."

Nan ran to the door before he could call to her to be careful. Before he knew it, what looked like the entire male population of Cape Girardeau filled the tavern talking at once while he still had a dead body on the floor, and who knew what above the stairs. Nan lit candles and attempted to draw attention to Baptiste's fate. Nate wept quietly at her side. Some listened; others peered in corners as if looking for the Sullivans.

Phillip climbed to the second step and raised his voice of command—a rare useful gift from his worthless father. "Give me your attention. The men who did this are ruthless, cruel, and likely not gone." The room went quiet and he continued. "Thank you all for coming to Miss Archer's aid. Shall we deal with the immediate situation, and then reconvene here to discuss plans to deal with this?" Nan's grateful face gave him strength. "What is the custom here for dealing with deceased friends?" he went on. The entire crowd turned to the sight some of them had been avoiding, the body under the tablecloth.

Before Nan could speak, a man he recognized as Ezekiel Wadsworth, the carpenter, spoke up. "I generally make the casket. We lay them in Poirier's barn until the circuit preacher can hold a service—usually at the tavern. Except in summer, of course, then we bury 'em fast." He glanced at the body. "Papists usually get taken over to the church in Kaskaskia."

"Miss Archer?" Phillip waited for Nan to decide what should be done.

"I would be grateful for a casket, Zeke. Would you hold him in your back room until you get it made? We'll lay him out here and send word. Father LaPlante might come over here for a funeral."

"Before we do that, we need make sure our perimeter is secure. Monsieur Jolie, please help me check every room upstairs. The rest of you pair off and search the shed out back and every corner around Archers' Roost where they could be hiding." Phillip stepped down into the room and took both of Nan's hands in his. "I know this is hard, but would you sit with Baptiste while we check for danger?"

She nodded. "It's my place to do it," she said.

Nate looked fit to rebel. "It's my place to secure the upstairs. Archers' Roost is—"

"Your responsibility. I know. But we can't leave your sister unguarded. Stay with her, please," Phillip said.

That soothed the boy's ruffled feathers.

She shocked Phillip with a swift hug. "Thank you. When we 'reconvene,' as you call it, I'll have ideas." The steel in her voice made it clear she wouldn't be brushed aside in the defense of her place and her loved ones.

Fair enough, Miss Archer.

CHAPTER EIGHTEEN

LUKE RETURNED TWO days after they found Baptiste, announcing that Gordy, "the weasel," lit out the first day after they started up the Missouri and never came back.

"Your lame duck turned out to be a fighting cock," he said, grudgingly impressed by the way Artie had organized the people of Cape Girardeau into patrols, and set up a security perimeter for Baptiste's funeral.

Nan stood with Luke on the porch of Archers' Roost watching for the arrival of the priest. A faint smile replaced her worried frown. "He has at that. A bit pushy."

Luke snorted. "That kind are. I thought dukes got up in fancy gear and paraded around palaces though. This one has guts."

As if summoned, Artie himself emerged from the tree line on the path along the river. The wind ruffled his chestnut hair, distracting Nan. He adjusted his long stride to the man at his side. Father LaPlante, like most men, stood a head shorter. Though Artie still appeared slender, no one would mistake that for weak. The trousers he wore fit like a second skin, and his plaid shirt clung to solid shoulders. He had muscled up nicely in recent months.

Very nicely, she thought as the two men approached. She pushed the distraction aside. They had sad business to attend to. She found it increasingly difficult, however. His comforting embrace, given in the midst of catastrophe, had imbedded itself deep inside her, body and soul.

Emil LaPlante reached for Nan's hand and gave it a pat. "Bad business this, Nan. Bad business." He offered his arm, and she led him inside. Luke and Artie peeled out in opposite directions, checking the security no doubt.

Chairs lined the public room, and the tables had been removed. A rough wooden casket lay atop two sawhorses in the center of the room. Nan herself had cleaned and dressed her friend's body, while her tears rained down into the casket with him.

The people who had gathered rose to their feet. Father LaPlante greeted many of them who were familiar to him, Catholic and not. Luke came in through the back, and Artie the front at the same time. There was no point in delay. The priest raised his hand for quiet and began to recite the Latin funeral prayers.

"*Requiem aeternam dona eis Domine, et lux perpetua luceat eis...*"

Yes. Eternal rest, perpetual light, Nan prayed. *Poor Baptiste deserves it.* She glanced at Artie, his eyes downcast, sorrow marring his face. She had been so wrapped up in grief and danger, she hadn't taken time to realize he had lost a friend as well.

The service droned on. "*In paradisum deducant te Angeli...*" *May the angels lead you into Paradise.* She prayed the all too familiar words. Life as she'd known it carried danger and death. So much of it. She suspected Artie had seen his share of grief as well. *Perhaps, but not like this. Not violent death.*

Father LaPlante sprinkled the casket with holy water and gestured to Pierre Jolie and some of the others, who lifted it onto their shoulders and carried it out.

An open grave awaited them in the little cemetery above town, and Baptiste's casket was lowered into it.

Nan sighed with relief. The ladies of Cape Girardeau had laid out a meal in her kitchen, and she was anxious to get back to it, to leave all this behind. Father LaPlante began a final prayer, and she had scooped up a handful of dirt to drop into the grave when a shot rang out.

Shouts followed and the crowd in the cemetery began to surge, some ducking, some reaching for their weapons, some peering at the ridge above them, the direction of the shot.

"Watch our flanks!" Artie's voice cut into the chaos. "Luke, take some of the men and get the women and the priest back to Archers' Roost." The two men stared at one another defiantly. Blood ran down Artie's cheek, leaving no doubt to any of them who had been the target. He didn't wait for Luke to do as he said. He charged off in the direction of the shooter, taking the route that provided a bit of cover. *Thank God.* Nate and Pierre Jolie ran beside him.

Nan's instinct to follow them was quickly suppressed as Luke and his men herded them all back to the tavern. Luke sent men with long guns to the second floor, with windows in three directions. He and the others locked the doors and shuttered the windows. Nan glanced around, stomped a foot in frustration, and set kettles on for tea and coffee while the others set a few tables back in the public room.

"We may be in for a long night. We may as well feed people," she announced. Her mind and her heart, however, had run up that ridge with Artie.

NOTHING. WHOEVER FIRED that shot had better evasive skills than aim. Phillip located crushed brush and footsteps where he'd knelt to take his shot, but little else. His trail went cold at Poirier's farm where it could have veered off in three different directions.

Phillip stared off in the direction he thought most likely, one leading into wilderness. "He could have doubled back, too," he mused.

"Or they," Nate said, alert to any movement. "We aren't sure it was one man."

Phillip nodded grimly. "We don't want to be lured any farther away."

It was dark when they returned to Archers' Roost empty-handed. He didn't expect a hero's welcome, but he didn't expect Nan's hard shove to his chest either.

"Did you have to go so damned far? We could have been under attack. You could have been dead!" She choked on those last words, in obvious distress. He took an entirely inappropriate pleasure in that.

"I'm sorry if we distressed you," he murmured, cupping her cheek to study her face.

"Quit mooning over the man, Nan, so he can talk," Luke barked. He handed Phillip a mug of beer.

Phillip drank deep and started to explain what they found—and what they didn't.

"Hired hand, most likely. He could be anywhere by now," Luke muttered.

"Leave the man be, Luke!" Nan gave Phillip another shove, this time into a chair.

"Sit still and let me tend to that gunshot wound. There's blood all over your face. You could have passed out, running off like that," she grumbled.

Luke pulled up a chair close by and the others hovered around while Nan cleaned the blood from his face and dabbed at the deep scrape along his scalp. He yelped when she poured some of her raw rye whiskey on it. "Are you trying to finish the job?"

"Do you want infection to do it for them?" she retorted. "Another inch or two and you would be lying stone cold in that cemetery."

"Are you ready to hightail it?" Luke asked.

Phillip's attention remained on Nan. Her distress on his behalf was a kick in the belly, the touch of her hands, peace personified.

"I mean it. Are you heading downriver to New Orleans or

coming with the rest of us to Pa's cabin up the Missouri?" Luke demanded.

"Who said we're running to Pa?" Nan asked, her sharp tone jolting Phillip from his abstractions.

"You go, but I can't outrun them. They'll come looking for me wherever I go, and I would just drag them after you." Phillip held Luke's gaze, determined to convince him. "You take Nan and Nate and get out of here."

"No." Nan and Nate spoke simultaneously.

"Then you head downriver to New Orleans. Go back where you belong," Luke said.

"And leave them to come after you? I'm not leaving until I testify—until I bring them down if that doesn't do it." Phillip glanced at Nan and back at her older brother.

"They'll come at us again if we make a stand here. We can pick them off one by one." Nate's words startled Luke as much as Phillip. They stared at him.

Nan put an arm around the boy. Luke opened his mouth to argue, but she spoke first. "Nate's right. If Artie won't leave, it is the only way."

Luke snorted.

"Archers don't run," Nate muttered, glaring at his brother.

Phillip squeezed his eyes shut. *Damned fool woman. The Sullivans are evil and don't care who they hurt.*

Nan went on as if they'd all agreed on a plan. "First, we need to get the innocent out of the firing line. Sullivans don't care about the rest of the folks in Cape Girardeau. This is our problem."

"They'd burn the town to the ground to get to Artie, and you saw what they did to Baptiste. They're a menace to all of us; it is our fight too," Pierre Jolie said.

"He's right. If you're making a stand at the Roost, they'll have to come around and through us," another villager said, less confidently. An argument broke out in the room.

Phillip rose to his feet, batting Nan's hands away. "I'm not leaving. Those men need to be taken down. The Archers can make their own decisions. Either I go over to Kaskaskia and endanger more people there, or I make my stand here. What other choice is there?"

"The farm?" Nate suggested.

Keeping you and Nan in the line of fire. "Jamie claimed it's harder to defend," Phillip reminded him.

Nan glanced at Luke. "I suspect Jamie was right. We stay here until he comes back, and consider it then."

Luke rolled his eyes. "Thank goodness it's January. The roof will stay wetter when they try to burn us out. How long do you think we can hold out?"

We. The damned Archers were going to stick like burrs. Phillip studied the crowd, peering from face to face, some determined, some fearful. "I suggest those of you that have places you can take your families, do so. Lock up and leave. Those of you that plan to stay, remain. We need to inventory our weapons and manpower." He glared over at Nan who stared right back, a stone wall of determination greeting his opposition.

CHAPTER NINETEEN

A WEEK LATER, there had been no attack, the farm was no longer an option, and the news was worse. Sitting around the kitchen table, while men guarded both doors and two more patrolled the upper windows, Nan's heart sank to her shoes.

Jamie had returned, exhausted and furious. He'd come across on the ferry and brought two more muskets, a stash of gunpowder, and bad news.

"Squatters. Squatters with paper. Either the Sullivans pulled another fraud and sold it, or Pa really did sell us out. They locked me out of my own house. Locked the livestock up, too. There's cash buried under the kitchen floor. We have to hope they don't find it." Jamie glowered at Luke. "Did Pa plan this?"

"Could have. I heard him threaten, but he never told me he was doing it," Luke said, shaking his head. "His money, he said, and he needed it. How'd you get the weaponry?"

Jamie shrugged. "Hidden in the rocks by the creek, like we were taught. If Artie here still plans to hold off the damned Sullivans, we'll need 'em."

"It's likely the Sullivans took the farm, trying to pen us in," Artie mused. "That option is off the table. They must have been planning to come after us as soon as they heard Luke took Gordy, before we even spoke to Welling. It isn't too late for all of you to head upriver and leave me to it."

"Travel will be nasty till spring," Luke murmured, peering at his hands casually.

"It appears we're all staying, Luke. You go if you must. Tell the old man to stay gone if he sold the farm out from under us." Nan lifted her chin defiantly.

Luke's lip curled up. "I never could run from a fight. This looks to be a good one. How about some coffee for Jamie here? He had a long trip."

It was on the tip of her tongue to say, "Get it yourself," and the twinkle in Artie's eyes told her he knew it. This wasn't time for family conflict, though. She brought the pot and refilled all of their cups, bringing a clean one for Jamie. She slammed the pot down on the table. "Enjoy it while we have it. When you're done counting bullets, we need to talk about food. And water."

"Are we entirely under siege?" Jamie asked.

"As good as," she said. "Artie sent a patrol into the village last night to raid McGregor's general sundries. He and his family left town, but we'll owe him when he gets back. Nate has rabbit snares in the garden—so far without luck. The well is where it always is. Fifty feet from the kitchen door."

"And?" Jamie prodded.

"No shots were fired since the funeral, if that is what you mean," Luke said. "So far, no sign of a frontal attack."

Nan peered into her coffee. "I think we're taking the wrong approach."

"What do you mean?" Artie asked.

"We've barricaded the doors, turned away paying customers from the river, and generally acted like scared rabbits. I suspect the Sullivans' minions are waiting for one clear shot." She glanced around the table. "I'm tired of waiting already, and I don't plan to hole up here until spring."

"No! No you don't. Don't even think about it." Artie surged to his feet, leaning both hands on the table and glaring at Nan.

"What?" Nate peered around the table in confusion.

"I suspect our sister wishes to be bear bait," Luke said, frowning at her.

"Bear bait? You mean like a goat carcass tied to a tree?" Nate gasped.

"Not tied to a tree, perhaps," Luke drawled.

Artie waved the discussion away. "We aren't even going to discuss this!"

PHILLIP WATCHED NAN from the corner of his eye while he finished Nate's morning lessons. He could no longer resist the sight of her; he had to force his mind back to the lesson. The boy had been belligerent lately, egged on no doubt by Luke's obvious disdain for book learning, but they'd managed to find a daily rhythm, and the lessons helped in more ways than one.

Boredom, ever a hazard of siege warfare, had taken its toll as one week passed, and then two more with no sign of gunfire, strangers, or movement of any kind. With little to do, Nan had taken to reading in the rocking chair she'd placed near the kitchen window—too near, in Phillip's opinion. The sight of her there gave the illusion of peace, however, one he relished. She burrowed herself deeper and deeper into his soul every day.

Phillip, with surprising support from Luke, had set up guard duty and foraging patrols. Luke himself took over the water supply, taking a partner when he went to the well under cover of darkness. One of the upstairs guards was assigned to watch it during the day, lest the Sullivans attempt to foul the water.

Jamie led forays to check rabbit snares, sometimes accompanied by Nate. They brought down a deer unlucky enough to wander from the woods, fooled by the quiet. By general agreement, Phillip stayed inside so as not to be a target. That rule applied to Nan as well, over her vociferous objection.

He rose from the table with words of praise for Nate. The boy had begun reading *Julius Caesar* in his room at night again, bringing questions about words he failed to understand to Nan or Phillip in the morning. "Well done indeed," Phillip said. "Tomorrow we'll talk about the Punic Wars, and Hannibal's elephants."

"Elephants?" The idea startled Nate.

"War elephants. Just you wait." Phillip grinned at him. Unable to suppress a longing glance at Nan, he left the room quickly. Days of proximity were eroding his gentlemanly instincts where she was concerned, and he could only be grateful for the presence of her three well-armed brothers.

He climbed the stairs on leaden feet to relieve Jolie who had guard duty at the rear windows on the second floor. It was deadly boring to stand for hours staring out the window, unable to read or do anything constructive because of the alertness required.

Perhaps Nan was right after all. We need to lure them in. Not that he—or her brothers—would permit Nan to set herself up as bait. He took the musket and shot from Jolie and pulled the chair closer to the window.

An hour passed in silence. Phillip surveyed the tree line to the left between the tavern and the boat launch over and over until the contrasting colors of fir and pine, the shapes of leafless branches, and the places where paths opened in the undergrowth were all images imbedded in his mind. To the right, a well-trodden path led uphill past thick briars to the village. Directly behind the tavern, the vegetable patch, the shed, and the well sat in open territory.

He jumped up once at movement from the briars only to see a rabbit run out, chased, no doubt, by a fox. With luck, it would find Nate's snares in the garden patch. He sighed and sank back.

Either jumpy or numb. This is not working. His mind began to wander, images of the vast lawn of Woodglen overlaying the Roost's little kitchen yard. He tried to envision Nan, swathed in silk or fine wool, strolling up the circular lane toward the stately edifice that was his childhood home. He failed.

Another movement shortly after brought him to full alert, made his blood run cold, and sent him running. Nan came out the kitchen door, striding purposefully toward the well as if his mind had conjured her.

What the devil is that woman thinking?

He leapt down the steps, passing Nate trying to walk up, and Jamie guarding the front door. "Your damned fool sister," he shouted as he went by the bar where Luke leaned, chatting with Pierre Jolie.

By the time he burst out the back door, she was almost to the well, and he surged forward. Something to the right, barely glimpsed from the corner of his eye, set his instincts bounding into action. He flew forward with one great leap, knocking Nan to the ground just as a shot passed overhead.

Breathing heavily, he covered Nan with his body while he heard other shots come from the direction of the kitchen. "Damn it, woman, lie still," he hissed. She did, relaxing under him. For a moment, her closeness was his only thought. He clenched his jaw. *No time for that, you idiot,* he told himself.

"Move before he reloads," she whispered.

"Luke and Jamie are covering us. Just stay down," Phillip said. "Do what you're told for once."

The heat in her eyes turned from something mysterious and feminine to a pure flame of fury. He stared her down. There'd be time to argue later. He tossed his musket to the left of the housing around the well and wrapped both arms around her before he rolled them both behind the well. It was meager, but shelter nonetheless. He reached for the gun.

Jamie dove down next to them, Nate's pistol aimed in the direction of the shot. "It came from the briars," he said.

Phillip nodded. "Where's Luke?"

"Dropped toward the river to go around and get him from behind. Stay here. I'm going the other way."

"He's gone." Nan's voice was muffled against Phillip's shirt. "He'd have fired again if he was going to." She wiggled beneath him, setting his blood on fire. "Let me up.

"You might be right," Phillip said. "But we're staying here

until they give an all-clear." He loosened his hold and she slipped from beneath him. He grabbed her arm to keep her down.

Jamie swapped the pistol for the musket Phillip held and crept toward the briars, coming at it on the town side.

Phillip rose to his knees, chanced a glance over the well housing, and pulled Nan close with his left arm, breathing heavily, her back to his chest, his right hand gripping the pistol. "They'll either kill him or catch him," he murmured.

When Nan sagged against him, he kissed the top of her head. "This can't go on," she said.

He started to apologize for the inappropriate familiarity, but realized she meant the siege, the shooters, and the Sullivans. "I need to stay alive long enough to testify," he murmured in her ear.

A sharp elbow hit his ribs. "Idiot."

"We could get them first." He shrugged.

"We need to rid the territory of those vermin so folks can live in peace," she signed. "And you have no business acting like a martyr throwing yourself to the lions."

When she spoke, her body moved against him, filling his with a delicious surge of lust, and an erection he couldn't control. *She has to feel that. This can't go on, indeed.* He tugged her a bit closer anyway. He had to protect her, didn't he?

She sighed and relaxed into his arms, nestled quietly there while long moments passed, his blood flamed, and erotic images tormented his imagination. "You'll go home when this is over. Once the Sullivans are no longer a threat," she said at last, pouring ice water over him body, soul, and imagination.

"Perhaps. I—"

"You have your land. You don't plan to farm. We both know you're no tavern servant. Once you testify, there is nothing to keep you here. You can pay what you owe us with interest once you reach Philadelphia," she said.

"Land speculation is off the table. I plan to invest in trade. I came here to make my fortune, and I won't leave until I have."

He tried to sound determined, but it was halfhearted. He knew what she really meant. There could be nothing between them. Nothing honorable at least. He would leave. After the trial or after he set up a going enterprise in Saint Louis. It made no difference. As warnings went, her words were brutal.

"But you—"

"If you two are finished having tea, you might want to get yerselves back into the cover of the house," another voice broke in. Luke stared down at them.

Nan wiggled free and surged to her feet. "Did you get 'im?"

"Get yerselves inside. I have words for you." He looked from face to face. "Both of you."

They did as he said. Nan spun around inside the kitchen door. "Did you get 'im or not?"

"This one; they'll send another." Luke shook his head sadly. "It was a young Indian, probably Winnebago from the looks. Sullivans either promised 'im the moon or threatened his family. He can't tell us now. Jamie shot him when he came after me."

When she tried to walk away, her brother grabbed her arm. "You need to stay put when we tell you. You coulda been killed. Or I could have, and it would have been on you."

She shook off his hand. Before she could speak or stomp away, he turned on Phillip with icy blue eyes sharp as knives. "As for you, you have our thanks for knocking the fool woman down before she got shot. But If I see you hold her like that again, I'll have your man parts off and food for catfish before you can blink."

Luke attempted to saunter off, but Nan ruined his exit. "Mind your own business, Luke, and pay attention. We need to rethink what we're doing. You have to see it now. This isn't working. The sooner we bring it to an end the better."

Luke glanced at Phillip and back at his sister. When he nodded in agreement, Phillip suspected Luke Archer meant to end more things than the siege.

CHAPTER TWENTY

"How long are we going to keep up this pigeon shoot?" Nan demanded once they were all gathered around the table. Artie sat at the head, Jamie and Nate along the sides with some of the others. Luke leaned against the bar, and Pierre Jolie stood behind Jamie while Nan paced, gesturing.

"This isn't like before, during the war. Then we knew what to expect; war parties and the Brits were up and down the creeks, and we knew they were coming. This is a war of nerves. It has been over a month with no word from Welling and the authorities, and two attempts at Artie." Nan wasn't positive they were both aimed at Artie, but she suspected they were. The shooter waited until she came out, knowing he'd chase after her like she was the bear bait. It had been stupid, and she felt like a fool.

"It sounded like Welling knew where the Sullivans were and they could swagger on in and nab them," Jamie muttered.

"It did to me, too," Nan murmured. "Doesn't seem like they did, and the Sullivans plan to shut Artie up for good before Welling gets off his arse to stop them."

"Our shooter or shooters have been hired hands," Artie agreed. "I'd bet my whole estate the Sullivans are parading around Smithland believing they are untouchable."

His "estate?" She shuddered to think what that might mean.

"Smithland's in Kentuck," Nate said. "Welling won't have the authority to arrest them there."

Luke snorted. "If he has backbone, he'll send men across to drag them into Illinois and arrest them."

"I don't entirely understand your jurisdictional boundaries," Artie said. "But he more likely stationed people to watch for them if they decided to cross. The warrant is in Illinois. The Sullivan brothers are smart enough to stay where they are and assume the law can't touch them. Nan is right, though. Waiting here with a target on my back is worse than useless. It's fraying everyone's nerves, and putting all of Cape Girardeau in danger."

He rose to his feet and stretched, muscles rippling across his back and shoulders. When he pulled himself to his full height, Nan's breath held. His face was set like flint, and the air of command he'd assumed after Kaskaskia settled over him, drawing all eyes. "If Welling won't bring them in, I'll have to."

Nan believed him. He would try it. "Not alone."

"We don't know for sure they're in Smithland," Luke said, rubbing the stubble on his chin.

"You can't attack them there anyway. They'd be surrounded by miscreants happy to do their bidding," Artie said. "Better I go alone."

"Right idea, wrong conclusion. We can't march in with your little army, that's true, but a man alone might slip in," Luke said. "Come at that cesspool of a town from the land side. A man who knows the land that is. That ain't you."

"We'd need good scouting. Maybe we could catch them at Cave-in-Rock or somewhere less full of bully-boys," Jamie suggested.

Luke frowned.

"What are you thinking, Archer?" Artie said.

"I'm thinking Jamie's right. I can go downriver and up the Ohio as far as maybe Elizabethtown. There's likely talk at McFarlan's Tavern there," Luke said. He met Artie's eyes and held. "You can't do those things. You're a tougher man than I gave you credit for, but you don't know the land, the river, or the kind of people you'd meet. I do. You sit tight and keep this bunch organized."

"And if you find them?" Artie demanded.

"One person won't be enough. Not if you have to bring 'em from Kentuck," Nan said. Artie's flash of gratitude warmed her. "Come back, and we'll decide from there. We can handle the pot shooters they send here."

Artie let out a breath and hung his head for a moment before looking Luke in the eyes. "I agree, but if you aren't back in two weeks, I'm going to Kaskaskia to confront Welling."

"Who'll guard Nan then?" Luke demanded.

Artie must have read her mind, because he spoke her thoughts. "She'll be with me," he said, his fierce gaze daring her brother to argue.

Jamie broke the tension in the room. "And I'll be guarding Nan from Artie."

Nan through up her hands in disgust. "I don't need a chaperone."

Luke saw it differently. "I'll be back in two weeks," he said, pushing away from the bar. "Help me pack."

WORD CAME FROM Kaskaskia before Phillip was forced to act. It did not come soon enough. Messages arrived on the day of the fires, four days after Luke left.

Nate saw fires start in the yard from the upstairs window, but Phillip ordered them all to sit tight, to let the shed and the ice house burn and increase their vigilance. He struggled to keep Nan from bolting out when the wood housing around the well burned.

"We can rebuild it over the hole as long as the villains didn't foul the water," he shouted, restraining her with an arm around her waist until she nodded in agreement.

Before they could formulate a plan, the smell of smoke increased. Smoke filled the top floor and filtered down the steps. The two Cape Girardeau men standing guard at the windows ran down to the public room, shouting "Fire on the roof!"

Archers' Roost, at heart a log structure with a wood shakes roof, was vulnerable; the interior, all wood, would go up easily. There was no choice; they had to get out.

"Do we know where they are?" Jamie asked, leaning his back on the front door. "I've seen no movement."

Phillip peered around at the anxious faces. "Whoever set the fires was out back, but we don't know where they are now."

"You think there's more than one?" Nate asked.

"Whoever they were, they mean to pick us off if we run out," Jolie said.

"We need to get the fire out!" Nan cast anxious glances upward.

A loud crash Phillip believed was the sound of roof beams falling into the upstairs put a period on that idea. "Too late for that. We have to get out."

Whoever started the fire could be anywhere, but he decided to gamble the attackers were still out back.

"We'll divide into four groups. Jamie, you and Nan go out the front and run left. Nate, follow them, but run right. The rest of us will divide into two groups and do the same out back. It's me they want. I'll go out first."

Pierre handed Nan a musket from behind the bar. The others were already armed.

"Nate, wait." Phillip reached behind the log holder by the hearth and pulled out a lethal-looking axe. "You're going toward the boat launch. Make certain any craft moored there is useless," he said, handing the boy the axe.

"You take my pistol then, Artie. You're more likely to meet them close up."

The courage and trust on Nate's face, humbled him when they traded weapons. Nate put the axe at his waist and hefted the musket. Phillip touched the knife at his belt to reassure himself.

Nan appeared ready to argue, and it was all he could do to keep from kissing her senseless, the daft woman. Phillip nodded at Jamie, who took Nan's arm. The sound of crackling fire from above and increased billowing of smoke down the stairs gave them all a burst of urgency. They did as Phillip ordered.

The Cape Girardeau contingent had already moved into the kitchen, and they all needed to run. He pushed the kitchen door open and threw out a chair. No gunfire. Either they'd moved or weren't fooled. "Now!" he shouted.

Phillip ran toward the village path above the briars, toward where they'd found the shooter last time. Behind him, the others scattered. He made it to the shelter of the briar patch and hunkered down, looking back to see flames billowing out of the roof of Archers' Roost. How Nan must feel at such a sight tore at his heart, but he had no time to think about it.

He crept around the thickest briars and onto the path Luke had shown him when they caught the shooter. Every sense alert to sound or movement, he walked slowly toward the previous spot only to come on a clearing further back, one with the remains of a campfire. He stooped down to feel the coals and found them recently doused but still warm.

Luke's tracking skills would have been a blessing now, Phillip thought as he combed the circle for some sign of their direction and found nothing.

Fearing the arsonists might have guessed they'd come out the front where he'd sent Nan, he started in that direction. The sound of gunshots sent him rushing through the undergrowth, pushing branches and bushes aside with his free hand, pistol gripped tightly in the other. Twigs and thorns lashed his arms and cheek. At the sound of a scuffle, he crouched down.

"Let her go!" Jamie's voice.

"Tell that eastern fancy pants to come get her," a deeper voice growled. "So I can do him like I done you. Only I'll shoot for the heart when I do."

"You already fired your musket. How are you going to…" Jamie's voice faded, weakening. *What has the dastard done to him?*

Phillip crawled close enough to see through the brush; the sight chilled him. Jamie lay on the ground bleeding, his weapon next to him, likely fired in the confrontation and useless now until it could be reloaded.

The man who shot him gripped Nan around her waist, a long, lethal-looking knife at her throat. Phillip recognized the pond scum as one of the men who'd beaten him.

Primitive rage overtook his fear, and the world around took on a red haze. The monster threatened Nan. For the first time in his pampered life, the desire to kill a man took over.

"Got a pistol in my belt, don't I? Ain't fired that one," the brute growled, dragging Nan toward her brother and giving Jamie a kick where he lay.

Phillip struggled for control. The beast held Nan in the way of a clear shot at the man. Phillip could only force himself to wait for his chance.

"Damned weak puppy done fainted—or died. We'll have to wait for your fancy man. We'll jist wait here til Davey rounds up t'others and brings 'im." An ugly grin split the monster's face. "Mebbe I'll have some fun while we wait. Pat said to use you as bait, but he never said I couldn't have fun doing it," he said, bringing up his hand to squeeze one breast, the knife at her throat never wavering.

Phillip swallowed hard, desperate for something to distract the animal, to make him turn. Icy resolve replaced his burning fury, and the solution came to him in a flash. He drew his knife, ten inches long and honed to a fine edge, from his sheath with his left hand and aimed the pistol with his right. He didn't dare aim close to Nan; he pointed the pistol toward the brute's left shoulder, close enough to feel, but far enough from the woman he held. Phillip would only have a second. He rose to his feet and aimed again before he was seen.

The shot flew left and the man swung that way. At that same

moment, Phillip tossed his knife to his right hand and threw it as he'd been taught, hitting the attacker in one side of his neck, imbedding it so deep the tip came out the other side. The fool grabbed for it in a panic, dropping Nan. His hand reached the handle and gave it a yank that only pulled the blade sideways, cutting through skin and sinew. Blood spurted from a severed artery as he fell, the knife still imbedded cockeyed in his neck.

Phillip spared him the least glance. He leapt over the brush to pull Nan into his arms. The kiss he gave her held back neither his relief nor the passion he'd struggled to keep in check these weeks, plundering her mouth with his while he gripped the back of her head and pulled her possessively against him. "Thank God," he murmured at last, breathing hard. "I thought I'd lost you."

She pushed a hand against his chest. "Jamie!" she cried, falling to her brother's side.

"He's alive," Phillip murmured, checking for a pulse, "but bleeding heavily."

Nan was already standing and yanking up her skirt to reveal a cotton petticoat. Phillip looked away while she pulled off the petticoat and tore it. She pressed a wad of cotton to her brother's side. "Looks like it came out the back. Pray he didn't hit a vital organ," she said.

"There is at least one more of them," Phillip whispered.

"I know. Do what you need to do," she said without looking up from Jamie.

Phillip went over and pulled out his knife from their tormentor, wiping it clean on the man's shirt and stuffing it in his sheath. He stared down at the swine's remains, shocked at his own lack of remorse, but there was no time to consider it.

The ugly-looking pistol at the man's waist was indeed primed and loaded. Beat up as it was, Phillip doubted its reliability, but stuffed it in his sash anyway. The man's pouch held powder and shot. Phillip used it to reload Jamie's musket, the one their attacker had fired, and the pistol Nate lent him. He set Nate's pistol next to Nan.

"He took the gun I had. It's in the brush over there. I fired it. I would swear either Jamie or I hit him, but either he has the skin of a gator or he has tin under his shirt," she said.

"Tin, I think. I felt it." Phillip cupped her cheek and forced her face toward his. "Are you truly well? There's blood—"

"His. I'm perfectly fine." The shaking in her hand put that to a lie, but he did her the respect of not mentioning it.

"I'm sorry that happened to you. Sorry you had to see what I did."

She smiled tremulously. "That was quite a throw. Luke will be impressed," she said.

The sound of guns on the other side of the Roost drew both their gazes. "It sounds like they got the other one," Nan said.

"Or he got them. Are we sure there was only one more?" Phillip asked.

"It sounded like it, but…" She shook her head.

Noise along the lane closer to the river alerted them, someone rushing through the brush. Nan reached for Nate's pistol, and Phillip drew her to her feet, pushing her behind him and holding Jamie's musket in front of him.

"Who goes there?" he shouted.

"The law," a voice called back.

Nan moved to Phillip's side, but both kept their weapons at the ready.

Two men came through the undergrowth, weapons pointed directly at them. Phillip held his breath.

"That you, Miss Archer? We come with a message for you from Josiah Welling." The young man glanced around the clearing and shook his head. "Came at an interesting time. I'm constable Johnny Carter. This is Constable Smithers. Welling sent us to tell you he got 'em. The Sullivans are in custody."

"Thank the good Lord," Nan sighed, dropping her gun and sagging against Phillip.

"Don't faint on me now," he said.

"I never faint," she retorted, and she proved it by ordering the constables to help move her brother.

THEY BURIED THE Sullivans' hired killers above town next to a rubbish pit. Artie's grim face made Nan fear he had regrets. He shouldn't; when he flung that knife, he saved her life.

Jolie had taken down the second attacker, the one called Davey. Another man glanced at the mutilated throat of the man Artie killed. "I've seen that one in McFarlan's Tavern in Elizabethtown. Goes by "Bear."

Artie identified them both as the Sullivans' creatures, the ones who had beaten him.

"Welling'll be delighted to hear that bit, I can tell you. He'll get the Sullivans on attempted murder or worse," Carter had said, glancing at Jamie.

Murder or worse? Violence and destruction. Will it never end?

After burying the vermin, they gathered on the lawn in front of what was left of Archers' Roost. Jamie lay out a blanket that smelled of smoke, one they had recovered from the house. Once she stopped the bleeding, he stabilized, but she feared for him. Nate had cuts on his cheek—from running through the woods, he said. So did Artie. Jolie's apprentice took a shot in his arm. She tended to their wounds as best she could from what she retrieved from the ruins of the kitchen.

Tending wounds and dealing with the dead distracted her for a while. Now, nothing kept her from facing the wreck of her life's work and dreams. Archers' Roost had been Nan's place in the world, her freedom from her autocratic father, her home, her independence, her peace. *Gone—all gone.*

Carter whistled low and slow, following her gaze to the smoldering ruins. "You can't live here for sure. Good thing Welling plans to put up the duke here in Kaskaskia."

"We'll see about that. I told you, Carter. I go where the Archers go," Artie said.

Nan never took her eyes from the wreck of the Roost, but the pain in her heart at his words sharpened. *He should go.*

"What will you do now?" Artie's question came from behind her left shoulder and his breath warmed the side of her head.

She squelched the instinct to throw herself into his arms and beg him to take care of everything, but Nan Archer was made of sterner stuff. "See what we can salvage. Tear it down and start over." *We've done it before. Built something up from nothing. We'll do it again, when Artie—Phillip—Tavernash—has taken care of the Sullivans and left.*

They'd even sort out the business with the farm. It was what Archers did. She stiffened her back and turned to look him in the eye. "Don't worry about me. I'll pick up the pieces and go on."

"I mean today. We need immediate plans."

His intense gaze made her knees weak. What was it? Pity? Respect? Other things she didn't want to consider at that moment. She feared he might kiss her again. Right on the lawn in front of everyone. Her body still throbbed from the one in the woods. She took a step away and wiped her hands together. "Find a place to sleep; I have to get Jamie under cover and warm."

Neighbors, the loyal band that had stayed, offered Nate, Jamie, and Nan shelter at least for a bit.

"Welling says the duke needs to be under guard until the trial is over and the Sullivans are done," Carter insisted.

"We could have used protection a month ago, constable," Artie spat.

Carter had the grace to appear shamed. "Can't be helped now, sir," he said.

"Those vermin aren't above using Miss Archer as bait. She needs protection more than I do. As I said, I go where the Archers go." He stared the constable down and turned to Nan. "Can Jamie make it across the river?"

She tipped her head and considered the matter. A decision as rash as it was unexpected took over. "If we bundle him warmly and keep him still—and if we act quickly." She glanced at Carter.

"We're coming, constable, as soon as I fetch a few things. Welling will have to deal with all of us."

She glanced back at the Roost, and felt Artie give her a side-arm hug. "We'll come back. We'll face it then," he murmured.

She pulled away, but she let him help her retrieve her stash of coin from under the kitchen floor. They packed what little they could salvage and were on their way lit with lanterns in the fading light. Nan turned her face to the river and a future as murky as its waters and as cloudy as the smoke from Archers' Roost.

CHAPTER TWENTY-ONE

FOLKS BEGAN TO gather three days before the trial, and Kaskaskia, Illinois's new state capital, was crowded to its rooftops. Some folks camped outside of town in spite of the cold weather.

Phillip could see the swelling crowds on the street beneath his window in a hastily constructed hotel. He paced the room in which he'd been confined, for—he was told—his own good. Welling didn't want to lose his prime witness. Armed deputies took shifts in the hallway between his room and Nan's. Earlier in the week, they'd gone to look in on Jamie, well-armed and accompanied by their guard. Nan's brother had been housed with Doctor Bingham, a local physician, who assured her Jamie would recover. Nate had been assigned to stay and look after his needs.

The crowded streets made forays riskier, and Phillip had been inside for two days. The boredom was as wretched as it had been under the siege. The only relief came from an interview with the prosecuting attorney that took the better part of one afternoon.

He welcomed a knock on the door—anything to relieve the silence. Carter's voice through it said, "The tailor's here with your gentleman suit."

At Welling's insistence—and apparent subsidy—a tailor had taken his measure the day they arrived. He was, he'd been informed, to appear respectable and not "like some scruffy river ruffian."

Phillip opened the door to let the man in. Across the hall, Nan stood at the door to her room, a book clutched to her lush chest. He could only smile with what he hoped was care and commiseration, keeping a tight leash on the temptation to ask her to join in the fitting, something sure to horrify the tailor and get back to Welling.

An hour later, he studied himself in coat, waistcoat, and a plain cravat reflected in the mirror while the little tailor hemmed his trousers. The ensemble would see him, if not barred from Whites, spoken about with sly comments and disparaging tones behind his back there. Two years before, he himself would have turned up his nose at it. Today, after four months in homespun shirt and cotton trousers held up by a remainder of rope, he stood a bit taller and felt more like himself.

He turned this way and that. Welling might be determined to turn the trial into high drama, but Phillip had to admit to the man's wisdom. He would impress a jury in this outfit, at least a jury on the fringe of civilization. A random thought made him grin at himself. Where would he carry his knife in this suit?

By the time the tailor tucked the suit, pressed and ready, into the tiny closet shrouded in cotton against the persistent dust of Kaskaskia, Phillip had enough.

He watched the tailor on his way out and turned to Carter. "When you bring Miss Archer's supper, bring it—and yours too—in. We'll eat together for once."

The constable appeared conflicted, as if unsure what to think, but in the end, he agreed. Phillip went back in to tidy up.

His Grace of Glenmoor plans to entertain, he thought with a rueful grin.

DINNER WITH ARTIE, even overcooked hotel food, was a joy. Far better than eating alone, Nan thought. Even if they had to put up with Carter. At least, she enjoyed it until Carter said something positively stupid.

"So tomorrow it is," Carter said. "The big show."

"Is that all this trial is? Some sort of traveling stage show, with jugglers and a trained dog?" Nan shook with enough outrage to make the rickety table wobble. "People died. People were beaten, cheated…"

Carter held up a hand to stem the flood of words. "I—"

"I hope you're wrong, but it does feel like some sort of provincial playhouse fare, with me as the trained dog. I'll be glad when it's over." Artie frowned into his soup.

"Don't get me wrong. It's the biggest trial in state history," Carter said.

Nan glared at him, her eyes narrowed at that bit of nonsense. Illinois had been a state for two months.

Carter went on without noticing, since he addressed his words to Artie as if she were not of any account. He sat back and put his thumbs in his belt. "We mean to clean up this country. There's no room in a proper state for the kind of no-goods who prey on honest folks. We plan to drive them all out. The Sullivans? Welling means to see them hang with your help."

"I will testify. I stayed nearby in spite of great danger to myself and Miss Archer's entire family, as you well know. This trial is no comedy. Justice will be done, one way or another."

Nan met his eyes, stunned by their fury and his grim words. *He means to take the law into his own hands if the so-called authorities fail. Luke would be impressed.* He'd said it before. This time, she believed him.

"None of that. We won't tolerate mob justice. We have laws and—" Carter said, looking from one to the other.

"Constable, in England, a man who put violent hands on a duke would be summarily hung. He could find himself transported to the antipodes for much less. I don't plan to tolerate any less punishment here in your so-called civilized state." Artie glanced at Nan. "Not for the attacks on me nor for what was done to Miss Archer and her property. You may tell Welling that."

Dinner had ended, and it appeared the conversation had too. "We'll see you in the morning, dook. You'll see. We'll do right," Carter said, opening the door.

He held it for Nan, but she lingered, studying Artie, a smile lurking at the edge of her mouth. "Summarily hung?"

"After a trial," he said without returning her amusement. "But hung. Yes. And you deserve no less justice."

It sounded bloodthirsty, but she thought something else lay behind it—the need to protect with whatever power he could bring to bear. He stood and took her hand when she rose, bowing over it as if she were a fine lady. Artie, her employee, the man who owed her money for room and board, had been transformed into something utterly foreign—a duke, a man of power and authority from far away. She'd been trying to ignore it, but here it was in front of her.

Worse, all doubt left her. If she hadn't before, she'd tumbled totally in love the moment he sent his knife flying and leapt over the brush to take her in his arms. She loved this man, and there wasn't a damned thing she could do about it.

She retrieved her hand, smiled at him sadly, and swept past Carter. Tomorrow, the trial, drama or not, would begin. They'd deal with the Sullivan threat, and then he would leave. Tears pricked her eyes, but she refused to let them fall.

CHAPTER TWENTY-TWO

PHILLIP WASHED, SHAVED, and dressed with more care than he had in months. He'd even polished his nails, ragged from hard work. He could do nothing about the calluses. Peering at himself in the glass, he gave his waistcoat a tug and smoothed the well-tailored coat. *Not bad.* He was glad Welling had sent a barber up, too. A skilled trim tamed his unruly hair into some semblance of his normal self.

A vague sense of unease had him patting his inside pocket to find it empty. *Not quite normal.* He had no calling cards, no wallet, no money, and, he remembered, no signet ring. Of the four, the ring could be had.

He went to the door and found Carter and another deputy waiting. He paid them no mind. The sight across the hall fixated him—Nan studying him in wide-eyed amazement. Of course she was. She'd seen him in rags more than she'd ever seen him in a suit—which was exactly never. He drew breath, but no words came out.

"You—You cut your hair," she murmured, her eyes tracking him from his hair to the pair of new boots on his feet. He hated those boots. He hated the look on her face.

"I'll need my ring, Nan," he said.

She reached under her collar and pulled on the ribbon around her neck. His eyes dropped to her chest where his ring nestled against her bosom. He blinked with a sudden realization and forced himself to take a good look.

While he stood there in his new finery, Nan still wore the skirt she wore the day the tavern burned down, washed now but still grayed from the smoke. She wore a new blouse, a simple blue one with little trim. She had few enough coins; she wouldn't waste them on clothing. He longed to give her silk and lace, but suit or no suit, he was, for all intents and purposes, penniless. Never in his entire life had he felt so powerless. Not even the day the Sullivans got him. She deserved more, and he couldn't give it to her.

She handed him his ring, still warm from her body and still on a red ribbon. She wouldn't meet his eyes; he wasn't sure he could meet hers anyway. He untied the ribbon and stuffed it in his coat pocket.

He began to put the ring where it belonged. "Damn!"

She glanced up then and saw him trying to put the ring on his left ring finger. "You'll have to wear it on the smallest finger," she murmured.

He put it there and then fisted his fingers to keep it in place.

"When you get to London, you can have it fixed," she said, turning to Carter. "Are we ready?"

His instinct was to offer his arm as a gentleman should. She didn't wait, but then they'd never walked arm-in-arm. A seed of misery took root in his belly, one he had no time to examine. The Sullivan trial awaited.

The courtroom resounded with conversation as people crowded in, eager to see the trial. Welling, who would prosecute the case, stood at a table in the front. Nan disappeared into the mass of people. Carter joined men Phillip recognized as deputies in closing the door before standing against it.

As Phillip walked to the front, he recognized the Sullivan brothers. The men who ordered him beaten, the men who took his clothes, his money, and his very identity, sat at a table to the right of Welling's, smirking and laughing with jurors. Rage best left in check rose in Phillip. He clamped his jaw shut against it.

Welling studied him momentarily and pronounced him fit. "You will do, Yer Grace," he said. "Ignore those two and act confident." There was no time for additional conversation when a bailiff called for silence and a black-robed judge emerged. Clifford Manley, Phillip had been told, was a longtime attorney in the territory.

A hammer of a gavel brought silence, and Phillip found the process more orderly than some he'd witnessed in England. "A jury of citizens has been seated. Does either counsel have cause to challenge the make up?"

The man for the defense asked a few jurors questions about whether they ever had "dealings" with the accused. He appeared to be looking for possible victims of the Sullivans' perfidy. He didn't find any.

Welling rose and walked to the jury, searching faces. "You there," he said, pointing to a man sunk down in his seat in back, "stand up." The man did as he was told, his gaze shifting around the room. "Where do you live?"

"Prairie Roché," he muttered.

"Does not!" Someone in the back of the room shouted it out. "I'm from there. Saw that one once when I was down at the tavern in Elizabethtown. He and some rough types were on their way home—on the Kentucky side. River rat, that one."

Welling respectfully asked that the juror be removed. He was replaced by a respectable citizen of the newly-minted state of Illinois in short order.

"Get on with it Welling," the judge said impatiently.

Welling complied by laying out the charges: theft, cheating the good people of Illinois out of their property, extortion, intimidation, assault, kidnapping, attempted murder, murder.

"Plan to prove all that, do you? We'll be here a week," some-one shouted.

The judge called for order. "What do you have to say, Goodman?"

The Sullivan brothers' attorney rose. "My clients are respectable businessmen; they did none of it." An undercurrent of snickering from the observers greeted that announcement.

"Call your witnesses, Welling," the judge said.

As he had warned Phillip, Welling had two additional witnesses; he planned to save Phillip for last. One was a farmer the criminals had attempted to swindle. One was a man who'd observed intimidation and violence in a tavern by the river. "On the Illinois side," he swore. Goodman, the attorney for the defense, challenged both, pointing out hearsay and inconsistencies, leaving Phillip dissatisfied, but Welling unruffled.

After a break for lunch, in which Phillip was hustled to a room in the courthouse where Nan was escorted soon after. "You needn't worry, Yer Grace. The lady is under our protection. You just tell the whole story." Welling used the time to repeat his earlier admonitions about testifying, leaving Phillip frustrated. He only wanted to be with Nan.

The break ended quickly, and then it was Phillip's turn. He rose and went to the witness chair, feeling the eyes of a hundred people boring into him, and swore to tell the truth.

"Kindly state your full name for the jury," Welling said.

Phillip, standing tall, raised his chin, and recited the familiar words. "Phillip Roland George Arthur Tavernash, Sixth Duke of Glenmoor, Earl of Wentworth, Viscount Gradington, Baron Walsh," he pronounced.

⊱⟫⟫⟫⟪⟪⟪⊰

NAN WIGGLED ON the hardwood chair at the back of the room to get a clear view of Artie—Phillip—the duke—sitting in the witness chair in his finery. When they asked his name, his answer drew gasps and a few laughs. She might have laughed once, Luke certainly had, but no more. Not since he took command during the siege. She'd always known he didn't belong in her world, and never was that more obvious than today. Pride in the man she knew warred with grief that her "Artie" was slipping away. Yet, she found herself determined to keep him simply Artie, at least in her own mind, as long as she could.

"And would you tell us your place of residence?" Welling asked.

"My home is Woodglen, an estate in Dorset, England. I currently reside at Archers' Roost in Cape Girardeau, Missouri."

Temporarily… Nan blinked back wetness and listened.

"Can you describe your journey here?"

Artie's voice never wavered. He described his route, his departure from Pittsburgh, and his encounter with a stranger in Mount Vernon, Indiana.

"Do you recognize the man who called himself Carpenter?" Welling asked.

"He is sitting at that table behind you," Artie said firmly. "The one to the right of the attorney."

"The jury will note that the witness has pointed out Patrick Sullivan," Welling intoned. Nan was glad she could only see the back of Pat Sullivan's head because some jurors who turned to peer at him quickly looked away, squirming. She had no desire to gaze into the face of evil.

Welling went on relentlessly, coaching Artie through his story, with the defense attorney objecting periodically to verify the location and the court's jurisdiction. Artie didn't waver in his answers, and he spared neither his dignity nor the sensibilities of listeners, describing the betrayal, the beatings, the broken fingers, and the pressure brought to bear to sign over his land grant—all of the ugliness the vicious rats in front of him caused. When questioned about the arrival of the counterfeiter, he pointed out Michael Sullivan without hesitation.

Goodman objected when Phillip concluded that he had been left for dead. "How do you know the intent was for you to die?"

"I was stabbed and thrown into the Mississippi unconscious." That reply drew uproarious laughter from the jury and the people who had gathered to watch. Even Nan laughed—attempted murder was obvious to any sensible person. The judge had to gavel for order.

"If you were unconscious, how do you know?" the lawyer shouted over the uproar. "Can anyone verify that?"

"Luke Archer," Artie said. "Or Miss Nan Archer. They are the reason I'm alive."

The damned attorney scribbled that down. Nan feared she'd be forced to testify.

The judge called a recess to settle people down, and Nan tried to make it through the crowd to Artie. She was waylaid by someone she didn't expect. A woman she recognized as someone working in Doctor Bingham's house.

"Is everything well with my brother?" Nan asked without preamble.

"I'm not the one to say, miss, but that young one and the doc said as how you should come."

Nan didn't wait. Jamie needed her, and Artie could handle himself. She wiggled through the crowd to the door without waiting for a constable and ran down the street.

She was halfway there when she was dragged from her feet and a dirty hand covered her mouth. No amount of kicking and attempts to bite freed her. Another pair of hands fastened a gag around her mouth and tossed a bag over her head to blind her. Sometime later, she was tossed to the ground, her head was freed, and she found herself alone, locked in a room as dark as it had been inside the foul-smelling bag. She lay on a cold stone floor and tried to think calmly.

Whoever took her meant for her to live or they'd have killed her outright. The Sullivans might be on trial, but she had no doubt that they were behind it. Instead of bear bait, she was being used to trap Artie—or to buy the criminals' escape, though she couldn't figure out how. Welling wouldn't let them go. She forced her breathing to slow down. Luke would find her; he always got her out of scrapes. Even more certainly, Artie would. Patrick and Michael Sullivan were dead men.

She hoped.

CHAPTER TWENTY-THREE

PHILLIP SCANNED THE crowd for Nan when he followed the bailiff back in. She hadn't joined him during the brief recess, and he needed to see her, just to gaze on her face before the whole circus started up again.

She must be somewhere in this sea of people! His brow furrowed when he didn't see her, but he told himself not to be a fool. She probably met someone she knew. The court demanded his attention, and soon enough, he was back on the stand testifying about Welling's laundry list of charges.

They began with his signet ring, which was passed from hand to hand by the jury while Phillip described how it was taken and how it was found.

"And you are certain this ring is the same one?" Welling asked.

"Most certainly. It was custom made in Paris by a superior gem cutter."

"Yes, the amethyst is inscribed. Can you explain the design?" Welling prodded.

Phillip described his family coat of arms, including the fox over trees on the ring. "The fox is a traditional symbol of intelligence. My father particularly liked identifying with the sly beast. It can also mean a refusal to be captured. I never appreciated that before. Lately I do." He glared at the prisoners while a ripple of chuckles circled the room.

"And the trees?"

Phillip shrugged. "Symbols of strength." *I undervalued that until lately, too. Nan. Nan is an example of strength.*

"Why three?"

"My great-grandfather designed the badge. I'm not sure what point he was making, but he did nothing halfway."

Goodman stood. "Are you positive this ring was taken from you? Is it possible you merely lost it?"

Phillip held up his left hand while his anger held by a thread. "My two middle fingers were broken when it was taken. Patrick Sullivan ordered it done. I'm lucky they didn't cut it off." He glared at the prisoners.

Welling took over again. "And how did you find it?"

Phillip told them about Luke Archer finding it on Gordy, who was given it by Michael Sullivan. Again, Goodman objected. "Hearsay! Where is this 'Gordy?'"

Welling acknowledged the point and went on, prodding Phillip to describe the snipers and attempts on Phillip's life, concluding with the horror of Baptiste's death.

Goodman rose to his feet again, shouting objection. "Can you prove any connection between some roving criminals and Michael or Patrick Sullivan?" he demanded.

"None I can prove," Phillip muttered.

"Is there a point to all these stories if you've no proof, Welling?" the judge asked.

The prosecutor addressed the judge formally. "We're establishing a pattern of intimidation and terror, your honor. I'll get to proof. You can be sure of that." He tossed a formal glance at the Sullivans.

While Welling was talking, a furtive little man Phillip didn't recognize handed the deputies a message. It was given to Goodman, who passed it to Patrick Sullivan, raising Phillip's sense of menace in the air.

Welling ignored the byplay. He rocked back on his heals and

announced, "We come finally to the fire at Archers' Roost. Please describe it."

Phillip did, but feared he couldn't possibly imbue his words with sufficient sense of the terror of that day.

"You were lucky to escape it," Welling said.

Phillip merely nodded.

"Did you discover who set it?" Welling asked.

"We found them."

"Where are they now?"

"Dead." Phillip couldn't entirely keep the satisfaction from his voice. Silence greeted his pronouncement, and Welling paused to let it sink in.

"But you recognized them?" Welling asked, never taking his eyes from Phillip.

"The one called Davey and the one called Bear. I could never forget either one. They were the same two men who beat me and left me in the river. The ones who were with the Sullivan brothers that day."

"And what did you hear this one called 'Bear' say?"

"That he'd been ordered to kill me. That he'd been ordered to use Miss Archer as bait to lure me out," Phillip said, his bile rising at the memory.

"And who did he say ordered him to do it?"

"Pat."

Goodman was on his feet in an instant. "Did he specify which 'Pat' that was."

Phillip glared right back. "He didn't have to. I knew exactly who he meant because I heard him say 'Pat' the day they assaulted me."

Welling rested his case. Goodman asked Phillip a few questions, prodding for examples of hearsay or mistaken identify. He called no witnesses. As a defense, it was an oddly lame attempt, and it made Phillip distinctly uneasy.

The judge addressed Phillip formally, and to his surprise, correctly. "Your Grace, do you have any doubt these two men were behind the shootings and killing before the fire?"

"None whatsoever."

The judge gave a firm nod and turned to the jury foreman.

"Barry, it is all yours; any questions?"

"Does arson constitute attempted murder?" Barry asked.

"That's for you to decide," the judge said impatiently. "You come back and tell us what the law requires."

As the jury filed out, exhaustion piled on top of Phillip's tension. He needed to share what had just happened with the one person who mattered. *Where the devil is Nan?*

Welling clapped him on the back and told him he'd sent out for a bottle of rum while they waited in his office. He shrugged off Phillip's unease. "She'll turn up. May have all been too much for a lady, retelling all those bad stories."

They didn't have to wait long. The jury, grim-faced to a man, filtered in. None of them looked at the Sullivan brothers; Phillip didn't know if that boded well or ill.

"Do you have a verdict?" the judge asked.

"Guilty," the foreman said. "Of murder and the rest. Stealing from honest citizens. All of it."

The courtroom exploded with applause, laughter, and arguments. Mike Sullivan surged to his feet and spittle flew as he yelled. "You damned fools. You'll regret this."

The judge commanded deputies to subdue the prisoner and called for order, but it took some time. All the while, Pat Sullivan sat quietly, sneering at Phillip, his eyes hard.

Mike Sullivan sat, but he tossed off the hand of the deputy who tried to hold his shoulder. A few more boisterous people were tossed out, but they established order eventually.

The judge set down his gavel and addressed the accused. "Stand, the both of you." They did, Mike with a nasty glower that would have curdled milk. "Michael and Patrick Sullivan, I remand you to the county jail for three days, at which time you will be taken to the statehouse square and hung by the neck until you are dead. This court is adjourned."

"All rise," the bailiff shouted as the judge stomped out, and the jury members rushed out, still not meeting the eyes of the men they had condemned.

The sneer never left Pat Sullivan's face. "We'll see about this, Welling," he said. "It ain't over."

Phillip's stomach clenched. He had to find Nan. He'd only taken a few steps when Welling called, "Ignore them. It is over. They'll swing in three days."

Running down the courthouse steps, Phillip ran straight into Luke Archer.

"Artie! Thank the Almighty. I came as soon as I heard they caught them. What the hell happened at Archers' Roost? Why are you all suited up? And where's my sister?"

⋙⋘

MUFFLED SOUNDS ON the other side of the door brought Nan to her feet. She had no idea how long she'd been locked in. She'd stopped thinking of it as a room. She could reach the walls from side to side in all directions. It was a hole, a fruit cellar, she suspected, empty but still smelling vaguely of rotten potatoes. The floor was damp and even sticky in spots.

She ought to fear what was outside, but what worried her most was whether the thick door let in enough air. It already felt stuffy. If it opened, she could at least breathe deeply. As it started to move, she took a step back and came up against a wall. A lantern blinded her; she could hear but not see.

"Did he say a finger, Marty?" The rough voice sounded uncertain.

"Said that or something so's they'd know we have her." The other voice was firmer.

A finger? Dear God! She tried to calm her mind, frantic to think of something to offer them—anything—so they spared her hands.

"Who wants proof you have me? What for?" she demanded.

Laughter met that. They raised the lantern to her face, blinding her further. "You din't hear, did you? Trial's over. Fools think they can hold Pat and Mike Sullivan for hanging. Won't happen. You're the insurance. If Welling won't let 'em go, that man of yours has to take back his testimony. Tell 'em it was all a lie."

Would Phillip do such a thing? Terror warred with determination to see the Sullivans pay.

"It won't work. Welling wants them dead and the duke doesn't give a fig about me. His precious pride won't let him take it all back," she said. "You'll end up dead along with them if you do this."

"Do you think—" the one called Marty began.

"Don't be a damned fool. Nobody messes with Mike and Pat Sullivan without paying for it. Don't listen to 'er. She's just a female anyhow. What does she know?"

I know more than these two idiots. She stiffened her shoulders. Her mind was her only weapon. "If you let me suffocate, what will you use as a hostage?"

"Suffiwhat?" Marty said.

"I can't breathe in here. Can't you keep me someplace better?"

They pulled the lantern back and she could just make out two dark figures in a dim room. A hurried discussion occurred in incomprehensible whispers.

The taller one grabbed her arm and pulled her out. "If you cause trouble or try to run, we'll have you back in there," he said. Not Marty, this one.

"What is your name?" she demanded.

"None of your business, woman. Now get over here. We need to—" He had her to a table before she cut him off.

"Listen to me, None-of-your-business, before you get in trouble so deep you either hang or rot in prison for the rest of your worthless life," she said in the voice of command that always worked with unruly brothers.

He put the lantern on the table. "What do you mean? Pat

Sullivan said—"

In the circle of light, she could see she was in some sort of warehouse or work room. No light filtered in so she suspected it was night. She gave the man her fiercest frown.

"Pat Sullivan is a lying weasel who will toss you over in a heartbeat or kill you if it suits him. He's going to hang. Count on it. You cut off my finger and your life won't be worth spit for attacking a woman. Luke Archer will see you dead and that's a promise." *Only if he has to; if the law doesn't do it first.* She hoped that was true.

"I dunno Frank…" Marty said.

Frank! "All you need is proof you have me, right?"

The two fools nodded.

"Here's what you're going to do. Hand me a knife."

Marty started to hand it over. "Hey!" Frank shouted, taking the knife. "Are you crazy?"

"Fine. You do it." She lifted her skirt, pointed a dainty toe, and showed the edge of the cheap petticoat she bought with her new blouse. Her best one had tended Jamie's wounds. "Cut off a piece of that lace trim. It is my own special creation, and my brothers will recognize it right off."

Both men stared at her petticoat for a while before Frank shrugged, knelt down, and sliced a piece. "This enough?" he asked.

Bear and Davey's deaths must have left the Sullivans scraping the bottom of their barrel of minions to find these two dolts. They didn't even recognize plain eyelet from a general merchandise store.

"Good," she said. "Now this." She held up a lock of her hair. A small one. It wouldn't hurt to be sure. She grimaced when it came off with a yank. "Easy!"

The hair and trim lay on the table. Frank pulled a crumpled envelope from a dirty pocket. "He said to send it in this." She saw the writing on the front. *If you want to see Nan Archer alive, get Pat and Mike Sullivan out of jail and out of the state.*

"How did he get that to you?"

"Ha! Behind the back of the jail guards. I acted like I were going to be sick, and Pat, he handed it to Frank and told 'im what we had to do. Gave us a five-dollar gold piece and promised another one when they got loose." Marty clearly found this reason to be proud.

"So is one of you to take it to them now?" She tried to keep the hope from her question. If it was down to one—especially if it was Marty—she might get away.

"Not till morning," Frank replied.

Marty nodded. "Overnight gives them time to know yer gone and get real scared. More likely to cooperate that way.

Damn. Nan sighed dramatically, trying to project greater calm than she felt. "Is there tea or coffee to be had? And some food. I've been in there for hours. Do you want me to starve to death before you get your money?"

Frank sent Marty for coffee and biscuits.

Nan gave Frank her best displeased older sister glower. "Do you have any cards? It's going to be a long night."

$$\cdots \!\!\!\! \langle\!\!\!\langle \cdot \rangle\!\!\!\rangle \!\!\!\! \cdots$$

CHAPTER TWENTY-FOUR

STANDING ON THE courthouse steps, Luke glared at Phillip. People continued to file out, staring at the two of them wide-eyed. "What do you mean she disappeared?" Luke demanded.

"From the courtroom. She may not have wanted to hear us go over the fire and what happened after," Phillip said, running an agitated hand through his hair. He hoped he was correct. Something about it didn't sit right.

"The fire. Tell me you got the bastards that set it," Luke said.

"And the ones that sent them," Phillip answered, glancing back at the courtroom. "I'll tell you later. First let's find Nan. She needs to hear the Sullivan brothers were found as guilty as sin and will hang for it."

"When did you see her last?"

"There was a recess after a bit of an uproar. She disappeared into the crowd."

"Looking for your sister, Mr. Archer?" The familiar voice caused both men to swerve to face Father LaPlante.

"I saw her speaking to one of Doctor Bingham's servants. She left in a hurry looking worried. Is someone you know a patient of the good doctor?" the priest continued.

"Her brother Jamie," Phillip replied, glancing at Luke. "I hope his condition hasn't worsened." He didn't wait for Luke to reply.

Luke caught up with him in three steps and LaPlante bustled

along their side. "In case I am needed," he murmured.

"What happened to Jamie?" Luke asked as they hurried along.

"Shot. Sullivan's men." Phillip didn't pause.

"Slow down, Artie. Is there something you aren't telling me?"

"Nothing concrete," Phillip answered, climbing the steps to the surgery. "Something about Pat Sullivan made my skin crawl."

Bingham's manservant answered their knock, opening the door wide. "Mr. Artie! What news from the trial?"

Phillip, Luke, and LaPlante all entered the reception area.

"Is Miss Archer here?" Phillip demanded.

"Is my brother well?" Luke asked at the same time.

At the sound of voices, Nate came halfway down the stairs to their left. "What news, Artie? Did we win? And Luke! Jamie will be glad to see you both."

"Is Nan here?" Phillip demanded.

Nate's stunned reaction was his reply.

"Barker, did the médecin send Flora Downing to bring Miss Archer?" Father LaPlante, who knew Bingham's staff well, and who was thinking more clearly, asked.

"Flora? That one left at mid-day when that ruffian of a brother of hers turned up. Doctor Bingham is ready to dismiss her. Is there a problem?" the manservant asked.

People began talking at once, which brought Bingham out to investigate.

"Let's calm down and think," Phillip said. "Is there somewhere we can sit without disturbing your work, Bingham?"

As it turned out, the day had been slow. He suggested the reception room.

"Jamie will want to hear this," Nate pointed out.

Phillip looked at the doctor, but Luke interrupted. "No point in getting him riled up. He needs to stay down."

LaPlante, Bingham, and Barker, the manservant, all joined them.

"What do we know?" Phillip began ticking things off on his fingers. "First, Nan stayed for every moment of the trial until this afternoon's recess. She was gone when they called us back out."

"How long ago?" Luke asked.

"Three hours give or take. Second, the last person she was seen with was Flora Downing. We assume she was tricked into coming here, but is it possible the Downing woman needed help?"

No one had an answer for that.

"And third, neither has been seen since. It isn't much to go on."

"We also know Flora's worthless brother came to get her," Barker reminded them.

Luke was on his feet. "We can't sit here talking. Where will I find the brother?"

"I agree," Phillip said. "But let's follow all the leads. Barker, can you lead us to Flora's residence? Does her brother live there?"

"I can lead you to her place, but I don't know about the brother. Someone there may know."

"Luke, Barker, and I will go there. Nate, you're very sharp about detail. I want you to follow her probable route from here to the courthouse and back. If she thought she was coming here and was diverted, you may be able to find something."

Phillip glanced at the priest. "There is likely gossip and rumor out there. I suspect your flock may have access to what's being said. See if you hear anything—anything at all—that will help us. Bingham, would you question your employees? If they are fond of Flora, they may be reticent."

"Unlikely," Barker muttered, rising and fetching a coat.

"We'll meet back here at two hours if we can and compare notes," Phillip told them.

Flora Downing lived in a walk-up on the backside of a commercial building. When no one answered their knock, Luke forced the door. There was little enough to search.

Phillip gazed at the narrow bed in one corner of the single room that constituted Flora Downing's world. "I doubt the brother lives here," he murmured. They found no notes, none of

Nan's possessions, nothing to provide the tiniest clue. *All we learned is that Flora is miserably poor. And gone.*

As if he read Phillip's mind, Luke said, "Poverty makes people desperate, and desperation makes 'em dangerous."

The three men fanned out to question neighbors. The business on the street side, a tobacco shop, was closing when Phillip pushed the door open to prevent it from being locked. "Sorry. I'll only take a moment. Are you the owner?"

The man nodded warily.

"Do you know Flora Downing?" Phillip demanded.

"Rent to her, don't I? What's she done?"

"We don't know yet. Kidnapping perhaps. Perhaps more."

The man hissed his disgust. "Mixed with her damned brother again, I'll warrant. I warned her to stay away from him."

"Do you know where we can find him?"

"Good luck with that. I turned him off from here and told him not to come back," the proprietor said. "Lives hand-to-mouth. Try every tavern you find. He'll be in one of them, or on the street outside. Now, if you'll excuse me, I have dinner waiting."

"What is his name?" Phillip asked, holding the door open.

"Marty Downing. Skinny little fellow with long hair and shifty eyes." The man shooed Phillip out, locked his door, and left.

Neither Luke nor Barker had gotten any more from the neighbors. No one had seen Flora all day.

Marty Downing might be known in any tavern in town, but no one admitted to seeing him that day. They made an odd couple between Luke's dirty buckskins and fur hat, with his lanky stride, and Phillip in a businessman's suit, with his upper-class accent. They drew curious stares. Phillip found their partnership confounding as well. It may have kept some from coming forward.

Things were no better back at the surgery. None of their friends had found out more, though Nate did confirm that three people saw Nan with Flora Downing near the courthouse. After that, they both disappeared.

"We need more people searching," La Plante said, rising to leave. "I'll put out a call and meet you here tomorrow."

"Can you talk to Jamie, Nate? Bring him up to date?" Luke asked.

"I'll help him," Bingham put in.

"I'll tell him about the trial, too. Congratulations, Artie. I should have said sooner. You won." Nate grinned.

Phillip had almost forgotten. There's been little time for elation. "I'll see Welling first thing and be back here at nine," he said.

"Damned city," Luke complained on their way out. "If they had Nan in the woods, I'd have the vermin tracked down by now. This isn't my world."

City? It was no London. Or Nottingham. Or Weymouth come to that. "Are you saying it's my world? You're wrong there. I'm as lost here as you are. Let's backtrack to one of those taverns and talk."

Two pints of beer later, Phillip finished his tale about the day of the fire. Luke's eyebrows rose when he described Nan being held by Bear. "And thank you for teaching me to throw that knife, by the way."

Luke studied Phillip from his fashionably cropped hair, past his city suit, to his new boots. "In that outfit, I can't picture you toting a knife. Hell, I can't picture it at all. You took out his throat?" he choked.

"For my sins, yes. Miraculous shot. And I feel naked without it. I'll have it with me tomorrow, count on it. Let's see if Nate will give up the pistol. Will you come back to the hotel? You can probably have Nan's room."

"You still know nothing, do you? They aren't letting me into their fancy new hotel looking like this, and I have no way to clean up. I'll camp by the river. I left my canoe near the boat launch. I'll put my ear to the ground down there, too. I may pick up something. We'll start this up again tomorrow." Luke rose and shook Phillip's hand. "You're not at all what I thought you were," he said.

"I'm not who I thought I was either," Phillip said. *Now if I can just figure out who I am.*

Left alone as Luke disappeared into the shadows, fear almost choked Phillip. Nan was out in the darkness somewhere, alone and frightened. He tried to force the images away. *Things will look better tomorrow.*

When he reached the hotel, there were no longer deputies at the door to his room. He tried Nan's door, and found it cold, dark, and empty as he expected. His heart plummeted all the same. He couldn't bear the thought of losing her, he admitted to himself. That thought terrified him, because he didn't know what to do with it. He wanted Nan Archer, wanted her for life, but saw no way to make that happen, different as their lives were. *Want her? Hell, I love her.*

Tomorrow, Glenmoor. Face it tomorrow. He went to bed wondering why he'd called himself Glenmoor for the first time in weeks.

⁂

CHAPTER TWENTY-FIVE

WELLING FROWNED AT Phillip, who sauntered into his office in his loose trousers, colorful tunic-like shirt, and a wide French-style sash, his knife sheathed at his waist. Phillip's information didn't improve his expression. "Gone? What do you mean?"

"I mean no one has seen her since the middle of the afternoon. Her brothers and I looked everywhere. Even the priest was out looking." He described their efforts so far, including Flora's disappearance.

"Marty Downing, you say? The man's a public nuisance and a drunk. He doesn't have it in him. Did you send someone to Archers' Roost? Feisty, she is, and proud of that damned tavern. She might have gone back to keep an eye on it now that we have the Sullivan boys in custody."

Phillip shook his head. "Unlikely. It wouldn't hurt to send someone over, though."

He was mulling that when Welling's nervous assistant knocked. "Sorry, Sir, but this just came, and I think you'll want to see it."

One glance and Phillip confronted the assistant before he could open the envelope, dragging him halfway to the door. "Who brought this? Where is he?"

"It was a boy, about ten year—"

Phillip was on the street before the clerk could think, looking both ways for a boy. A matron came down the steps a moment later. "Did you see a boy run out?" he demanded.

"Only Bobby Green," she laughed. "He never walks when he can run. What has he done now?"

"Made a delivery. Thank you for your help." It wasn't much, but LaPlante might be able to find Bobby Green. Phillip trudged back up to Welling's office.

"Do you know a Bobby Green?" Phillip asked.

"Is that who brought this thing?" Welling asked, nodding at the envelope and its contents spread on his desk. "Lying little guttersnipe. Likely just the messenger."

If you want to see Nan Archer alive, get Pat and Mike Sullivan out of jail and out of the state. The words were no less dreadful upon a careful reading. The contents, however, were not as horrifying as he feared. He dreaded seeing Nan's ear or some other body part on the desk. Instead, it was a scrap of lace and hank of hair.

"I assume that's Miss Archer's hair?" Welling asked.

Phillip touched it with one finger. The piece was almost too small to tell, but the flimsiness of the evidence was a clue in itself. Nan was just the sort to talk them out of whatever they planned. "Yes, it is," he said.

"We aren't letting them go," Welling said.

Phillip's first instinct was to argue, but Nan wouldn't want them freed. Still... "We need to question them."

Welling nodded grimly. "You may not want to sit through it. It could get...messy."

Phillip ignored him. He followed the man to the jail behind the courthouse, a square stone building with no pretense of being anything other than it was. Bars covered every window.

Welling waved the message in Pat Sullivan's face. The weasel grinned. "Good to know people out there still care. I wonder who sent it?" He glanced sideways at his brother.

"Marty Downing didn't write this. He's illiterate. I wonder who did?" Welling demanded.

Phillip thought he caught a flicker of something—shock? fear?—at the mention of Downing's name, but it disappeared quickly.

"How would I know? I don't associate with reprobates who live in the bottom of a whiskey barrel." Pat Sullivan glared at Phillip defiantly.

Phillip broke contact to address Welling. "Tell me when your boys have answers from these two. For now, I'm due to meet the Archer brothers to continue searching."

"See here!" Mike Sullivan shouted. "You can't—"

Pat spoke at the same time. "Wouldn't if I was you. Whoever sent this means business."

Phillip spun back to him. "As threats go, that would be stronger if it didn't come from behind bars."

He made it across the street before Luke ran up to him. "Looked for you up at Welling's where you said you'd be." Luke glanced at the jail. "Get anything out of them?"

Phillip shook his head, but described the note.

Luke's curses would shame a sailor.

"You were supposed to meet at Bingham's surgery. What's your hurry? Did you find something?" Phillip asked.

"Heard, more like. We need some men. Hell, we need Jamie. I wish he was on his feet," Luke replied.

As it turned out, he was. Jamie paced the reception room of Bingham's surgery refusing efforts to get him to sit. When Luke and Phillip entered, he demanded, "What's the plan? Do you have a lead?"

Luke told them what he'd gleaned along the waterfront.

"Boatshed? Warehouse? Barn? It's logical," Father LaPlante said. "Shall we search?"

"What do you think, Artie?" Luke asked. All eyes looked to Phillip: Bingham, Barker, Father LaPlante, two men who seemed to be with the priest, and the Archer brothers. It felt good to know Nan's older brother relied on him for strategy at least.

"If we alert them, they may run," Phillip said. "We need

someone to guard the boats and two to watch each of the roads. If we find them, there'll be more than one. We'll need two or three to confront them. I suggest, Father, you and your friends take the roads. Nate and Barker, spread out among the boats. We'll leave the good doctor to his practice. Luke and I will flush them out." *One way or another.*

"I'm going with you," Jamie said, chin raised defiantly.

Phillip peered over at Bingham.

"It's better if you don't, Jamie. But the dressing is fresh and you seem to have some of your strength. Go if you must, but don't overestimate your strength and stamina," Bingham said. His gazes aimed at Luke, frequent and telling, seemed to say, "See to it."

Luke nodded.

"Good luck, gentlemen," Bingham said at last. "I'll be waiting for you here when you bring her."

Bring her to the doctor? Phillip hadn't considered that. His heart beat even faster, the pounding making it hard to listen to Luke's information as they stalked toward the river.

⇥⇤

"THE WOMAN'S A card shark," Frank growled when Marty came back from his delivery. "She took me for every coin I had, even the five-dollar gold piece. I took it back, though." His evil grin would have frightened children. The vicious knife he used to clean his nails struck Nan as much more terrifying.

"A cheat as well as a kidnapper. I should have known," Nan said from her place at the table. Tired, hungry, and fed up with the dirt and the stink of the place, Nan felt her defiance weakening in the face of Frank's threats.

"Quiet you. Tell me how it went, Marty," Frank said.

"The boy and I went over like you said. He went up, told me he give it to the swell in Welling's office," Marty said.

"Are you sure they got it?" Frank demanded.

"Walked over to the jail not fifteen minutes later, din't they? They got it all right."

"Did you wait for a message from Pat?" Frank asked.

"Hell no. There was law crawling all over the place after that. That swell what testified against them Sullivans left, though, him and that mountain man, her brother," Marty said, nodding toward Nan.

Frank cursed. "Law crawling all over means Welling won't do the easy thing. It'll be on that swell of yours, missy. He goes back on his testimony, or you are disappearing for good."

Nan's swell of hope when she realized Luke had returned quickly faded. Artie would never let the Sullivans go, and she couldn't blame him. She could only hope for rescue.

She'd had no luck freeing herself. She had tried the ploy of needing to relieve herself, only to face the humiliation of doing so in a dark alley with Frank nearby. The gleam in his eye made her sick. She attempted to sweet talk Marty until Frank threatened to hit her. Her effort to buy her way out after she won his money had been lame. He merely took it from her. Neither left her alone long enough to try the door, or climb on boxes to the windows high above her head.

"When's that sister of yours bringing breakfast, Marty?" Frank asked.

"She run off. Took the money we gave her and made for Saint Louis. Said she din't want to mix herself up in kidnapping," Marty said.

"Damn. Then you need to fetch vittles," Frank said.

"Why me? You been sitting here since sunup when you sent me off. It's your turn," Marty said.

"She's too smart for you, Marty. You'll never be able to keep her here," Frank said.

Nan held her breath, fearing Marty would suggest that they lock her in the dark closet, but he wasn't clever enough. His shoulders sagged and he slouched toward the door.

"Don't take long," Frank said. "I'm hungry."

"And don't forget me," Nan called.

It felt like an eternity with Marty gone and Frank jumpy as a bug on a hot rock, and Nan was relieved when the door handle jiggled.

"What took—" Frank leapt to his feet mid-sentence when Marty, hands bound and mouth gagged, was tossed to the floor. Luke entered before Frank could blink, a pistol in his hand. He was fast, but not fast enough. Frank had his knife at Nan's throat by the time Artie and Jamie followed him in.

Nan swallowed hard. "Let me go, Frank. There are three of them. Harm me and they will cut you up into tiny pieces and feed you to pigs."

Jamie moved relentlessly to Luke's right and Artie to his left, forcing Frank's gaze from right to left. He stepped back to keep them in sight until his back was to the wall. None of her rescuers took their eyes off Frank's knife. Luke took a silent step forward down the center, and then another. Frank's attention was riveted on Luke, but Nan saw Artie's knife hand come up.

Royally sick of the Sullivans' pestiferous followers holding her at knife point, she shouted, "Don't think you can do Frank like you did Bear, Artie? You can't—"

The roar of Jamie's pistol deafened her, but she kept the good sense to push Frank's knife hand away. She'd tricked him into glancing toward Artie just long enough for her brother to get a clean shot. Same ploy, different weapon.

Frank dropped to the floor whining and moaning, clutching his left hip. Luke dove at him and Artie dove at Nan, dragging her into his arms and kissing her, as he had in that clearing the day of the fire.

"Enough!" Luke roared, and Nan jumped back. He glowered at Artie, who examined her neck with trembling fingers.

"Did they hurt you?" Artie murmured. She shook her head.

"I'm bleeding," Frank whined.

"If you're lucky, they may get a doctor for you at the jail,"

Luke said, giving him a kick. Frank fainted. "Artie, go fetch Nate and Barker to help us drag these two worthless carcasses to the jail. One of 'em at least can't walk."

Artie glanced back at Nan, and looked as though he intended to argue. He didn't.

"Wait," Nan said. "How did you find me?" Her eyes were on Artie.

"Luke heard rumors about the waterfront," Jamie told her. "Artie had identified Marty over there as one of the men we wanted—did some investigating yesterday. We were snooping around here, and tried the nearest tavern. We'd hardly told the barkeep what we wanted when he waltzed in. Barkeep gestured with his head, and we took him. Easy as that. It was only a bit harder to get him to tell us where you were."

"That's the gist of it," Artie said. He studied her sadly until Luke cleared his throat. "I'll be right back."

Nan spared Luke a quick scowl and narrowed her eyes on Jamie. "You should be in bed."

"I couldn't miss the fun." He grinned.

"You need to get back; Bingham said not to overdo it," Luke growled.

Jamie smiled angelically. "I didn't."

Artie returned with the others and the men busied themselves about dragging her captors from the floor and off to jail. Artie never looked at her again. First that heart-stopping kiss, and now he wouldn't even meet her eyes, not in front of her brothers.

Just as well, she thought. *Once the Sullivans swing, he'll leave.*

CHAPTER TWENTY-SIX

THE DAY AND a half between her rescue and the hanging depressed Nan. A hanging, even of evil men, horrified her. Artie insisted on seeing it, needing to be certain. Luke went with him. They refused to let Nan and Nate see it, and ordered Jamie back to bed. She was happy for once to be spared. The men returned grim-faced and refused to say more than, "It's over."

Artie, her Artie, had disappeared. In his place stood a duke, one willing to work side-by-side with her brother Luke, but a duke nonetheless. When he had come through the door to the warehouse, dressed in his old clothes, armed to the teeth, he'd been her Artie. But as soon as they reached the hotel, he had changed clothing, and his very self with it. His manner became as stiff as his clothes and he took to calling her "Miss Archer."

Enough, Artie, I get your message, she thought as they sat over dinner planning their next steps. They would rebuild, of course, though Jamie needed two more weeks to recover at the very least. Nothing held the rest of them in Kaskaskia. They were experiencing a February thaw, and the Archer siblings all agreed that Luke had to go upriver and confront their pa about the farm. Artie kept his eyes on his ale and stayed out of it.

Nan herself was determined to return to Cape Girardeau in the morning to begin rebuilding. She nattered on about who among her friends might help clear the debris, and whether it could be done by the time Jamie could help fell logs to rebuild. Luke surprised her by suggesting he float logs down the rivers, trees being more plentiful in the hills. She battled tears at that. Luke had never supported her determination to run Archers' Roost before. When Jake laid the foundations, he had objected.

Nate made a list of tools they might need, but Nan expected some at least would have survived the fire in the shed. "What we need we can get in Cape Girardeau. No point in trying to haul them home. I did order tents. They'll be on the ferry landing," she said.

"Tents?" Nate frowned. "I was hoping Jolie would take us in."

Nan shook her head. "They've done enough."

"What about you, Artie? What do you plan?" Luke asked. Nan thought his gaze a bit sharper than needed.

"I'll return and help Miss Archer rebuild, of course. Where else would I go? I still have no money. The only things I own are work clothes, a good knife, and one suit of clothes."

One suit that fit him perfectly and fed dreams Nan hadn't known she harbored. As to the haircut, all city trim and fine, she longed to run her hands through it. She longed for a far sight more than that. She almost missed the rest of what he said.

"At least until I hear from back east. If the British envoy replies to my letters, I'll know what sort of immediate options I have. If he sends sufficient means, I can pay Nan back and begin putting plans into place upriver. If he sends only enough for fare back to Philadelphia, I'll have to go there to make arrangements," Artie explained.

"What plans?" Nate asked, wrapped up in the conversation.

"I told you I won't leave until I build something I can be proud of," he began. Nan wasn't listening. One thing was very clear. As soon as he heard from this "envoy" of his, Phillip Tavernash, Duke of Glenmoor, would be on his way as he intended from the beginning, and Artie would disappear like the wisp of a dream.

PHILLIP WASN'T SHOCKED when Luke pulled him aside as they left the surgery, urging Nan and Nate to go ahead and pack.

Phillip had expected it for a while. He'd come to respect Nan's mountain man of an older brother, but he didn't relish trading punches with him. *Especially not in a suit*, he thought wryly.

"Look, Luke—" he began.

"Hurt Nan, and I'll kill you myself," Luke said. As an opening salvo, it was effective.

"I would never hurt her! I…" *Love her.*

"You're going back to what's left of Archers' Roost with neither Jamie nor me to keep an eye on you, nor even Baptiste and Sal. How long before you can't stop sniffing under her skirts? As soon as you hear from that envoy of yours, you'll be off like a shot, leaving her mourning or worse."

Worse? He means with child. "I would never!" Phillip said.

"I saw what happened when Jamie shot that worm, and I've watched her face. She's already more than half in love with you. Take it any farther and there's no going back for her," Luke said.

"She needs help." Phillip knew that much. He couldn't let her face the ruins of her tavern with only Nate for company.

Luke peered upward with a dramatic sigh and back at Phillip. "I can't deny it. She'll need protection too—until Jamie or I get there. Just keep your hands off her, Artie, or whoever the hell you are. Don't promise what you can't deliver, not in words or any other way." He shoved Phillip's shoulder so hard he hit the side of the building.

He's right, damn it anyway. My father may have been a reprobate, but I'm not. I don't ravage innocents, and I don't take advantage of women under my protection. I love her, but until I can formulate a future, Luke is right.

Luke stalked away and Phillip didn't see him again before Nan, Nate, and Phillip gathered at the ferry landing at first light.

Nan, Phillip noticed had three tents. Neither she nor he commented on it, but she clearly had expected him. Neither spoke.

Late day sun beamed down on the tavern clearing when they reached Archers' Roost, showing the charred timbers and broken windows in stark relief. Nan arranged their bundles under the trees by the river and set out some bread and cheese she'd packed. She turned her back on her brother and Phillip. "I'll start seeing what I can salvage," she said.

Phillip hurried behind her. She refused to look at him. "Start with the well. We'll need water," she said without turning. It was as practical as it was dismissive. He had packed his suit carefully, anticipating that he would need it before long. He had changed to his work clothes before they left, however, and got right to it, doing as she directed.

Within three days, his industrious Nan accumulated an impressive collection of salvaged material. Piles of dishes and a box of utensils lay next to pots, pan, pewter mugs, and what-not, all waiting to be washed clean of soot. Linens fared far worse, but even there, Nan managed to find some worth saving, listing and lamenting the cost of replacement.

It was unlike anything in Phillip's pampered life. In his world, if so much as a cup was chipped, a replacement appeared. He never thought to ask the cost or the fate of the damaged item. Sheets and coverlets? They appeared mysteriously as he needed them. If he didn't like the weight or color or size, another appeared through the intervention of his efficient housekeepers at Woodglen and in London. Watching Nan's sheer force of will to rescue what she could and her delight when she found something she could salvage, he was both impressed and shamed.

My Nan is an astounding manager. His Nan. He thought of her that way more and more. He managed to keep his word to Luke and his hands to himself. His eyes and heart were entirely different. *Don't promise what you can't deliver, not in words or any other way… I can help rebuild the Roost. I can promise her that much.*

He turned from watching her count towels and went back to

building a brick circle around the well, enough to keep the dirt from falling in, repeating Luke's words to himself. She needed money for materials and to replace the Roost's inventory more than anything. If only help arrived in response to his letter to the British envoy, he could pay for the whole thing. Helpless, and frustrated that what he had to offer lay a thousand miles away— and more another three thousand more miles across the ocean— he forced himself to work harder.

He managed days when their work kept them largely apart. Nights were another matter. She worked herself to exhaustion and fell into a bed roll in a tent every night; he could do nothing to ease her burdens. He lay in his own tent, warm enough—too warm thinking of Nan—and listened for the sounds of her sleep, thinking of everything he wished he could give her—and the love he ached to make with her.

The fourth night, he couldn't stand it. He'd have rolled in the snow if there was any. He crawled from the tent and went to the river's edge, tempted to plunge in to cool his blood but wise enough to stay put, leaning against the big elm.

He didn't hear her approach, but he knew when she came to stand behind the bench and gaze on the moonlight reflected in the water. He held his breath, certain she could not see him in the shadows. Several moments passed.

"What keeps you up, Artie?"

Damn. She knew I was here. He could hardly say, *"Lusting for you."* Not when watching her outline in the moonlight made it worse. "Thinking of all we have to do. It is daunting."

She sighed deeply. After another moment, she turned his way and took a step toward him. "Would you kiss me, Artie?"

So unexpected that it took his breath away, the question froze him in place. He held himself rigid.

"One kiss. I'd like one kiss in the serenity of the night. One that isn't a survivor's kiss prompted by horrific violence. One just for the simple joy of kissing."

He swallowed hard. "Nan, I don't know what is going to

happen to me. I don't want to promise what I can't deliver."

"I'm not asking for a promise," she said tartly. "I'm asking for one kiss."

"A kiss can be a promise," he murmured. It would be. It would promise everything he desired but couldn't have with any kind of honor unless he let it anchor him to Archers' Roost. He wouldn't let it, and that wouldn't be fair.

"It doesn't have to be." She walked toward him. "I know you'll leave. This place isn't for you. You don't belong in a rough tavern much less a tent, wearing homespun, working with your hands. I suspect I know it better than you do."

She came to stand a foot away, still bathed in moonlight. He could feel the longing in her, the heat radiating from her. His heart pounded; his breath came fast and hard. "So," she whispered. "One kiss. No promises."

He touched her check with the knuckles of one hand and she leaned into it, making a soft noise, and he was lost. His hand went around her head and his other arm around her waist, pulling her until they touched gently, chest to chest. She lacked only an inch or two of his height; he needed to bend only the smallest bit to reach her mouth, her glorious mouth. And so, he did, running his fingers up into her hair.

What constitutes one kiss? He wondered. Was it when lips touched lips and then done? How long dare they hold? Was it when his tongue traced the seam of her mouth? When she opened for him? How much exploration constituted just one kiss? He stopped caring, and kissed his way across her cheek to the spot below her ear and down her neck, his mouth wet and needy against her skin.

She moaned, gripped his shoulders, and slipped one hand around his neck, pulling him closer, her body thrusting against his, their closeness now neither gentle nor tentative. He plundered her mouth again and she followed his lead.

A rush of cold air when she ran her tender fingers under his shirt, caressing his chest, forced him to his senses, awakening his sleeping conscience. She moaned in protest when he pulled his mouth from hers. He set her head to his shoulder with the shaking fingers of one hand while the other caressed her back. "One kiss? That promised quite a lot, I fear, Nan. More than either one of us plans to make good on. We could make love and then what?"

She pulled back. "No. I—"

He didn't let her go entirely. "You what? Are you telling me you will lie with me once, or twice, and then we'll go our ways? I don't think I can do that. Yet, you said yourself I don't belong at Archers' Roost. Can you picture yourself coming to England with me?" *God, Glenmoor, the vipers of the ton would tear her apart.*

"For a visit. Maybe. But no. This is my place." Her tremulous voice faded to silence, and she pushed against his chest half-heartedly.

"Your kiss promised much, Nan. Beware what you promise." He took her hands and pulled them away, sliding past her. He left her there and sought his own bedroll and a sleepless night.

CHAPTER TWENTY-SEVEN

"TELL ME AGAIN how long Artie said he'd be gone," Nate said, pulling more charred timbers and piling them in the clearing. They planned to have one last bonfire to finish it all off and start clean, now that they had salvaged what they could and stripped the main building down to its stone foundation. Three of the furthest guestrooms had proven to be livable. Shelter was a blessing, but the last three, smoke-stained as they were, would go too once the main tavern was up and they started on the extension. The neighbors had helped and were helping still.

"A week, I think," Nan replied. She bit back her irritation. The fool man had kissed her until her knees gave and she almost melted in a puddle at his feet, and then he ran like a scared rabbit. The next morning, he announced he had some idea he didn't see fit to share and took off promising to return. *For now. Remember that, Nan Archer. Sooner rather than later, he'll leave for good.* He didn't take his suit. She took comfort in that.

The week ended yesterday, by her counting.

"That's the last of the chair pieces," Jolie said. He knelt and began poking chair rails and broken legs under timbers for tinder. "My kitchen is filling with cakes and hot dishes," he said over his shoulder. They had decided to make a late winter feast of it, as February, milder than expected, came to an end. They may as well celebrate the end of threats and the return of their friends.

Two hours later, the sun sank to the horizon behind the Roost, and Nan stood with clean hands in her new blue shirt while villagers watched Jolie open the tinder box.

"Artie's back!" Nate shouted.

Walking up from the river road, Artie's broad shoulders filled out his old jacket in ways that made Nan tingle. He appeared fit and whole, and the last rays of the setting sun found golden highlights in his deep chestnut hair, taking her breath away.

Soon enough, Nate reached him for a welcome slap on his back and neighbors surrounded him. "Just in time," Jolie called.

He approached her, Nate at his side, his eyes darting around the clearing and coming to rest on the pile. "What is this?"

"We're giving the old Archers' Roost a proper send off," Nate said.

"A funeral of sorts," Jolie added.

Artie gazed at Nan, searching for answers.

"No point in grieving. We'll get rid of the wreck so we can start over," she said. "Where have you been?" she muttered under her breath for his ears only.

"Later," he said with a quirk to his lips, his eyes on Jolie who struck the flint and lit a spill, putting it to the dry moss in among the chair parts. It took instantly. Fire crawled along beneath broken furniture, half burnt logs, wooden roof tiles, and broken boards at the bottom of the massive pile.

Neither Artie nor Nan looked away from the fire, but she felt his long fingers skim along her hand, searching for hers. She gave it freely, their clasped hands at their side hidden in her skirts while fingers of flame began to climb higher through the layers of wood.

A cheer went up when the fire flickered to the top, and a fiddle came out.

THE DANCING INDUCED by fiddle and fire bore no resemblance to anything a dancing master tried to teach Phillip. Toe-tapping music had people leaping and galloping, swinging one another by the waist, or cavorting individually. It was certainly no funeral. These were no Maypole or Morris dancers either. He'd attended a few village harvest fairs in Nether Abbas near Woodglen, but he had seen nothing like this. Then again, people tended to treat their duke with awkward reserve. God only knew what went on after dark when he left.

Jolie swung Nan out into a raucous dance, and Nate grabbed her for another while Phillip stood tapping his toe to music that seemed to call every part of him to move. He asked Jolie what it was.

"French. Maybe a bit Cajun," Jolie said with a shrug. He passed Phillip the whiskey jug making the rounds, adding to the uninhibited behavior.

At a pause between numbers, Nan came toward him, her steps taking on dance rhythm as the music started up again.

God but she is glorious. It was, he realized, a prayer and true thanksgiving. Nan Archer's very existence was a blessing. *You love her.* Whether those words came from the Almighty or his own soul, Phillip couldn't say, but he knew them to be true.

But it can't be! He still had no idea how there could be anything permanent between them. His panic met only silence; there were no answers. But there it was. He loved her. For that reason alone, he should stay away before he hurt her.

Nan, as always, had other ideas. She took both his hands and led him into the midst of the reveling villagers, swaying in front of him and casting a spell over his senses. Soon she had him moving with her and all thought fled. They danced twice before Nan was pulled into a circle of women holding hands and revolving in step while laughing. Artie joined the others, taking a swig of whiskey whenever the jug came his way, his eyes straying to Nan wherever she was.

The fire died down, and in the gloom, he'd begun to wonder

how he could get Nan alone, perhaps under the trees for a kiss or two. Thoughts of more danced in his imagination. If he could find her. She seemed to have disappeared. He didn't have long to consider the matter. His lascivious thoughts were interrupted.

A woman came down the village path banging a pot with a spoon, another lighting her way with a torch. "Food's on!" the women called.

A cheer went up and torches were lit from the dying fire. Nate and another young one were ordered to, "Mind the fire doesn't spread," and promised food.

Phillip froze in place. Nan, he realized, must have gone up to help prepare the feast. His unruly, whiskey-fueled imagination had left him hot, aroused, and in no fit state to socialize with the respectable ladies of Cape Girardeau. He shooed the boys off. He may as well see to the fire.

He sat on one of the salvaged chairs, lost in thought. He had anticipated a quiet welcome from Nan and Nate. He had hoped his news would please her. He had planned to be polite, reserved, and respectful, all dishonor under control. He had planned to be useful, but keep to himself. She'd asked him to kiss her before, and it couldn't happen again, not after the speed with which the passion between them grew out of control. What he found instead was a bacchanale that tossed inhibitions to the wind.

You love her. The words came back. *What do you plan to do about it?* What could he do? He might persuade her to come to England as a duchess, but even the thought felt uncomfortable. She wasn't a porcelain doll to be dressed up and shown off. The *ton* darlings would make fun of her, and she would hate the hypocrisy and superficiality. He did, too. He was certain he did not want to go back to that life.

They could live quietly at Woodglen, with its dozens of bedrooms, multiple withdrawing rooms, dining salons, and ballroom, with its dining table set with porcelain and six silver forks at each place. The two of them would rattle around the place. And do what, exactly?

Nan was a woman of purpose, he realized. That was one of the things he liked about her. Liked. Not instead of love. In addition. He enjoyed spending time with her, working side-by-side. The Woodglen idea bore no attraction. He would help rebuild Archers' Roost, but then what? Spend his life as her assistant in the tavern? No. Other ideas were taking shape, but had no real form, at least not yet. An urgency to settle them came over him.

Footsteps approached, and Phillip pushed his morose thoughts away. When he had word from back east, he would know his real options. There was no point in fretting until then.

"Do you plan to sit there all night?" Nan's voice came out of the darkness.

"I'm watching the fire," he said.

"A bucket of water will take care of it," she retorted, and he saw with a start that she was correct. While he sat in his own puddle of worries, the thing had burned down. She had obviously come prepared. She handed him a bucket, and held a second one. They worked in silence. One trip to the river and back and the fire was safe to leave.

"Come and eat, Artie," Nan said. "There's plenty left and you have to taste Cecile Jolie's cake."

Still, he hesitated.

"I won't attempt to ravage you, you know. Your honor is safe," she said.

He felt a fool. The crowd was what he needed now.

"Let's go then," he said.

They hadn't gone three steps when she hit him with her question. "Where were you?"

"Kaskaskia."

"What on earth were you doing there?"

"Loading and unloading boats. It isn't Saint Louis, but there's a fair amount of boat traffic there, and work to be had." *And much that is useful to learn.*

"Why?"

He took her hand in his then and turned it palm up. He dropped coins in it. "For the rebuilding fund," he said.

"I—I don't know. I—" she sputtered.

"Thank you is the usual response."

"Thank you," she whispered.

"I'm going back day after tomorrow. This time for two weeks." He was glad it was dark. She was probably marshalling arguments to keep him here, her face all adorably scrunched up. "I can chop wood, serve ale, and load barges, but I have no carpentry skills. I'm more useful to you this way." *And safer.*

She had no answer. They walked on in silence.

CHAPTER TWENTY-EIGHT

FEBRUARY PASSED INTO March and Nan gave thanks every day it had been a mild winter. Jolie and McGregor had put in a wood box stove in the middle of the three thin-walled guest rooms they sheltered in—another debt she couldn't pay, at least not for a good long while.

Luke arrived after a thaw as promised, floating a raft of fine logs. Nate, God love him, led his friend Josef to the big woods and hauled back more. Twice. Jamie had come home, but hewing trees was still beyond him. Still, he did what he could.

They were building back in the French style as it had been, *poteaux-sur-sole,* the logs fixed vertically, close together on a timber sill laid down over the foundation stones. Folks who wanted a log structure had to look farther afield every day, and building in the area was giving way to board built timber frame, post and beam, and many preferred it. Nan wanted logs as she'd always known, even if each log took two men to raise and going was slow. She couldn't afford milled boards anyway, and was already worried how she'd pay for roof shakes and window framing and enough boards to cover the eaves and floors.

It was the need for milled framing that concerned Artie the last time he'd been home. She still stubbornly called it home when she spoke to him. It was her home if not his. He'd been home twice since the night of the bonfire, bringing much needed coin each time, and gorging himself on her cooking.

Today he sat on a rickety chair by the iron stove in the little room they'd designated the sitting room, where he slept on a pallet when he was home. Luke had cobbled together some flat wood as a table, and Artie counted out their hoard of coins. "Tell me again how much milled board we need?"

She'd measured as closely as she could. "I want two extra windows if we can manage it," she said, giving him the number. "It'll be less without those two. Inside doors can wait. Closets too. These three guest cottages will do until we can rebuild the wing."

Artie glanced at Jamie. "Any idea what the lumber will cost?"

Jamie frowned. "Goes up and down. With so many folks moving into Illinois and nearby, the cost keeps rising. When I built the barn…" His frown deepened to utter gloom. The farm was still a painful problem, one they'd yet to solve.

"There is more than one mill. Competition should help," Artie said.

"True. There's a new one below Cahokia, one in Sainte Genevieve, and one in Prairie Roché, but that's too far overland," Nan said.

"One in Saint Louis, too," Jamie added.

"Two," Artie mused. He glanced up at her and answered her unspoken question. "That's the word in Kaskaskia. There was talk of building another there. The competition may help. We ought to check prices. Luke, can you do Cahokia? I'll get myself to Sainte Genevieve before I go back to work."

"Back? It appears to me you've more than paid me what you owe. We could use you here," Nan said.

"My dear Miss Archer, innkeeper, I can never repay what I owe you," the daft man said, glancing at each of her brothers. "All of you. I mean it. But I will someday."

"So you keep promising," Luke drawled, rising to his feet and slapping Artie on the back.

"You know nothing, Luke Archer. Mind your—" Luke's cheeky wink stopped her. He'd gotten fond of Artie himself these last months.

"Still no word about the farm?" Artie asked, taking the conversation off one painful subject and sticking his finger in a bigger wound.

"Pa insists he didn't sell it. Welling promised to send deputies to check the papers, but he said with the Sullivans gone, he had a lot of fraud to look into." Jamie held his mug up for coffee and Luke refilled it. "When we get the Roost rebuilt, if there's still no word, I'll go evict them myself."

Artie nodded solemnly. "First things first. Continue getting the logs up. Check prices of lumber. Get best price. Begin framing. Reopen the tavern to paying customers and move upstairs. Gradually finish the interior. Rebuild the guest wing, then deal with the farm. Do I have that right?"

"Farm before finish work or guest wing," Nan said, peering at Luke and Jamie, who nodded.

Artie left again the next day with little but the clothes on his back and that vicious knife. She packed him what food she could spare. He returned in a week this time with more coin. He and Luke worked out a price list for lumber.

"We should check Saint Louis. We could build a flatboat and bring it that way," Jamie said.

Artie jumped at the idea. "Construction will be dead in the water if we don't do something soon. Let's go up and buy what we can. If the price is high, we'll come down to Cahokia or Sainte Genevieve."

It was agreed, and Jamie and Artie left a few days later, well-armed, and taking most of their money.

Two days there, she reckoned, watching them push Luke's canoe into the river. A few to build the flatboat and one or more back. A week perhaps. The Roost might be livable in a month. Maybe. She'd convince Artie to stay home this time, just a bit longer.

A week later Nan's world upended when a vision the like she'd never seen came up from the boat launch: two men, one pulling a sledge with a large trunk and some bags.

"Is this Archers' Roost?" The taller one, a vision in red regimentals, glanced around their construction, and asked with a curl to his lip. His entire face reflected as much disbelief—and disapproval—as his voice.

Her heart sank. Artie's past had caught up with him.

PHILLIP LAY ON his back and let the sun warm his face and still his racing mind for once while Jamie poled the flat boat. They'd done very well in Saint Louis, negotiating the best price on the river. Negotiating lumber was one reason he'd been glad he brought the blasted suit. Even better, the land office had been much more forthcoming with information when he wore it.

The entire visit had prospered. Jamie had been patient while Phillip poked up and down the water front, asking questions and taking notes. After a while, Jamie had taken real interest in life along the waterfront himself.

Phillip had been surprised that Jamie planned to build their flatboat. "No point in hiring someone," he announced. "I've done it before, and if I run into a problem, there are folks to ask."

Jamie had been puzzled, but didn't ask questions when Phillip branched along the Missouri as well as up the Mississippi, ideas beginning to come into focus in his mind. Now they followed the current south in companionable accord.

"We'll be home soon," Jamie called. "Nan will be happy to see what we brought—enough to finish the rough work and get under the roof."

Home. Nan called it that, and why not? It had been his only home for months. Woodglen had been a palace where he grew up, but had it been a home? He now knew the difference—it wasn't.

They floated past Archers' Roost toward the boat landing,

both of them with eyes glued to the shore.

"Progress!" Jamie's palpable delight was understandable. The log walls were up and the spaces between were being filled with mud and clay. "Look down on the lawn!"

Massive log roof joists had been laid out ready to raise. That would take all hands, even Phillip's. When he glanced that way, he saw that the tents had been raised again, and a flash of red brought him to high alert. There was no time to ponder as the current brought them past and their view was cut off.

Moments later, Jamie beached the flatboat at the landing, and both men leapt off. Two old sledges leaned against a tree for the use of travelers. They loaded two bundles of roof shakes onto them, left the rest, and pulled them up the path to the Roost.

Nate saw them first and came running. He took over Jamie's sledge, concerned as always about his brother's recovery. "Famous! You got the roof. How did we do? Do we have enough for the outside?"

"That and the floors," Jamie answered.

"Nan will be ecstatic," Nate replied. He sobered when he glanced over at Phillip. "You have company, Artie. Some fancy Brit soldier from back east. His uniform has Luke and Nan in a dither. Wanted him to take it off."

Word at last and in person. I ought to be overjoyed. He wasn't. Phillip had, in fact, hoped for a letter, funds, and more time to study his situation. If Sir Charles sent an equerry, he would have to face decisions before he was ready.

Nan met them halfway, her nervous glances toward the tents telling him everything he needed to know. Her smile when she peered at the roof shakes was a long stretch away from the joy he expected. "Your friends came looking for you," she said.

He sighed and peered down at his homespun shirt and dirty britches. "I'll need my ring, Nan. They'll never take me for Glenmoor in these clothes," he said.

He watched her pull his ring from her bodice with a tender smile, and untied the ribbon when she handed it over. He stuffed the blue satin ribbon in his pocket to keep it safe. If he needed a keepsake in the end, it would be a precious one.

He slipped his signet ring onto his smallest finger and marched over to what had become a British encampment. Three tents stood in a precise row with an improvised table and chair in front of one, as the commanding officer's aide-de-camp might have. Laundry hung neatly on a line behind; a bicorn lay on the table where a man in regimentals wrote something.

"Welcome to Archers' Roost," he announced. "I'm Glenmoor. I understand you were looking for me."

The soldier, an ensign from the looks, knocked over his chair in his eagerness to stand and greeted Phillip with a gaping mouth from which no sound emitted.

Phillip found his own mouth twitching. The humor of the thing drove out all his concern. "Perhaps this will help." He held up the ring. "The Glenmoor signet. Would you like me to recite my pedigree? The oath of allegiance?"

The young man, red-faced bowed deeply. "Forgive me Your Grace. You didn't, or rather I didn't expect—that is Archers' Roost..."

"Isn't what you expected either. We had a fire." *Understatement, that.* Phillip had no time to explain. Another figure emerged from the tent buttoning his coat, an officer about Phillip's age—thirty-two years or so.

Tall, austere, and frowning, the captain studied Phillip carefully. His bow was shallower than the ensign's but sharper, in the military manner. "Captain Sherrod Lord Fitzwallace at your service, Your Grace. It appears your situation is even more dire than Sir Charles anticipated."

Fitzwallace. He must be one of the Duke of Awbury's sons. Phillip didn't miss the inclusion of "lord." He recalled Awbury as a man as high in the instep as they came. Phillip swallowed a groan.

"Sir Charles" was of course Bagot, the envoy to Washington. Suddenly, Phillip was awash in peers and expectations. He squared his shoulders and lifted his chin with as much dignity as he could under the circumstances. "Well met. The Roost has not always been quite so primitive," he said, wondering at his need to defend the place. "It was attacked by the same men who almost killed me."

Fitzwallace blanched.

"No need to fear. The danger has passed. The men responsible were tried and executed. I was able to give testimony."

"That must have been uncomfortable. Colonials are not respecters of rank," Fitzwallace said.

"No, they are not," Phillip agreed.

"We're here now. We'll bring you back to civilization safely." The captain's smug assumptions grated.

"I assumed so, but perhaps not just yet."

It was as though Fitzwallace didn't hear him. "We've brought proper suits and linens, if you wish to dress first. However, we also have mail and papers from Sir Charles."

"The clothing can wait—perhaps until we are in more suitable accommodations?" Phillip couldn't see himself in Nan's little drawing room in silk trousers and an embroidered waistcoat.

"Where are you lodged at present?" Fitzwallace asked.

"With the Archers, of course."

"In those squalid little cabins?" Fitzwallace gasped.

I'll give you little, but hardly squalid. Not on Nan's watch. "We contrive," Phillip replied, determined not to give Fitzwallace's arrogance any slack. "May I assume you also brought the funds I requested?"

"Of course. And badly needed, no doubt."

"I'll take them now, and the messages, if you please."

Fitzwallace glanced up at the construction site and the swarm of workers, some openly staring, and back at Phillip. "Is that wise, Your Grace?"

"That's for me to determine. Now please."

Phillip caught a glimpse of a large trunk and some smaller luggage in the tent on the far end. It explained why there were three. The captain emerged with a valise and a money pouch.

Fitzwallace clearly wanted to argue, but thought better of it when he saw the determination in Phillip's eyes. He handed them over. "Yes, Your Grace," he said.

"We'll speak tomorrow, Captain." Phillip walked back across the lawn toward Nan carrying a valise full of letters and other documents. He also hefted a pouch containing a small fortune over his shoulder.

CHAPTER TWENTY-NINE

"ANGELS ABOVE, ARTIE, that's enough to tempt a saint!" Nan stared into the pouch on her table in flickering candlelight. "No wonder you kept it over your shoulder all day. Why didn't you leave it with yon army to guard it?"

Artie shrugged. "I enjoyed shocking Fitzwallace. And I trust the lot of you completely."

Yet, he'd waited until her brothers retired to squabble in their sleeping quarters before he showed it to her. She'd made up his pallet by the stove when he had asked her to linger. He clearly wanted to share it with Nan alone. Her heart sped up.

"You best keep it between the two of us for now lest you be overheard. Bagot sent more cash than I expected. The bank credit in the valise came with a warning to explain why. Banks are failing, Nan. All over your country. I'll have to take care what bank I use in Saint Louis," he said.

"That pouch has more money than I could hope to see in a lifetime." Shock and awe almost choked her.

"We have plenty here to pay for windows and to replenish your furnishings and inventory," he said.

"You don't owe us that, Artie. You've already worked off your debt," she said. She wouldn't be beholding to any man, even this one. *Archers don't take charity.*

"I owe you my life! Do you have a price for that?"

She waved his words away. "Even if I let you spend all that, there is way more than it would take in that pouch. What do you plan to do now?" *And what are you anyway?* She couldn't get the size of the fortune in that pouch nor his cavalier attitude about it out of her mind.

"I haven't decided. Will we raise the roof trusses tomorrow?" he asked.

"With you back, we should have enough men. I doubt those fine prancing officers would help." *The worthless interlopers are naught but trouble.*

"They will if I order them to."

Nan gasped. "You can order that tin soldier and his toady around?"

His laugh, bitter and harsh, surprised her. "Duke. Remember? I could and they would, but it might be better not to antagonize Fitzwallace quite so much for now.

Uncomfortable silence stretched until Nan thought she should leave, but was unable to pull herself away from this man she thought she knew well, one obviously more of a stranger than she had guessed. The heat in his eyes made her wiggle uncomfortably in her seat. That at least was familiar.

"Sit with me a while as I read the messages in the valise," he begged. She couldn't resist. If he was slipping away from her, there may not be more chances like this.

"Is there anymore in Luke's jug?" he asked.

She poured him a dram of whiskey while he pulled two letters from the valise. "I thought you said there was bank business in there," she said.

"There is. Also, letters assigning Captain Sherrod Fitzwallace as my equerry—bodyguard, secretary, and assistant in one. He's to stay for one year or until I return to Philadelphia, whichever comes first."

Her temporary servant had a servant, and a high-class one at that. "That man isn't staying in a tent for a year," she said. The very idea was ludicrous. "You'll have to buy a house in town."

She didn't want the redcoats hanging around Archers' Roost in any case.

"I'll lodge him in Saint Louis."

Her breath caught. The idea made her eyes go wide. "You want to spend a year in Saint Louis?"

He shrugged in that noncommittal way of his. "Sir Charles Bagot, the British envoy, wishes me success in my endeavors, whatever they are. He also sent some requests."

"What sort of requests?"

He leafed through the valise. "Let's see… Reports on settlement and population. More on the volume of trade. He sent letters of introduction to the Chouteau brothers and to Governor Clark. He expects me to meet with them."

Casual reference to meeting the most powerful men in the territory shocked Nan down to her toes. She shot a prayer of thanks he didn't look up to see it on her face.

"All reasons to go to Saint Louis. Anyway, as I said, I should lodge the captain there." He waved the two unopened letters. "What I want you here for are these two. They are from my brother. Please sit with me while I read them."

She poured herself a tot of whiskey, thinking she might need it. "Tell me more about your brother." He'd hardly mentioned the man since he'd first arrived.

Artie swallowed. The subject made him unhappy for some reason. "He's older. When he came to us, he was twelve and I was eight. He…" Artie blinked as if looking for words. "He protected me. He was kind to me."

"Protected" struck Nan as an odd choice. *From whom?*

Artie went on. "Our father resented him. Treated him badly." He shook his head. "He treated all of us badly. He sent Gideon away when I was at school. He told me he was dead and that should have been the end of it."

"Obviously, that wasn't the end of it." Suddenly concerned, Nan leaned forward and took one of his hands in hers. "What happened?"

"A year ago, my stepmother and I located him. He had been sent to my father's mine in Wales, meant to die there. Instead, he prospered. We found him wealthy and content."

"Then why do you look so miserable? Weren't you pleased to find your brother alive?"

"Oh yes! Thrilled to have him back. He's a wonderful man. We discovered something else, though, the reason our father treated him badly. I told you some of this before. Gideon was the son he left in South Carolina after the American rebellion. Father returned to Dorset and conveniently forgot about him when he came into his title. Then Gideon turned up at Woodglen, and Father declared him a bastard and a 'half-wit colonial.' He's none of those things. Gideon's mother was legitimately married. And that meant mine wasn't."

He confused her with all that. "What do you mean? The man married again while his wife still lived?"

"Exactly. I'm the bastard. Gideon should be Duke of Glenmoor, but it was confirmed on me—signed and sealed by the Crown—and we can't do a damn thing about it. The Crown does not like to be told it made a mistake."

It was more than Nan could sort out, but one thing struck her right away. "Don't tell Fitzwallace. You'll never be able to keep him in line."

That at least brought a grin and the old Artie up to the surface. "True enough. I need to exploit what I have when it is useful." He pressed her hand where it held his. "The thing is, Nan, Gideon was given nothing, and yet he made a fortune on his own. I was handed everything. I've never earned anything. The difference in our lives shocked me out of my complacency. I came here to make something on my own. Something I could be proud of."

"You admire your brother."

"More than I can say. Admire and love." He picked up his letters. The first, obviously a short note, made him laugh. "He wrote this when he got my missive telling him I was leaving

England. Some of his language is indelicate, but he wasn't happy I asked him to look after the estate."

"Estate?"

He waved one hand casually, staring at the page. "The family manor, the investments, the whole business, everything attached to the title. He hated it, but I've made sure it all will belong to his son one day, as it should. I knew he couldn't look away." He tapped the other letter with one finger. "I wonder if he went? Shall we see?"

He read the much longer letter in silence, occasionally reading out a sentence. "He says it was a blessing in the end. 'It brought me Mia,' he says. He's remarried! To a local woman." Further on, he laughed. "He and my old steward are quite a pair. He says, 'Marshall can't read. If you knew, you might have warned me—' I didn't know, by the way, the rascal. Trust Gideon to ferret that out. 'Now that we have that in the open, we've become quite a partnership. Fillmore is still frosty. Mia is melting him slowly.'"

"What is a steward and who is Fillmore?" Nan asked, the impact of all this slowly dawning on her.

"The steward manages the land, the tenants, the stables, the farms. The butler—that is Fillmore—the house and all its servants."

Nan stared at this man she thought she knew. Even the title and authority hadn't made some things as clear as they were becoming. "How much land, Artie?"

He hesitated. She suspected he was tempted to lie. He didn't. "Somewhere between ten and eleven thousand acres. There are over five thousand in smaller parcels around the country." He clamped his jaw shut, waiting for her reaction.

Nan considered the Archer farm. Her pride in their full section. It would fit in this Woodglen's kitchen patch. Truly they were from different worlds. Artie may as well have come here from the moon. Something else hit her. "How many servants?" Her words came out a croak.

"In the house? Twenty-five or thirty normally. More when needed." He frowned and went on. "There are twenty bedrooms in the guest wing alone. It takes—"

"Merciful saints!" Nan soared to her feet. "You've been sleeping in my attic. I knew you didn't fit there, but—thirty servants. Merciful saints!"

He rose and reached for her hand, but she wasn't having it. "No. I have to leave. You have to leave, Artie. Your Grace."

His words followed her out the door. "Not until we rebuild Archers' Roost."

PHILLIP SAT LONG after the candle guttered out going over Gideon's letter in his mind, and over Nan's horrified reaction to her first real glimpse of the reality of his life. He hadn't meant to delude her ever, yet perhaps he had. He could see why she might feel like it.

He had no choice at the beginning, and he did tell the Archers he could pay his debts—repeatedly. He'd given them glimpses of the duke, but pulled back into "Artie," their friend and assistant every time. There was no way they could know the extent of it, not if he didn't tell them. Why didn't he?

In the darkness, he couldn't hide from himself. This interlude at Archers' Roost had been a relief from his confused feelings about his life, his legacy, and his shame over the title. Though uneasy at first, he had enjoyed being Artie. He had enjoyed being part of a courageous, affectionate family. Taking down the Sullivans verified his manhood; Luke Archer's respect, hard won, gave him pride. The drive to rebuild The Roost filled him with the satisfaction of creating something of value.

Behind it all there was Nan. As long as he was Artie, he could be her friend at the very least, if not the lover he longed to be. As Artie, his life had worth. But it could not last. He had known deep down she would react the way she did if he let her see his reality.

He forced himself to admit that wasn't the whole problem. He had pushed the burdens of the title onto Gideon without the privileges and gone off on an adventure like some would-be Gulliver. Had he been playing at it? Was he toying with Nan Archer? This world was her very existence. It was no game, and she deserved total honesty from him. He hadn't given it. He owed her total honesty. He owed it to all of them.

He couldn't hide behind Artie any longer.

CHAPTER THIRTY

"SUN'S UP, ARTIE. We have a roof to raise. Move your lazy bones." Luke's voice echoed through the little sitting room. Phillip rolled over toward the wall and squeezed his eyes shut.

He couldn't block out sound, though. The Archer boys trooped in. Clanging pans signaled Nan's presence too, and it was impossible to block out the smell of porridge and coffee.

Phillip groaned and turned on his back.

"Ah, he's alive after all," Jamie joked. "Lord Artie may even be some help."

Phillip couldn't block the previous night from his mind either. He'd only come to one conclusion in the depths of it. Artie was as much a fraud as the Duke of Glenmoor. He pushed himself to a sitting position and put his aching head in his hands.

"Did you hit Luke's liquor last night, Artie?" Jamie asked.

"Couldn't sleep," he said, stumbling up and dropping into a chair with a groan.

"Maybe those strutting peacocks in the tents upset your sleep. They're enough to give me nightmares," Luke said.

Close enough, but not for the same reason. He didn't answer.

Nan slammed mugs on the table. "Mayhap they reminded him who he is." She didn't meet his eyes.

"Ooh," Jamie cooed. "Sorry, Your Grace. We forgot."

"Stubble it, Jamie. What's the plan for today?" Phillip asked.

"Jolie should be here before long. He plans to round up any-one who can help. That and block and tackle should do it, but it won't be easy. Any chance you could get those soldiers of yours to help?" Luke asked, spearing him with his sharp gaze.

Phillip downed his coffee and reached for the pot. "One of them, for certain. Fitzwallace wouldn't be worth the trouble."

Nan put porridge in front of him without meeting his gaze or speaking. He stared into the bowl and ate silently, rising before the others.

"I'll go down and roust them," he said. He burrowed under his bedding and pulled out the pouch of money and the valise and tossed them over his shoulder. He had hidden Gideon's letters in the sack he used to store his suit from the trial and the few possessions he had owned two days ago, before the real world caught up with him.

"What's with the bags, Artie?" Nate asked.

He hurried out the door and pretended not to hear. He didn't hear Nan reply either. *Thank God.* He'd have to deal with the Archer boys later.

"Heads up in there. I thought soldiers rose with the sun!" Phillip waited only a few moments before the ensign came out, dressed if a bit rumpled. He bowed properly.

"Good morning, Your Grace. How may I help you?" the young man said. He didn't appear to be much more than a few years older than Nate.

"What is your name, Ensign?" Phillip asked.

"Evan Fitzwallace, Your Grace."

"Fitzwallace?" Phillip voiced his surprise.

The young man colored slightly, glancing at the captain's tent. "We're by way of family of a sort." He stumbled over his words.

By-blow, no doubt. Awbury's or one of the sons'.

"Is that uniform all you have to wear, Ensign Fitzwallace?"

"No, Your Grace, but I've nothing proper for…" The ensign

glanced around helplessly.

"Is it appropriate for physical labor?"

The young man nodded.

"Good. Where is your captain?" Phillip asked.

The solder shifted from one foot to the other. "Preparing for the day," he said.

"Kindly inform him I wish to speak to him and then change your clothes."

The ensign was in the captain's tent so long it confirmed Phillip's suspicion that Fitzwallace still slept, and that the younger man served as valet as well as secretary.

Fitzwallace appeared, shaved and immaculately dressed. A clenched jaw and narrow eyes made his displeasure obvious, but his bow and greeting were punctiliously proper.

While the ensign slipped behind him and darted into the smaller tent, Phillip accepted the obeisance as his due, chin up.

"I require the service of Ensign Fitzwallace. I've had a good look at the contents of these," Phillip said, handing the money pouch and valise toward the captain. He spared Fitzwallace the overt insult that he counted the money, but he had. "You may stay here and guard the ducal treasures, Captain. We'll talk later."

The captain accepted the valise and pouch with a curt bow and took them into the baggage tent. He didn't reemerge.

Avoiding me.

The boy, Evan, changed quickly and emerged smiling and eager. "Will I do, Your Grace?" he asked.

Phillip smiled back and led him up to the house where workers had gathered. He called to the youngest Archer.

"Nate, this is Evan Fitzwallace. He plans to help. Can you show him what to do?" He turned to his companion. "Evan, this is Nathaniel Archer, one of the family that owns Archers' Roost. We're all here to help them restore their tavern and home. Today, we're raising the roof beams."

"I'll do my best, Your Grace."

At the title, Nate's eyebrows rose, and Phillip noticed curious glances from the villagers. He'd considered asking Evan to avoid use of the title, but he'd put deception behind him. He'd deal with Jolie and the others after the roof was on.

Nate led Evan away, and Phillip scanned the crowd, his eyes unerringly finding Nan on the far side, her face turned away from his with deliberate determination. He fell in to listen as Jamie assigned tasks.

BY THE TIME the sun had passed its high point overhead and begun its slow journey west, Nan thought with satisfaction that they might get the entire roof on before dark. The joists and beams had been raised, the rough lumber from the flatboat had been hauled up from the boat landing, and a crew was nailing boards to beams as the ladies stood at the path and banged a pot to signal the mid-day meal.

Nate and the other boys dismantling the remains of the flatboat gave a cheer. Artie's friend, Evan, worked companionably among them all morning and appeared to get on well with them all.

Artie's friend. Artie—His Grace. She grit her teeth, swearing to herself she would not talk to that man again until she could bring herself to call him by his title, like the arrogant, aristocratic—wealthy—Englishman that he was.

Even as she thought of him, the man himself climbed down a ladder from the roof. She'd been unable to dismiss him as the spoiled rich swell she wanted to believe he was. He worked too damn hard all morning.

In spite of the cool weather, his damp shirt hugged his shoulders, muscles rippling beneath the thin cloth as he climbed down. *When did his trousers get so tight? They positively cling to his—* Nan swung away, her back to the man, and marched uphill, joining their neighbors.

"Nan!" Jolie trotted up. "I've been meaning to ask all morning. That new young fellow calls our Artie 'Your Grace.' Do you know about that?"

"Aye. He never made a secret of it. But ragged beggar that he was when he came to us, he was too embarrassed to insist on his honorables, I suspect," she said.

"That's correct, Jolie. I thought you all knew." Artie's deep voice startled her from behind, rumbling through her chest and setting her heart racing.

Nan stopped, but only Jolie turned to face him, one hand scratching his head. "If you told us, I don't recall anything. Who are you anyway?"

"Promise not to laugh? I'll tell you what I told Luke the first day." She didn't hear Jolie's answer, but Artie went on with a self-mocking lilt to his voice, "I am Phillip Roland George Arthur Tavernash, Sixth Duke of Glenmoor, Earl of Wentworth, Viscount Gradington, Baron Walsh."

She glanced back as she hurried away, on time to see Artie's dramatic bow and Jolie's bark of laughter.

"McGregor," Jolie called. "You have to hear this."

Moments later, the men followed her into Poirier's barn for the meal, laughter and teasing still going on.

"Attention *Mes Amis*! Our friend Artie has just surprised us this day, has he not?" Nan saw Jolie with an arm around Artie. "Tell everyone what you told me."

Artie—the duke—caught her eye, and for a brief moment, he had the face of a condemned man. Just as quickly, it disappeared and so did Artie. In his place stood the Duke of Glenmoor.

He raised his hands to command attention, and every eye in the place, Archers and villagers alike, turned toward him. Jamie turned his gaze to Nan, questions she had no answer for in his face. Luke spared her a glance as well. Both began moving in her direction slowly.

"You may have heard my young friend Ensign Fitzwallace call me 'Your Grace' this morning. He was correct to do so. 'Your

Grace' is the customary form of address for a duke. When I first met Luke Archer—" He glanced about until he saw Luke, creeping closer to Nan, and gestured in his direction. "—I introduced myself to him as Phillip Tavernash, Duke of Glenmoor."

"Oh, tell them the rest," Jolie insisted.

The duke—she was determined to think of him as the duke—sighed. "Sixth Duke of Glenmoor, Earl of Wentworth, Viscount Gradington, Baron Walsh," he said wearily.

That brought both gasps and laughs.

"It is a mouthful, I agree." He returned the laugh and went on. "Too much for Archers' Roost. Artie sounded easier. Besides, I knew well by then that titles have no meaning in your country, so I saw no need to explain protocol or forms of address or any of the things that matter in my home place."

A brief silence fell before someone shouted, "Where's yer crown?"

The duke smiled. "Kings wear crowns. Dukes wear a coronet, a circlet of strawberry leaves, on formal occasions. Mine is home in the family vault."

"Is a duke better than a prince?" Poirier's fourteen-year-old daughter sighed.

"Princes rank higher than dukes. Then come marquesses, earls, viscounts, barons, and so on down the list."

Jamie sidled up to Nan. "What brought this on?"

"The little army camped on our lawn came to remind him who he is. That boy Evan calls him by his title," she said.

"Do you have a castle like a prince?" someone asked. Nan braced for his answer, wondering if he would prevaricate.

He didn't. "Not exactly. I have a manor house, though. Rather a large one, I fear. Parked on a large bit of land."

The young ensign chose then to chime in. "One of the largest in England," he said, blushing red.

"How much land?" She couldn't see who asked, but the question was inevitable. Land mattered in this territory.

"The duchy of Glenmoor's main estate is roughly ten thousand acres. We have five smaller parcels as well."

"Did you know that?" Luke hissed in Nan's ear while the duke answered more rude questions.

"I found out last night. I believe our Artie is as rich as John Jacob Astor himself. When he said he could afford to pay me back, he wasn't lying, but he wasn't telling the whole truth either."

"Don't suppose he had to, did he?" Jamie said. "He never lied."

"Let the man eat. He worked as hard as all of us!" Jolie spoke over clamoring voices, and the duke cast him a grateful glance.

"If you have any more questions about dukes, you might ask Ensign Fitzwallace over there by Nate Archer," he said before sitting down. The businessmen of Cape Girardeau jostled to sit with him, she noticed.

"I think we need to have a talk with our friend Artie," Luke said.

"You do that. I've had enough." Nan all but ran out of the barn and down to the river, veering toward woods when she noticed the red-uniformed soldier sitting by the tents.

CHAPTER THIRTY-ONE

MOST OF THE good people of Cape Girardeau slept late the day after the roof raising. Nan Archer watched the sun come up over the river from the newly reconstructed porch before getting to work. She hadn't precisely risen early; she had never gone to sleep. When she managed to push Artie from her mind, lists of tasks and worries over cost crowded in.

In the dawn light, she stepped inside the partially constructed Archers' Roost, pencil and papers in hand. With walls in place and a roof overhead, it felt familiar. Workers had laid the first level floor and the inside walls that divided the public room from the kitchen, servant rooms, and pantry as before. She could walk through and imagine it alive with guests.

I can leave the guestrooms to the boys and move myself into the kitchen here until they can build in the upper floor and stairs. Gaping holes where the windows would go were little more than a temporary inconvenience.

Nan was at peace with her world again, or so she tried to tell herself. It didn't work. *That blasted man has upended everything!*

Artie had already disappeared from her life, and she didn't know what to do with the duke who took his place. It was as if her wounded duck had turned into a peregrine falcon soaring above them. Nan knew for certain she couldn't fly that high no matter how badly she wanted to.

The builders had set up a bench behind the tavern, and she sat down to take stock of the work. Practical tasks always soothed her disordered moods. She listed the remaining structural issues, noting where they had material—flooring—and where they did not—window glass. The little stove in the guestrooms would have to do for now. Putting up stores would have to wait for cupboards, the bar, and cash. She frowned at that. She wasn't about to let herself become the Duke of Glenmoor's charity case.

"Hey Nan!" Nate, cheerful and energetic, approached munching what she guessed to be a leftover piece of cake from last night. He had a book under his other arm.

"You're up early. Ready to work?"

"I thought you said today was a rest day. I'm meeting Evan at the boat landing. Artie asked us to watch for a keelboat heading north and flag it over. We're going to read while we wait."

"Keelboat?" she demanded.

Nate shrugged. "He has some sort of business up in Saint Louis. He and Jamie have been talking about it."

Of course he does. And, of course, my brothers all know more than I do.

Nate went on his way. Nan sat for a few moments but couldn't concentrate. She wandered over to the makeshift sitting room, interrupting a conversation. Whatever it was, Luke, Jamie, and the irritating duke all stopped when she came in.

"I'm glad you're here. Luke's coffee is terrible," Jamie said into the silence that followed.

"Is that all I'm good for to you, James Phineas Archer?"

"Unruffle your feathers, Nan. He was teasing. We need you. Come and sit," Luke said.

"Yes. Luke's coffee is delightful," Jamie said with a dramatic shudder. "Unfortunately, we finished the remains of Cecile's cake," he added with a wink.

The men shifted so she could sit at the table.

"What is this all about?" she asked.

"Artie has to leave for Saint Louis. He has dealings with the governor," Luke said, waggling his eyebrows. "At least he's removing the British Army from our lawn. They're spoiling the view." He peered at her closely. "You don't seem surprised."

"About the governor? I'm not. It isn't our business," she said, darting a glance at the duke and back to focus on her brother.

"No, but I'm going with him," Jamie said.

"Whatever for?" she demanded.

"Window glass, a stove, lumber for cupboards, doors, and stairs. I'm going to build another flatboat," Jamie said.

"Come with us and buy furnishings," Artie said.

She glared at him. "We don't have money for that."

Her brothers shifted uneasily, but Artie never moved a muscle. He simply gazed at her, immovable and determined. "Yes. We do."

"I'm not going to Saint Louis and I'm not—"

Luke slammed a hand on the table. "Don't be a ninny, Nan."

⇒⟫⟪⇐

"IF YOU DON'T give me a list, I'll shop on my own and you'll have to take what I bring." Phillip glared at Nan across the table.

The woman was being stubborn as a mule. When he announced his plan to shop when he went to install his unwanted equerry—and deal with Bagot's assignments—in Saint Louis, she refused to come along. Given proprieties, he couldn't disagree, but he disliked the thought of picking out colors and patterns or even furniture for the tavern.

"I'd rather use Cape Girardeau people. McGregor knows what I usually order." Her voice sounded harsh, the product of a clenched jaw.

"Good thought. I'll speak with McGregor about linens and coverlets before I go. They may have your crockery, but the furniture will come from Saint Louis."

She glowered across the table.

They'd been talking in circles for two hours. Jamie had given up and gone for a walk a while ago. When Nate and Evan interrupted, it was a relief.

"There's a keelboat on the landing like you asked. The captain's pleased to take on more load, he says, but he can only wait one day. Can you be ready by tomorrow?" Nate asked.

Phillip looked at the ensign. "Evan?"

"We'll be ready early," the boy said.

Phillip rose with a weary moan. "I don't have time for this. I will deal with Fitzwallace and be back in an hour. Have the list or I'll make the decisions."

"I'd make that list if I were you," Luke said over his shoulder when he followed Phillip out.

"Damned stubborn woman," Phillip muttered.

"She doesn't want your money."

"I owe her that much at least," Phillip replied.

"It's trivial to you. It is a fortune to her. That rankles," Luke said. "People have pride."

Phillip paused. "I can't change who I am. Should I not do what kindness I can? I owe your family my very life."

"Do you plan to buy her some furnishings and disappear?" Luke asked.

Phillip considered explaining his half-formed ideas, but it was too soon. "I'll be back in a week or two. We can talk then if you like. After that you can drag me out and beat what you think I owe out of my hide, only I'd rather keep my face until after I see some people on business." Phillip gazed at him steadily.

"We'll do that. You know I can find you if you don't come," Luke said.

Phillip marched down to the encampment, Evan at his side. "We leave for Saint Louis tomorrow," he announced. Fitzwallace, who had been sitting idle, came to his feet languidly. His bow was just short of insulting. "As you wish."

The words met Phillip's back as he strode past into the tent housing his luggage. He flipped open his trunk without a by-your-leave. He didn't have to look up to know Fitzwallace had scurried after him. "It's best not to overdo the outfit on the river. Too much flash won't impress Americans and could draw the wrong sort of attention." He pulled out a coat modest by ducal standards and a rather nice embroidered waistcoat. "This will do. I'd like it aired, pressed if possible, and ready first thing in the morning. I'll come here to shave and dress before we go."

He glanced around the tent, spied a smaller trunk-like safe, and found it locked. He held out a hand. Fitzwallace didn't have to ask. He handed over the key. As Phillip expected, it held the money and the letters of introduction. It also held the pay packets for both officers. "Well kept, but I have business to conduct." Fitzwallace followed his movement as he picked up the money pouch.

Phillip met and held his eyes until the captain remembered his place and bowed. "As you wish, Your Grace," he murmured.

Phillip handed back the key. "You can't be too careful. I'll bring it back before nightfall."

Nate caught up with him as he passed the newly-roofed Roost. "Nan said to give you this," he said.

The paper was, of course, a list of provisions to restore Archers' Roost for living and for business, but no personal needs.

He walked through Cape Girardeau, aware of awed expressions, a few smiles, and inclinations of various heads, an American sort of bow. Silence greeted his entry into the general sundries store, but McGregor soon softened when he heard why Phillip had come.

"I'd have extended her credit, you know," McGregor said when they had finished.

"Now you don't have to." Phillip left an extensive credit line for the Archers, paid a deposit for things McGregor had to order, and paid in full for some urgently needed items to be delivered immediately. He also covered the bill for provisions "borrowed" during the siege. It might have been simpler to do the ordering himself, but Nan would want to support local business her own way.

He spent his last afternoon at Archers' Roost stacking lumber.

Early the next morning, he found Evan in the process of dismantling two of the tents while Fitzwallace stood by, impatient to leave. The tents belonged to the Archers and he'd as well ignore them.

Scion of the highest class, the man stood so high in the instep he ought to topple over under the weight of his own arrogance and snobbery. *Was I ever that narrow-minded?* Phillip very much feared he was.

"I prepared your clothing as best I could under primitive conditions," the captain said. "The ensign will assist you. I suggest we begin with barbering."

Phillip almost refused, time being short, but a haircut might be a good idea. Evan proved efficient as well as skilled. Trimmed and shaved, he followed the ensign into the privacy of the luggage tent. His clothing, only moderately ostentatious by ducal standards, had been aired and readied. He suspected Evan was responsible. Fitzwallace seemed incapable of doing anything except ordering the ensign to work.

Soft linen and silk felt good against Phillip's skin. Muscle memory set in and his bearing rose. "Here I am, the duke," he muttered to himself.

Evan helped him into his finest pair of boots, the ones he'd left behind in Philadelphia for fear of damaging them. *What foolishness!* He'd lost his second best pair to Sullivan's thugs and hadn't even considered the matter, but these! He had to admit his beleaguered feet reposed in comfort.

"One more thing." He approached the small safe and held out his hand. Fitzwallace gave him the key, and he put half the money in a small purse, adding that and his letters of introduction into an inside pocket before locking the rest up.

The clothes he'd come down in lay on the ground. "Put those in the small portmanteau, Ensign. You can launder them in Saint Louis. Pack this with them." He handed his knife to Evan, enjoying Fitzwallace's bug-eyed fascination.

They met the Archer brothers at the boat landing.

"Gol-lee!" Nate took in Phillip's appearance with wide eyes.

Phillip extended his arms to give the boy a look. "Will I do? For my business, that is?"

"Is this what a duke looks like?" Nate asked.

"Sometimes. Sometimes grander."

"I'd like to see that!"

"Who is this swell from out east, do you think, Luke?" Jamie drawled. The two of them eyed Phillip insolently. He saw no sign of Nan and didn't ask.

"I'll see you in a week as I promised. Probably less," he said, extending his hand to Luke.

Luke glanced at the hand and back at his brother. "I dunno, Jamie. Do you suppose this is proper? We wouldn't want to insult His Majesty."

Phillip gave Luke's shoulder a gentle bump. "Darned straight," he said, drawing grins from both brothers.

"We best get moving," Jamie said, heading up the gangplank.

Phillip turned to find Fitzwallace glaring at the Archers. He sailed past the equerry with a haughty lift of his chin. "Stow my bags below," he ordered, climbing the gangplank, leaving Evan and Fitzwallace to follow. He turned on the deck to see Luke Archer grin at him.

He winked back, but as the boat pushed away, he had to wonder if this trip would give him what he hoped, the beginnings of an answer to the questions that had plagued him. *Who are you anyway, Phillip Tavernash? What do you want out of life?*

He saw her on the river bank then, in front of Archers' Roost standing tall in the shade of the great elm, waiting for him to pass. Nan knew precisely who she was. He envied that. Until he had the answer to his questions, he couldn't meet her halfway. Watching the wind blow her honey brown hair loose from its binding and her skirts whip in the wind, he knew with absolute certainty that his answers lay with this woman. He wasn't sure how, but determination to work it out drove him.

CHAPTER THIRTY-TWO

THE NEWLY CONSTRUCTED **Pride of the West Hotel** shone with buffed floors and banisters, gleaming chandeliers, and finely polished furniture. If it lacked Archers' Roost's hominess and welcoming atmosphere, it far outstripped it in elegance. It was not, however, up to the standards of London or even Philadelphia and it lacked any pretense of old money. Fitzwallace sniffed at the place when shown to his room, his aristocratic nose quivering in distaste.

Descending the main stairs and crossing the entrance to the dining room, Phillip found it suited his purposes perfectly. He spied Jamie already seated at a table. A beaming host led Phillip to join him. The buzz of conversation quieted as he passed, and heads turned before the crowd, largely businessmen, settled back into their negotiations and planning, at least so it seemed to Phillip. The proprietor, clearly delighted by his distinguished guest, the Duke of Glenmoor, made sure the food and the service were excellent.

Jamie grinned at him. "Are you really going to leave your two keepers here for a year?"

Phillip gave his order to the waiter before answering, while Jamie dug into eggs, steak, and fried pork belly with gusto, oblivious to the fine porcelain.

"As soon as I have my report for Bagot ready, I'm sending

Fitzwallace east with it. Don't tell him; let him wallow in his misery over being stuck in this uncivilized place. His world view is a bit fastidious." Phillip flipped out his serviette and covered his lap, a gesture that would be ludicrous in Nan's tavern.

"Is that how you see it?" Jamie frowned.

Phillip smiled ruefully. "Hardly. Saint Louis booms with adventurers, fur traders, and entrepreneurs of all sorts seeking their fortune. It grows larger every time we visit. It bristles with life, the energy infectious."

"You sound like a man who might stay a while," Jamie said studying him closely.

"If I can find my place in it, I intend to," Phillip responded.

"Is that what all the questions along the docks are about?" Jamie sat back, trying to puzzle it all through.

"Fur trade is bustling, but there are already dozens of players—mountain men, trading posts, and so on—almost all of it funnels through the Chouteau brothers at the top of the heap. There's no room for competition. Salt passes through here. Lumber. Agricultural products. What do they all have in common?" Phillip glanced up at the waiter who laid his breakfast down in front of him, murmuring his thanks.

Jamie sipped his coffee, considering his answer. "They all travel on the rivers."

"Precisely. And there is no dominant force for shipping or boat building. I think there's room for one."

Jamie's eyes lit up, letting Phillip's suggestion sink in. "Yes. Furs may die out. The salt may play out. Something else may come along, but it will always need boats on the river."

Jamie's expressive face leapt from idea to idea as Phillip watched. Nan said curiosity was Jamie's besetting sin. Phillip thought it might turn out to be a treasure, at least to him. "Save those ideas. We need to gather more information."

"Is that why you're meeting with the Chouteau brothers?" Jamie asked, smiling when Phillip said "we."

Acquiring accommodations and obtaining printed calling

cards had taken up Phillip's first day in Saint Louis, but he'd found time to deliver his letters of invitation to the famous fur traders who dominated Saint Louis and the fur trade, and also to Governor Clark.

"Yes! They probably think His Majesty's government wants a piece of the fur trade. Bagot is more interested in cooperation between Canadian interests and the trade here, and I'll discuss that. My own interest is in how much they move along the inland rivers and how. It should be a productive meeting. If they'll see me."

Evan, his uniform now crisp and tidy, approached soon after and gave Phillip a perfectly correct obeisance in full view of the entire dining room. "A message arrived for you, Your Grace." He handed Phillip a note on a small salver before standing at attention with his hands behind his back.

"Auguste Chouteau expresses his delight. It will apparently be an honor to receive so distinguished a guest. I'm invited to tea at 2 o'clock," Phillip read, glancing at Evan and Jamie.

He urged the ensign to join them, but Evan said he'd come to order a tray for Fitzwallace, and scurried off to do that.

Jamie and Phillip finished their meal and left the dining room together. "I wonder how Auguste Choteau feels about steam-powered boats," Phillip mused.

"There's one in town now," Jamie replied. "I might just wander over and have a closer look at the beast."

⇛⇚

WITH ARCHERS' ROOST under roof, Nan's assistants thinned out. The town folk had lives and businesses to see to. Nate, of course, was enormous help, though he missed Evan. He and Luke finished up the shakes on the roof, covered the spaces left open for windows, and made shelves in the kitchen. Cupboard doors would have to wait.

She needed those shelves. Nan had moved her pallet and

scant personal belongings to the small servant's quarters adjoining the kitchen, and she set about making order out of what remained.

Deliveries began the day after Artie left, taking her brother, her list, and her heart. A good stew pot had come the first day along with toweling, crockery to augment what had been salvaged, and a fine set of wooden spoons. McGregor's joy when he told her of the size of her credit line softened her fury at Artie's high-handedness. He had at least bowed to her request to give his trade to Cape Girardeau.

This day, she went up to the store herself, reviewing McGregor's supply of cloth. A bolt of heavy cotton—not quite pure white—would do nicely for table coverings. None seemed suitable for the downstairs curtains, however. She ordered several lengths of chintz for that, the colorful flower pattern far finer than the ones she had lost.

She desperately needed some clothing: a blouse or two, a work skirt, and one for Sunday and personal linen. She had lost everything, but fretted at the thought of taking such things from a man. Still, she reckoned the line of credit was hers to do with as she pleased. All of Cape Girardeau already knew where it came from. She drew a line at ordering fine things from out east. What McGregor carried in the store would do her fine.

McGregor himself carried the big wash tub she bought down to the roost. Nan heated water over an open fire, shaved a newly acquired bar of soap, and began to scrub every precious item she had saved from the old Roost until it shined and found its place on the new shelves.

Every flake of soap, every smell of new lumber, every object arriving from McGregor's, however, reminded her of Artie. The damned fool had paid his debt and then some.

"I owe you my life! Do you have a price for that?" His words echoed in her heart and mind. She wanted to shout. *No! It is beyond price, beyond debt, beyond commerce. I love you; your life matters more to me than anything, even Archers' Roost.* That what lay between them might be reduced to a transaction left her despondent.

CHAPTER THIRTY-THREE

IN HIS SEVENTIES, Auguste Chouteau stood tall and proud with a shock of white hair and an air of authority. His carefully applied charm let Phillip know no continental title held any sway over his hard-earned place in the world. His brother Pierre, several years younger but equally formidable, joined them. There at its founding, they were without doubt the power in Saint Louis.

After a polite exchange, in which Phillip expressed his and His Majesty's admiration for what the family had accomplished, they got down to business, and the variance in their interests soon became clear.

"Yes, we are aware of the Hudson's Bay Company's fur trade interests in the north. All too aware," Pierre said dismissively. "You will find that the late war left many on this side of the border suspicious if not outright hostile to English interests. We don't fear their competition."

"Sir Charles mentioned the North West Company also," Phillip said. He forced himself to focus on Bagot's questions, keeping his real interests at bay.

He soon realized that, in matters of the trade, Pierre took the lead. He answered again. "The situation in the northwest is a bit uglier. The recent treaty allows for joint occupation of the Oregon Country, and we compete aggressively there, but the final border remains in dispute. If your envoy wishes to support cooperation, settling that matter might be in everyone's best interests. Clean borders make for cleaner competition."

Phillip captured it all in the notebook he carried. He noticed that Pierre didn't mention that the treaty he referenced had in fact settled a border between British possessions and the United States Territory all the way to the Rocky Mountains.

"You've been here through much change. What think you of the American regime?" Phillip asked.

Auguste shrugged majestically. "Peace is good. Order is good. Business prospers best when there is order."

"Is it true you have interests in banking?" Phillip asked, abruptly changing direction.

Auguste gazed at him warily. "We have dabbled. At the moment, banking in the United States is somewhat volatile."

If what Phillip heard from Charles Bagot was true—and he believed it was—that was an understatement. "I was warned to be careful where I put my money," Phillip said.

"Your money?" Auguste asked. His surprise appeared genuine. So did his interest. He leaned forward.

Phillip outlined his general deposits in London and Philadelphia. He saw no need to explain his reluctance to tap the full resources of the duchy. The amounts he described were enough to grab Auguste Choteau's interest. "I came with some cash assets, more than is comfortable to transport, as well as a line of credit on the bank in Philadelphia. What do you recommend?"

A half hour later, The Duke of Glenmoor became a client of Auguste Choteau's private fund organization, by far, Phillip suspected, the safest organization for saving and borrowing in the territory and several states.

His host relaxed into a wise and mellow recitation of real estate in Saint Louis and its surroundings—and farther distant. "Is your interest business, investment, personal? Do you seek to build a home here?"

He did. The thought that had been dancing on the edge of his consciousness came into focus. He wanted a home, one grand enough to enjoy but scaled to family life. One for Nan. But he had to ask her first, and before that, he needed more. He needed a place in the commerce of Saint Louis.

"Business to begin with. I would like to build a boat works." That astonishing statement brought both of the brothers to attention.

Pierre answered his questions about inland waters. "Our trappers and the peoples of the plains still bring the furs overland by horse and mule to trading posts, but yes. Eventually, it comes down to rivers—the Kansas, the Missouri, the Snake, and more. There will always be a need for boats."

"What is your opinion about steam?"

"It is the way of the future, but still risky. They blow up, not so? What do you know about steamships?" Auguste asked pointedly.

"As yet, I know little, but I know a man who does." Gideon certainly would, and he could direct Phillip to more. His excitement grew in the telling. "They are getting safer. So far, what few steamships I've seen on these waters come from the east. Saint Louis needs its own steamboat building enterprise. I plan to create one."

The brothers glanced at one another. Phillip could see they appreciated his vision; he suspected the ideas weren't new to them, but they were skeptical of his capability. He would have to earn their respect and convince them. He'd said enough for now. He changed the subject.

"What can you tell me about Governor Clark?" he asked. He expected to meet the man himself later that afternoon. Fore-warned is forearmed.

Again, the brothers glanced at one another, and paused as if choosing words carefully. Auguste spoke first. "He loves the country. By that I mean his eyes are on the territory, the vast open land."

Pierre studied his fingernails. "Open for now."

Auguste went on "He was Superintendent of Indian Affairs before Territorial Governor. He licensed traders, issued passports. Still does."

No wonder they are cautious; Clark has had great influence over how they do their business. "He's the crucial representative of the United States for the places on which you depend."

"We survived the Spanish, and the back-and-forth between them and the French, and then the United States. And war." Auguste shrugged. "We manage."

It was obvious to Phillip that the old fox did more than manage. "But what is the man like?"

"Typically American," Auguste said. "Promotes business. And settlement."

That brought a frown from Pierre. Phillip turned to him. "What do you think?"

"Auguste mentions the European flags. Also here are other peoples. This has been and most of it still is their land. We have dealt with them well for fifty years to their benefit and ours. Clark claims to respect and admire them. You'll see it if you visit him."

"His respect is real," Auguste said tartly.

Pierre grunted. "He tries in his small way to help them, but he is an expansionist. He seeks ways to protect native culture but fully supports the drive for settlement and exploitation of the land. He wants to have it both ways, but in the end, the peoples will be driven from their land."

Auguste frowned and appeared to turn the subject. "Do you plan to build here in Saint Louis, or do you too have your eyes on the west?"

"Here for certain. The river cities are wild enough for me," Phillip said, and it was true.

"Then those affairs are not your interest. Missouri will soon be a state with all the civilization and law that comes with that. Clark is no peacetime administrator. He won't be governor for long when that happens."

Phillip shook their hands moments later, delighted with Auguste's offer to meet in two days to look at property.

"YOU'RE THE WITNESS that struck down the Sullivan boys!" It had taken Governor Clark a half hour and a tumbler of rum to conjure up that insight.

Phillip's lips twisted into a self-deprecating smile as the governor poured him another. "For my sins, yes." As territorial magistrate, Clark would have heard of the trial. Phillip was happy with the change of subject. He'd managed the mission for Bagot—greetings and a few questions—in ten minutes.

"You've been out here a while then. When you presented your formal letter of introduction from the British envoy, I expected a tourist passing through. But then, if I heard the story correctly, your stay hasn't been entirely voluntary."

"It wasn't what I expected, no. Let's just say I've learned many things," Phillip replied. Glancing around the governor's wood-paneled study with its buffalo skin rug—head and all—and artifact-lined shelves, he knew he still had much to learn. The entire house seemed packed with treasures from the governor's travels, many of them artifacts from native tribes. It was a curious contrast to Auguste Chouteau's understated elegance.

"Do I hear correctly you were sheltered at Archers' Roost?" Clark asked.

"That is correct."

"Has old Amos Archer settled down there, or is he still running the hills?"

"I believe he has a cabin somewhere up the Missouri near Arrow Rock. How much further he roams—" He shook his head. "You'd have to ask Luke Archer."

The old explorer, in his prime at fifty, sighed. Phillip caught the longing in his expression. Auguste's comment that he was no peacetime administrator came to mind. "Is the son with you?" he asked.

"Not Luke, no. One of the other ones. He's helping me study the shipping traffic in and out of Saint Louis."

"You didn't mention that. Does your government have an interest in shipping?"

"Here? Not that I know of. My interest is personal," Phillip said. His business for the Crown had taken ten minutes and yielded little. He described the bare outlines of his ideas.

A slow, knowing grin came over the governor's face. "This country seduces, doesn't it?"

"I don't know yet if I can carve a place for myself, but I mean to try."

"As have many before you." Clark raised a glass. "Good luck to you."

A knock at the door disturbed them.

"Come."

"Sir, I—I'm sorry. I've interrupted." A boy about Nate's age stood in the doorway. Lanky, as if he hadn't quite grown into his height, with neatly trimmed black hair and warm brown skin, he intrigued Phillip immediately. *Is he Clark's son?*

"We were just finishing, Baptiste. Come and meet the Duke of Glenmoor, visiting us from England," Clark said, rising. Phillip rose with him.

Clark left out a few details about the duke, but Phillip didn't care. He inclined his head to the lad.

"Glenmoor, this is Jean Baptiste Charbonneau, my godson and ward. He stays with me when he is not away at school."

"I'm pleased to meet you, sir," the young man murmured.

Of course. French. Phillip suspected Native ancestry as well. "I'm pleased to meet you," he said, and the young man murmured the similar sentiments. Baptiste said little, but his bright, intelligent eyes took in much.

Phillip's innate manners came to the surface regardless of how much the boy intrigued him. "I will leave you two to your business. Thank you for your time, Your Excellency."

Clark took his proffered hand. "Please convey my regards to Sir Charles. Since you appear ready to stay for a while, perhaps we'll meet again. Bring Luke Archer if you come back this way."

Phillip left the house and walked back to the hotel with a lift to his step and hope in his heart. He swept through the entranceway and up the stairs to pound on Captain Fitzwallace's door. He paused only briefly before opening it. The captain slouched in a chair without a coat or boots, his shirt open at the top. A half empty bottle of very expensive brandy sat on the table next to him. He crawled to his feet and sketched a bow.

"Your Grace. I wasn't expecting—"

"Clearly not. I want you to make plans to travel."

Fitzwallace brightened. "How soon?"

Yesterday. "I will have the reports Sir Charles requested for you tomorrow or the next day at the latest. You may leave any time after that. Survey travel schedules. You may want to go via New Orleans. It is time at sea, but perhaps more comfortable than up the Ohio and overland. Take your choice."

Fitzwallace picked up his coat eagerly while Phillip spoke. "I'll investigate schedules and the cost of three tickets."

"One, Captain. Evan will stay with me."

One arm halfway to a sleeve, Fitzwallace stopped what he was doing. "You're staying here?" he asked in palpable disbelief, his brows lifted so high Phillip thought they would reach his hairline. "Here?"

"As I said, Fitzwallace. The ensign as well." Phillip didn't need an ensign, but Evan needed to be relieved of his overbearing half-brother.

An overtly scowling Fitzwallace stuffed his coat on, refusing to meet Phillip's eyes.

"Unless you want me to report your disrespect and insubordination, you will rein it in and do as I order. My choices are none of your concern. Am I clear?"

Fitzwallace gave a jerky nod. "As Your Grace wishes. I will go to the shipping office now."

Feeling lighter, Phillip left him there. He'd finish those reports if he had to stay up all night. It shouldn't come to that. Once he sent them with Fitzwallace—and alerted the envoy via the United States Mail in case Fitzwallace got sidetracked or chose to abandon his duties—he'd be finished with his obligations to the blasted title and free to pursue his own goals. His increasingly clear goals.

CHAPTER THIRTY-FOUR

"IF THEY DON'T come today, I'm taking Nate hunting," Luke said, putting away a massive portion of eggs.

"You may as well plan on it. We've not heard a word in two weeks," Nan sighed. She wondered if Artie would come back at all once Saint Louis society got a hold on him. Still, he promised, and without window glass and additional lumber, work on the Roost had come to a halt.

She had a guest to feed, a pleasant distraction. She'd been able to rent out two of the old guestrooms once she moved up to the tavern building. She packed up a good portion of eggs, toast, and coffee, and carried it over. Tom Fuller had been a regular before and promised to be again once they were fully up and running.

"Is it true that helper of yours turned out to be some bigwig?" Tom asked, taking the basket from her. "Sure didn't look like it."

"He is, in fact, an English duke," she murmured, stepping back to leave.

"Ha! Don't that beat all. I would have liked to see folks' faces when he told them. Must be odd in the brainbox, though, working in a tavern and hiding that he's some big man."

Nan gave him a pained smile. "Maybe." She stomped back toward the kitchen.

Except he didn't exactly hide it. Not really. I just didn't understand how important he was. She kicked an inconvenient stone out of her path. *I'm an ignorant fool.*

She leaned on the well housing and pulled up the bucket, sloshing a third of it in her angry march to the kitchen. She wet the big iron skillet and began to scrub.

I'm an ignorant fool. The duke may return, but Artie—my Artie—will never come back. The words echoed in her head. The closer she came to tears, the harder she scrubbed.

"Nan!" Nate called from the front.

She scrubbed her eyes with one soapy hand. "What do you need?" she snapped.

The boy burst into the kitchen. "We didn't get far. Saw a flatboat coming this way. It's them."

Nan could hardly breathe. "Are you sure?"

"It's carrying a big cookstove. Must be." Nate ran out as fast as he had come.

⟫⟫⟫⟪⟪⟪

FOR THE RETURN trip, Phillip hired a man who was teaching Evan Fitzwallace how to manage the poles so that Jamie sat with Phillip, the two of them with their feet over the side watching scenery pass. Jamie shook his head. "Amazing. Auguste Chouteau himself showed us property," he said as he had repeatedly since they left Saint Louis.

Phillip suspected Jamie was much more impressed to have met the famous trader Chouteau than he was with Phillip for all his fancy title, and for good reason. "I've been meaning to ask you something."

Jamie peered at him expectantly, head tipped to one side with a faint smile on his face.

"Are you ready to leave the farm behind?"

"The farm? Why would I?" Jamie's stunned expression almost made Phillip laugh.

"To build boats, of course. I can't start this enterprise alone. We'll hire people, but I'll need someone I trust to oversee construction. Your questions to that steamboat captain were intelligent and insightful. I think you knew as much as he did about how the damned thing worked by the end."

"I have ideas about boat design for the things too," Jamie mused, excitement taking root. "I've been thinking about it. But I don't know how the engines are made. I'd like to talk to an engineer."

"We might be able to hire an expert. You could apprentice and take over eventually."

"Would we have to go to England? Captain said the engine came from England," Jamie said.

"The engine might or might not, but boats like that designed for rivers are useless in England. The rivers and canals are too narrow for the paddles. Don't get me wrong. An English ship crossed the Atlantic last year, at least partially under steam, but the best builders of steam-powered boats for rivers are in this country. I saw them at work in Pittsburgh on my way out."

Jamie considered the new information. "Captain said one is building in New Orleans."

"Commerce so far has been largely from New Orleans east, but commerce on the upper Mississippi is just beginning to expand. I need to do this now, get in early if I'm going to do it at all. I want your support."

Jamie shook his head. "But the farm. I promised Nan."

"Hold those thoughts. We'll talk again," Phillip said, standing up. "Look there. We're almost home." They moved to the clearing and he saw Nan standing on the porch, shading her eyes from the sun while she watched. *Home.* To his delight, she took off at a run to the boat landing.

Moments later, Nate waved from the landing. "Welcome home!"

Luke bent to help them beach the craft. "Lumber, I see. Window glass?" he asked.

Jamie pointed out the wooden crates. "Three tables and chairs for them. And the stove, of course."

Phillip ignored the hubbub. His eyes were only for the woman who emerged, breathless, from the path to the Roost. She wore new clothes, simple but flattering. That she made use of the credit he had established at McGregor's warmed his heart. He dared hope the avid gaze she returned meant she felt the same. It took all his effort to stay on the boat and not run to her in front of her brothers.

"Nan. Look. An iron cook stove!" Nate exclaimed.

There was little enough room for conversation. It took all of them, including Evan and the boatman, to drag the stove up to the Roost and into the kitchen. A cast-iron step-top stove, it had a wood box under a six burner cook top to one side, and a box oven with two shelves on the other. Nan could only stare at it. She'd been cooking on a tiny box stove and open hearth. The wonder of the thing struck her dumb.

Phillip took solace in watching her glances dart from the stove to him and back, all the way uphill.

They wrangled it into her kitchen. "We'll have to build a stovepipe and chimney," Luke grunted.

"Artie thought of that. Pipe is packed on the boat," Jamie said.

Phillip couldn't speak, he could only watch Nan admiring her stove.

"Quit gaping and come and tell us where to put the tables," Luke demanded, herding them all back to the boat.

It took two hours to unload the rest. Phillip's attention never left Nan. Once she frowned over at him when she discovered he'd bought a decorative lady's dresser for her room along with a matching bedstead. The other beds and dressers were plain enough to suit her.

Once, she came close enough for him to lean in and whisper, "I bought you a present."

Nan's fiery red blush brought a frown from Luke, who glared at Phillip. "I saw the bedroom set," she hissed back.

"Not that," he said.

Her blush darkened, and she bumped him with her shoulder

and walked on.

He grinned to himself. He'd considered all sorts of inappropriate gifts a man might give a single lady—silks and jewels among them—but settled on something she wouldn't refuse.

When at last the boat was empty, Nate suggested they begin to dismantle it and stack the lumber.

"Enough!" Nan raised both hands to emphasize the point. "You can do that tomorrow. We haven't even welcomed them properly. They've tales to tell, no doubt. Come up to the Roost for a drink."

She didn't have to ask them twice.

They weren't halfway there before Jamie started regaling them with their adventures on the river and in the city. He started with his time on and around the steamboat. "And Artie bought a piece of property by the docks. A big piece," he told them.

They'd reached the front door by then. "What for?" Luke asked.

"I'll need it to build boats, won't I?" Phillip said, grinning.

Luke's jaw dropped, but before he or anyone else could pepper Phillip with questions, Jamie went on. "I haven't told you the best part yet."

"Hold off," Luke said, ducking behind the bar. "This is a bit new, but I think it will do," he said, pouring beer for Jamie and Phillip.

Jamie took a sip, gave it a look and a nod, and went on. "You wouldn't even guess this. Artie bought the property from Auguste Chouteau himself. The man came down to the river and showed us various properties."

"He must be really old. He founded Saint Louis, didn't he?" Nate asked.

"I think his stepfather did, but he was there. I think Auguste himself was your age when they arrived," Luke said, hefting his own beer to his mouth.

"He may be up in years, but he doesn't look frail. Dignified, though. Kind of serious," Jamie said.

Luke chuckled. "I hear he wasn't so stuffy years ago. Sitting on his money bags now."

"We had dinner with him," Jamie announced. Phillip suspected he'd saved that for last. Sure enough, it brought a gasp from Nate. Nan didn't look up. She'd been subdued the entire time.

"In Chouteau's big house?" Nate asked.

"No. At our hotel, but it was fancy enough. Everyone in the city knows him, too," Jamie said, preening.

Nan's unnatural quiet left Phillip concerned. He hoped it meant she was as anxious as he for a moment alone.

He put his mug down. He didn't see the box he wanted.

"Did you see the governor, too?" Nan asked, her voice strained. If he could get her alone, he'd demand to know what bothered her.

"I didn't, but Artie met him," Jamie said.

"What's he like, Artie? And what are you doing?" Nate asked.

"I'm looking for… There it is," he said, patting a big box next to the crates of glass. "Help me with this, Nate."

The two of them lifted it to the table. "It's my gift. To—to all of you who are interested. Perhaps Nan would like to open it."

She stared at it as if it contained snakes. "You open it."

"I'm the giver not the receiver," he said.

"Open the blasted thing, Nan," Jamie said. "Don't be a ninny."

"I am not a ninny," she shouted just before she turned on her heels and left the room as if chased by a hungry wolf.

"Damn." Phillip stared after her.

"That's been brewing for two weeks," Luke mumbled.

A second later, Phillip took off after her.

"Hey, Nan! It's books. A whole box of books!" Nate shouted after them.

CHAPTER THIRTY-FIVE

NAN MADE IT to the big elm before she stopped, wrapping her arms around her middle. She couldn't bear another moment in there. He'd come back as he'd promised with his load of bounty for Archers' Roost, winning her brothers' admiration and gratitude, like the grand beneficent lord he was. The night at least was moonless. It suited her mood.

"I knew you'd come here. Why are you running, you daft woman?" Artie's voice came out of the dark.

She felt him behind her, but she refused to turn. His breath came warm on the back of her neck.

"You're angry," he said. "What did I do?"

She answered so softly he had to ask her to repeat it. "Nothing you can help. When are you going back?"

He walked around her, but she turned away. "You aren't making sense, Nan. Help me understand."

"I don't know who you are."

"What?"

She turned and said it louder. "I don't know who you are."

"I'm—" He drew in a breath, and his fingers trembled as they touched her cheek.

"You were Artie who swept my kitchen. Now you're the Duke of Glenmoor who meets with governors, and buries my family in bounty," she whispered.

He took her hand and led her to the bench. "Sit with me. Please."

She sat at the far end, leaving room between them. He scooted closer. "First of all, I won't apologize for doing what I can to help restore the Roost."

She tried to move away. He wasn't having that. He pulled her up against his side with one arm around her shoulder.

"That's better. Warmer. Let's talk about this. You said you don't know who I am, and it is a fair question. I'm not, as it turns out, the Duke of Glenmoor. At least I shouldn't be. I told you that before," he said. When she didn't answer, he went on. "I left England, confused and adrift. Who am I then if I'm not Glenmoor? What value do I have?"

How can this man have any doubt about his value? She looked up at him then, seeking his eyes in the dark. He kissed the top of her head, but she wasn't ready for that. She stiffened and moved back as far as his arm would let her. "Go on," she said.

"I'm not Artie either, unfortunately, though I loved being that man. Your care healed my body. Archers' Roost healed my battered heart. Your family taught me how love works, done right. You let me know I wasn't as worthless as I feared. That sense of worth gave me courage."

"You have plenty of courage. The day you took down Bear, I—" He stopped the flow of words with his fingers, sending a tingling feeling through her whole body. Nan was in danger of melting into this man, but she needed to hear more.

"Yes. I discovered I had physical courage, and the moral courage to testify at the trial, but I mean something else. You gave me the courage to create my own place in the world. Until I met you, everything I owned had been given to me. I never had to work for anything. Do you remember what you said after the fire?"

"I said many things."

"You said, 'We'll start over. We've done it before.' You set about rebuilding your life. It shamed me. Restoring Archers'

Roost is the first time I've been part of an enterprise to build something worthwhile. I like that feeling."

A shaft of hope pierced Nan's darkness. "What are you going to do?"

"Come with me, and I'll show you."

Hope started to blink out. "Come where? To England? I can't do that. I already—"

"To Saint Louis," he said. "Did you listen to Jamie when he wasn't babbling on about Chouteau?"

"You bought property. You're staying?" she said, her voice betraying the longing of her heart.

"If I can," he replied.

"You can if you want," she said, her voice becoming thick with need. She lifted her head to his.

"I want," he whispered. "Oh yes, I want."

SHE HAD TURNED to him herself. When he took her mouth, he intended to reassure, to coax, to build a bridge between them. It quickly flamed into something else. She reached up and cupped his cheek as she leaned into the kiss, returning it fiercely.

Phillip snaked his arm around her waist and pulled her onto his lap, never taking his mouth from hers. His other hand stretched around her neck, into her hair, pulling her closer still. She wiggled to get comfortable, every movement sending his arousal higher.

When she tore her mouth off his, gasping for breath, Phillip kissed and licked his way down her chin to her neck. She tipped her head to give him access until he paused, his lips over her rapidly beating pulse. Nan moaned, and it was all the encouragement he needed.

He laid her back over one arm and worked the buttons at the top of her blouse with the other, opening her to his wandering mouth. Nan's restless hands wavered between caressing his nape and pulling at his shirttail in an effort to touch, her kisses moistening his shoulder. He laid her back on the bench.

When he found one nipple to lick and suckle, her body jerked under his. "Artie? What?"

He pulled back, trying to see her in the shadows. "I'm—"

"Don't stop," she whispered, reaching up to pull him back down.

"Wait," he said, working on the buttons with one hand, opening her to the waist, and caressed her magnificent breasts. *My glorious goddess.*

Her slender fingers had found their way under his shirt and her touch burned a path across his belly. He pulled up the front and leaned over her so that they touched, skin to skin, stretched out along the bench, kissing her deeply, while her hands moved to his back, exploring frantically.

His fingers moved down her hip, instinctively bunching up her skirt on one side until he touched the skin of her hip. Her questing mouth stopped and she went still.

A weak voice inside him asked, *what are you doing, Tavernash? Too much too fast. She's—* His Nan. She was his Nan, and precious beyond belief.

"Artie, I'm… I…" she murmured.

"I know. Me too. Delighted. Aroused. Confused," he said, giving her a quick kiss. "This isn't the time to carry this further." As he sat up, the clouds parted and he studied her laid out before him, her bounty open to his gaze. "You are a treasure," he rasped. "But we need to stop this." He tugged her up into his lap once more, pulled her blouse together, and wrapped both arms around her, laying her head on his shoulder with his cheek against it.

They stared at her beloved river, sparkling now in the moonlight, and let their breathing return to normal.

"I love this place," she said at last.

"Archers' Roost?"

"And the river and the land. I could never leave it."

Phillip set her aside and began to button her blouse. "We need to go back. Luke would kill me if he found us like this." Nothing had been decided between them. He still had hurdles to overcome.

She snorted. "He would never, and you know it."

"He loves you," he said. She didn't disagree.

"The governor wants to meet him. He wants to meet Amos Archer's children. That includes you." It wasn't entirely a bouncer. Clark did want to talk with Luke.

"I've never known you to lie, Phillip Artie Tavernash," she said tartly.

"Just come to Saint Louis with me. We'll talk then." He pulled her to her feet.

She kissed him then, fiercely. "Just a few more kisses, Artie," she begged.

He allowed himself one and then another. "No more, or I won't be responsible for the consequences."

NAN STRAIGHTENED HER clothing and his. She stole another quick kiss before she let him take her by the hand and lead her toward the Roost.

Her entire body felt restless with unsated desire. Her skin burned from the things he'd done to her. She wanted more, and knew what it meant. She may have been innocent, but she had grown up in a world that left her far from ignorant. Still, she suspected he was wise to call a halt. When she asked if he was staying, he said, "If I can." That offered hope, yet it hardly constituted a promise.

She'd gone a few steps when something else occurred to her. "Staying," meant not returning to England. It didn't necessarily mean Archers' Roost.

Chapter Thirty-Six

HARD WORK HELPED. Phillip could drop into bed exhausted every night, with a chance of sleep, in spite of longing for Nan. The first week, he slept in the makeshift sitting room in the old guest wing remains. Nan was across the yard in a room off the kitchen, where she had insisted on storing the precious books he brought until shelves could be built. He could easily imagine her there. Imagine her in inappropriate detail. There were no more interludes by the river.

Their first priority was installing the cook stove. A stone chimney on the south side of the building served two hearths, one in the kitchen and one in the public room as it had before. After some discussion, a decision was made to place the stove near the kitchen hearth and vent it to the same chimney rather than up a pipe.

By the third day, he sat and watched Nan hum to herself while she prepared breakfast on the new stove. Her honey-colored hair had been pulled up in a knot at her crown, giving him a view of her lovely nape. He now knew the feel of it and longed for a taste. Jamie came in to breakfast before he could succumb to temptation on the spot.

Jamie, by far their most skilled carpenter, framed out the windows, training Nate as he did. Phillip helped complete the upper floor; he and Luke began framing the stairs with Jamie's oversight. They kept Evan busy chopping wood, and the boy was beginning to fill out.

Phillip managed to steal a kiss Saturday afternoon when Luke disappeared for an hour. "Need to breathe the woods," he had said. That was one of many things Phillip wouldn't have understood a year before. He did now, but in his case, he needed to breathe Nan's scent. Actually, the smell of something sweet and delicious baking had filled the Roost.

He found her up to her elbows in bread dough. She'd taken to baking with a vengeance once she got the hang of the box oven. The smell of something sweet permeated the kitchen. Phillip came up behind her and put an arm around her waist, pulling her close and savoring that kiss to her nape he'd been longing for.

"Artie! I'm baking!" She turned in his arms, holding both hands sticky with dough up on either side.

"I noticed." He grinned. "The smell has been driving me mad." *You've been driving me mad.*

"I'll have tea and cookies in an hour," she said, dabbing his nose with dough from her finger.

"Biscuits," he said. "I don't know 'cookies.'"

"They'll taste good either way, now shoo."

He stole one more kiss—though to his joy, she gave it freely—and went back to work.

Nan insisted Sunday be a day of rest, even for Evan. She set out chairs on the porch, and led them in prayer to greet the Sabbath, choosing not to take the time traveling to Kaskaskia. Phillip knew some of them, and prayed silently when he did not. *I made an error with those books*, he thought. *I forgot to get that Bible.* He wouldn't make that mistake again.

Breakfast featured sweet breads. Raisins, currants, and nuts assuring him she made good use of the credit at the general sundries store made them all the sweeter.

"I made a list of the remaining tasks. We should be able to move in upstairs by the end of the week," Jamie said.

"No work today!" Nan said in her best governess voice.

"Yes, Nan," her brothers droned, laughing at one another.

"If we get the upstairs finished, maybe Jamie and I can go over to Kaskaskia and see about progress on the farm paperwork. Welling certainly has been dragging his feet," Luke said, piling potatoes next to his eggs.

"If the squatters are Sullivan people, they may have left. If they're plain folks who thought they bought it, it might be more complicated," Jamie said. "But we can't let it slide. If nothing else, we owe Pa his money back."

"Can it wait a few weeks?" Phillip asked.

"Probably. Why?" Luke asked. "I need to be getting back upriver. I'd like to settle the farm business before I return to Pa."

"I want you all to come to Saint Louis with me." Phillip put his fork down and his hands in his lap, gazing from eye to eye to draw their attention. "I'd like to show you all the property I bought, and explain my ideas."

Nate bounced with excitement. "Can we, Nan?"

Luke merely frowned.

"Luke, Governor Clark knew your father, he told me. He'd like to meet you." He gazed around the table. "Actually, he wanted to know about all of you and Archers' Roost."

"I haven't seen any sign of the steamer on the river. If it is still in Saint Louis, I'd like to take another look. I have more questions for the captain," Jamie said, turning to his brother. "You should see it, Luke—only a bit bigger than a keelboat, but an engine takes up the added space. Faster even downstream and easy going up."

"I have no use for the damned noisy monster," Luke said. "It'll drive me right up the Missouri for good."

"Did you know they've built a brick church in Saint Louis?" Phillip asked casually. The Archer boys ignored that as an irrelevant comment, but it was Nan's attention he hoped to catch. "They're importing art from France. If we're done with the upstairs by Thursday, we could be there for Sunday services."

Jamie perked up. "He's right, Nan. Three or four times the size of the log church in Kaskaskia. They call it 'Saint Louis King of France.' Nate, pass some of that bacon over here before you eat it all. Evan needs some."

"We'd have to flag a keelboat by Thursday or Friday," Nan muttered.

Phillip smiled into his coffee. He knew he had her interest. "Luke could put his canoe and gear on the boat and then leave for the territories from Saint Louis after he has a look at things. Or Kaskaskia first to ask about the farm, if he has to."

Luke grunted, which was about as much of an affirmation as Phillip could expect.

Nan began clearing the table. He rose to help her, drawing puzzled looks. "No work today, remember? Ought to apply to Nan, too."

She rolled her eyes, but she let him help.

No work today. What would I be doing in London? Probably sleeping off a night out doing things I'd rather not remember. Phillip smiled when Nan handed him a towel to dry the dishes. "What do you plan to do today?"

"I thought I might take a walk along the river. I want to see what wildflowers have come up," Nan answered.

If it was London, he'd take her for a ride through Hyde Park. *It is what a gentleman did, if he was courting.* And he most certainly was. A walk would do as well. "May I come with you?"

Her smile held invitation and feminine mysteries that deprived him of speech.

THEY HAD BEEN in the city two days when an invitation arrived while they were at breakfast. Every aspect of the hotel's management absorbed Nan, and breakfast service in the formal dining room was no exception. Well-dressed waiters and linen tablecloths were beyond her capability at Archers' Roost, but good food, flowers, and well-set tables were not. Civility she could manage.

Evan, who had reverted to his formal role, much to Nan's disapproval, interrupted her preoccupation and appeared in the dining room with the invitation on a silver salver.

Artie—she still couldn't call him anything else, even if he did tell her 'Artie' wasn't real—took it with raised eyebrows. He read it slowly and seemed to be considering the contents carefully. "It is from Governor Clark. He's having a reception tomorrow evening."

"Word is there are some big people from Washington in town. A senator and some Congress folk. The boat landing is buzzing with statehood talk," Jamie said.

He'd been full of riverfront gossip. After Mass on Sunday, Jamie had stayed behind to visit with the boatmen when Artie took them all upstream to the property he had bought just north of the city where he planned to establish a boatyard. While Artie explained his plans to Luke and Nate, waving his arms expansively and pointing, Nan tried to see his vision for the flat, empty land, but she struggled.

"He's inviting you to meet the bigwigs?" Luke asked. Nan assumed the same. They all gazed at Artie, breakfast forgotten.

Artie sighed deeply. "Let me read it. 'The governor begs the honor of the presence of His Grace the Duke of Glenmoor—' My own humble self." He raised a hand when Luke would have spoken. "He goes on, 'and his guests the Archer family at a reception at the governor's house on Wednesday next at six of the clock.'"

"We're *your* guests now, Artie?" Nate laughed. "I thought it was the other way around."

Luke rubbed his jaw. "He wants us to meet those easterners?"

"I think he wants to show them the people of the real Missouri," Artie said. "At least Clark's vision of the country and its folk."

"Are we supposed to turn up in moccasins and buckskins?"

Nan asked. Her words left a bitter taste in her mouth.

Artie ran a hand through his hair. "He may hope Luke does. You all just need to be yourselves."

"I won't go. I don't have proper clothes, and I won't be patronized like I'm some uncivilized countrywoman." She glared at him.

Jamie leaned toward her. "You need to show up, Nan. Get yourself a proper gown and show him who you really are."

Nan wasn't entirely sure the real her belonged in a proper gown, but Jamie's words and the gleam in Artie's eyes tempted her.

"What do you think, Luke?" Artie asked.

"He wants me as some trained bear," Luke muttered.

"He remembers your father—and his time exploring—nostalgically. These parts are filling up with farmers, and I think you represent that freer world, and he genuinely wants to meet you. I'd suggest we ask for a private meeting, but if he has important guests, he may not be able to."

Long moments passed, all eyes on Luke. "I'll go," he said at last. "But I won't dress up for him."

"You look fine the way you are," Artie replied. Luke had come up to the city dressed in loose trousers, his buckskins stuffed in a bag. He had moccasins on his feet. Artie leaned over and added in a hushed tone, "But don't forget that vicious-looking knife of yours for your belt." Luke almost smiled at that.

Nan glowered at them. "I'm still—"

"Which one of you wants to take Nan dress shopping? I'll take Nate to the tailor," Artie said, studying Nan, a dare in his eyes. Something else in his eyes, suspiciously like longing, made up her mind. If he wanted her in fine clothes, she would do it for him. Once.

Scarcely an hour later, Jamie dragged her to a dressmaker—on Artie's credit—and a flurry of measuring, poking, and prodding ensued. She was grateful he didn't come himself. It would have been hideously embarrassing. The soft fabrics the woman produced made Nan's heart ache. She couldn't resist. She refused frills and fussy ruffles, but as the dress took shape, she gave up the struggle. *I've been seduced by lace and silk.*

She pushed the thought away, seduced not being the most comfortable choice of words in this situation. Her characteristic honesty, however, forced her to admit she looked forward to Artie seeing her in a beautiful gown.

Everything else about Artie and this trip confused her and muddled her brain. She found the brick church, though still being completed inside, as lovely as promised, but it was only one piece of the city. When he took her by the hand for a walk every day, they spoke of inconsequential things, like the signs of spring and the beauty of the river.

The land he so proudly showed her had been empty, flat, and on the river. He appeared to see a factory bustling with boat manufacture when he looked at it. She saw a flood prone plot of land. He laughed and pointed out how far back his property stretched. A fair point. Nothing she'd seen so far felt permanent to her. Nothing appeared settled. Fine enough the property might be for making boats, but it wasn't Archers' Roost. Perhaps nothing ever would be.

"Miss Archer? Did you hear me?"

Nan bent with a smile to ask the dressmaker to repeat her question. She had a dress and a reception to look forward to. She let go of her fears and doubts and gave herself permission to look beautiful for Artie—and to enjoy it if only for one night.

CHAPTER THIRTY-SEVEN

"Y OU'RE BACK IN full duke display tonight, Your Grace," Nate teased while they waited for the others in the hotel foyer under the glow of candles.

"With help from our Evan. I hope this waistcoat isn't too much." Phillip glanced down at the object made of grey silk embroidered with elaborate flowers in silver thread. "You're looking rather splendid yourself," he added, studying the buff trousers, white shirt, and blue superfine jacket with a loosely tied navy blue scarf at his neck. Jamie, similarly attired, pulled at his cuffs nearby.

"There!" Nate exclaimed, mouth agape. Phillip glanced up and his heart stuttered in his chest.

Nan, resplendent in crème and gold, descended on Luke's arm. At Nate's exclamation, they paused on the stairs.

Candles from the crystal chandelier glittered off the tiny gold flowers affixed to the net overlaying her crème satin gown and the gold lace at her neck and around the fashionably puffed sleeves. The neckline scooped just low enough to tantalize. A gold band complemented her honey-brown hair arranged in a fall of curls around the crown of her head. His throat went dry. *Goddess indeed.*

"You look like a princess," Nate exclaimed.

"For once, I agree with my little brother," Jamie said, staring up at her.

Phillip, who was beyond speech, stepped up and offered his arm as she continued down, all but nudging Luke aside.

"Will I do, Your Majesty?" Luke's laughing words penetrated Phillip's daze, and he peered over at the man.

His brows lifted. "You clean up splendidly," he said.

Nan's oldest brother dressed in the French manner with loose trousers, long tunic, wide sash, and high laced moccasins. His shirt was brilliantly white, and his buckskin trousers appeared new. His hair was brushed back, hanging in waves past his shoulders. The final detail, a long hunting knife in its sheath, was tucked in the red sash. Phillip grinned. "Clark will love it."

Nan said nothing at all, but let him lead them to Governor Clark's house. The night being warm, they walked under the stars over boardwalks. "You are a wonder, Nan. Beyond beautiful," he whispered as they approached the house.

The house, a broad, rustic place with a wide porch and heavy beamed lintel, stood two stories high. As they discovered, it was deeper than it was wide.

Nan's hand trembled on Phillip's arm as the butler received them and led them down a central hallway. He put his gloved hand over hers to reassure her, even though he was a bit breathless himself. It felt very much as it might being presented at court, or at the Duchess of Haverford's annual ball. He glanced down at the vision of perfection at his side, and felt his raging nerves calm.

They were led to a room he hadn't seen before, a long sort of reception room to the back of the house, and their names were announced. At least a hundred people filled the space, most well-dressed, some that wouldn't be out of place in a London soiree, though perhaps not a court ball. A few were more casual. Phillip spied Baptiste Charbonneau dressed not unlike Luke, surrounded by people peering into what looked like a display case.

The room, Phillip realized, strolling to the side, was almost a museum, one dedicated to hunting, exploration, and Native cultures, not dissimilar to ones he'd seen in the houses of aristocrats who thought themselves scholars or explorers. Nate gawked at buffalo heads, beadwork, and tomahawks hanging on the wall. *In this case, a museum dedicated to William Clark.*

Clark, who was in conversation with two well-dressed gentlemen, looked up, spied them, and broke into a smile. With a comment to his companions, he approached.

"Your Grace, thank you for joining us. Miss Archer, may I say you look splendid tonight." He beamed.

So much for her fear that he wanted her as "some uncivilized countrywoman," Phillip thought with a grin. She still clung to his arm tightly.

Phillip made the introductions, and as expected, Clark was keen to speak to Luke. After a few words of small talk, he gathered Luke off to meet people. "There's a map that may interest you. I was showing it to Senator Harrison," he said.

"There. You've met the governor and lived," Phillip teased.

A cocky-looking waiter swung by and offered champagne. "Here you are, lady and gents. There're spirits too, if you'd rather. Refreshments are at the far end," he said with a wink.

Phillip handed Nan a glass. Jamie and Nate looked at each other and headed to the far end of the long room.

"Everyone here seems to be examining us," she murmured.

"Ignore the stares. They'll find something else to be curious about. Besides, interest can be friendly," he said, though experience in London ballrooms suggested otherwise. "Shall we survey Clark's treasures?" he asked.

They hadn't gone far when a fashionably dressed young woman approached and proved his words right. "Are you Nan Archer?" she asked.

Nan acknowledged the greeting. "And you are?"

The woman, so petite she stood just to Nan's shoulder, with blue eyes and dark hair, introduced herself as Emilie Chouteau. "My father tells me your family owns Archers' Roost." Leaving no doubt as to her family connections, she nodded toward

Auguste, who stood across the room speaking with other gentlemen.

"Miss Archer is the proprietor of Archers' Roost," Phillip said proudly.

"How utterly splendid! I so admire you," the woman said. She went on to describe a visit. "I have been in many inns and taverns on this river and west, but none so well managed as Archers' Roost."

Soon the two women were chatting amiably about Nan's challenges and women's trials in this land: from the difficulties posed by many brothers to problems obtaining quality goods from afar, to a woman's need for independence.

Phillip murmured his excuses and went to pay his respects to Auguste. When he looked back, another woman had joined them and they appeared to be enthusing over Nan's gown. He turned his mind to business.

He and Auguste had a few private—but satisfying—words before his new friend introduced him to several businessmen, a few of whom were potential investors. Phillip was leery about being beholden to too many strangers, but their interest affirmed his ideas.

As the evening wound on, he saw Nan on the arm of William Clark, speaking with one of the dignitaries. He left her to it, pride warming his heart. He saw Luke deep in discussion with one of the Chouteau sons over the large map in the display case. He listened for a while, fascinated by the knowledgeable additions and corrections they discussed. Sometime later, he found Nate and Jamie sitting in a corner quietly.

"I'm taking Nate back to the hotel to bed," Jamie announced.

Phillip agreed. "I'll tell Nan." He couldn't be sure, but he suspected Nate had been sampling the "spirits" the servant mentioned with negative results.

He turned to search for Nan to do just that, but didn't see her. He walked to the front of the room and inquired about her with Luke, who told him he'd last seen her speaking with the senator's wife. He walked the length of the room without finding her.

"Are you looking for Miss Archer?" Emilie Chouteau peered up at him.

"I am."

"My brother Gabriel offered to show her the garden." She got an amused glint in her eye. "He is flirting, but I think my new friend Nan is not the sort to be impressed."

He found them in the light of flaming torches. *At least the puppy hasn't lured her into the shadows.*

"Phillip! I was just thinking of you. Monsieur Chouteau was just telling me about his adventures along the Platte River."

Gabriel Chouteau shrugged with false humility. "We are searching locations for another trading post."

"Is it navigable?" Phillip asked, his interest piqued.

"To the forks, yes. After it is less reliable. The Shoshone tell us they manage," the man said.

"Someday, all the rivers west will need Tavernash boats," Nan murmured. Their eyes met and held.

Chouteau glanced from one to the other, and quietly excused himself. Phillip glanced around and swept her into the very shadows he had fretted about and into his arms. She rose to meet his kiss and returned it with all the passion he could have hoped for.

She whimpered when he nibbled the corner of her mouth, and he smiled against her skin, kissing his way along her chin to her neck and lower still to the spot that had teased him all evening, across the expanse of skin to the edge of her neckline.

He lifted his eyes to hers when his fingers danced along the edge and began to tug it down. When it didn't move far, he undid one tie in back, never taking his gaze from her eyes, wide and dark with passion. Another tug exposed more, and he kissed his way across the tops of her breasts while he cupped them with his hands, feeling her nipples pebble against his palms through her gown while his tongue slipped into the valley between them.

Joy and hope flared as high as his passion, but he pulled his hands away. *Not here. Not now. Not yet.*

He kissed her mouth, pulling her fully against him. "When then?" she whispered against his lips.

Had he spoken the words out loud? He gave her his answer. "Marry me, Nan."

She stiffened in his arms. "I—That is, I'm still …"

"You said that you didn't know who I was. I'm finally figuring it out, and I hoped this evening you would too. I won't drag you to England unless it is to visit. I hope you believe that. I won't drag you out to the edge of the wilderness like your father either. We can make a life here."

She dipped her head, her forehead against his shoulder. He put the knuckle of one finger under her chin and lifted it. "Don't answer now. Let me continue to court you. Do you ride?"

The apparent change of subject confused his beloved. "Yes," she replied cautiously.

"Then ride out with me tomorrow. I have more I want to show you." He prayed he'd chosen correctly and his last throw of the dice would be enough. She nodded silently and began to pull up her bodice.

He turned her to tie her dress, and couldn't resist a kiss to her nape. Viewing her in better light, he found her respectable enough to return inside.

Thank goodness I had the sense to keep my fingers from her coiffure. For now. But soon…

CHAPTER THIRTY-EIGHT

THE BON HOMME Road led west from the town, away from the river. Cultivation nestled closer to Saint Louis than it did Cape Girardeau, Nan noticed. *How long will it last as the town expands?*

"They call them ribbon farms, I was told," Artie said, riding amiably beside her. Dressed in loose trousers and tunic, he was her Artie again. He'd arranged a well-trained mare for her to ride, a hamper of foodstuffs, and blankets for a picnic. When he'd asked about side saddle, he had to describe it, confirming her suspicion that English ladies must be fragile—or their men thought they were. When she mounted astride and arranged her skirts, she left her ankle boots showing, and the gleam of heat in his eyes delighted her.

"Yes, the French lay out their properties long and narrow to allow all farmers river or road frontage," she explained. "The Northwest Territory, including Illinois, was surveyed in squares. We had to build roads as lands were allotted."

She took in her surroundings absently, still puzzling over his plans for the day. *Where is he taking me? It can't be about the Archer Farm? That's an Illinois issue.*

"Missouri has a stain on its soul," she murmured moments later.

He followed her line of sight to a group of black-skinned

workers bent over hoes in a field. "They may be freemen," he said.

"Unlikely. When the northwest territories became free states, many moved here in order to retain the vile practice."

His deep frown touched her. "Missouri may never become a state as long as it insists on enslaving people."

"I hope you're right. We'll have to fight it," she replied.

They had gone about an hour when the houses became fewer. They passed a narrow lane turning south. "Do you know where that goes?" she asked.

"I was told there's a village called Les Peres that way," he said.

The road had become a narrow lane, and they passed into a cool green woodland. Nan felt her body relax and she stood in her stirrups to breathe in the fresh air, scented with leaf mold. A patch of blood root and trillium in full bloom sent her spirits soaring.

"Thank you, Artie. I needed this," she said, joy bubbling out of her.

His smile mirrored hers. "There's more."

A short time later, the lane split in two directions when they came to a burbling creek running over rocks and lush with plant life. "Does it have a name?" she asked.

"This is the Bonhomme Creek," he replied.

"Let's stop here!"

"Just a bit farther," he replied. He took the north fork of the road and they followed the creek, ducking in and out of the trees, approaching and reapproaching the water, until they came to a clearing on the bank.

He dismounted then, in the dabbled light, and she slid into his arms, getting a swift kiss. He gave her only a moment to enjoy the place before grabbing her by the hand. He tied the horses where they could drink from the creek, and led her toward a path she hadn't noticed through trees and slightly uphill to find a stone house, solid with windows all around and a tile roof, presiding over a low grassy knoll surrounded by the trees. Someone had planted flowers by the door.

"What is this?" she asked.

"Do you like it?"

She met his intense gaze. The question mattered to him. "Artie, what is this?"

"Mine. Or it will be if you like it. The house is small, but can be expanded."

She blinked, absorbing that. "Expanded?"

"If we have children. We'll need more room."

She stared, mouth agape, and he babbled on. "We'd have enough acreage to protect the trees as settlement expands. There's a good well. It is only a two-hour ride to my boat works—potential boat works—if I trot briskly, but it would be a good place for a home. Auguste swears the house won't flood. The creek flows into the Missouri not far from here, so your father…"

She kissed him then as much to silence him as anything, and then kissed him again because it felt good. "What are you trying to ask me?"

"Will you marry me?"

She took a step back. She thought of Archers' Roost. She tried to envision herself in this place. She tried to envision those children. She thought of the night before, Saint Louis society and the people she met. And then the intense longing she saw in his eyes put all her anxiety to flight. They would figure it all out. Together.

He faltered and glanced away, up at the house. "You could make it a tavern if you rather, but…"

She pulled him into her arms and kissed him well and properly. "Yes, I'll marry you, you big goose. In that brick church in front of all those important people."

RELIEF FLOODED PHILLIP, and peace settled over him. *This. This is where I belong. Here with Nan. This is what I've been seeking.* He cupped her face with trembling hands and kissed her back. Excitement warred with passion. "Come, let me show you the house.

The rooms were not large, but there were four of them upstairs and four down. He pointed out where they might have a sitting room and the small room he thought to claim for a study.

She grinned when she saw the iron cook stove in the kitchen. "You do like to eat," she teased.

"I don't expect you to labor over me. We'll be able to hire servants," he said.

Laugher overflowed from her. "Artie, you know me. Do you think I'll be content to sit and knit all day?" She stood arms akimbo in the landing upstairs. "Four bedrooms? How many children do you expect?" she asked with dancing eyes.

"I thought we'd make one your private sitting room. A place to read." He grinned back at her. We'll build shelves for all those books I brought you."

She peered out the windows. Storage shed. Well. Necessary farther back, in the trees. "Have you tested the well?" she asked.

"Yes. But we can do it again. We'll need a stable," he mused.

"You've thought of everything," she said.

"I didn't want to risk you saying no. I need you, Nan Archer, like I need air to breathe. With you at my side, I can build something good. Without you? I'm nothing."

She snuggled against him. How could he resist? He tucked her in close. "You were never nothing, Phillip Artie Tavernash. You are mine," she whispered.

Her heated kisses sent his arousal flying. He glanced frantically around at empty rooms and hard wooden floors, and said, "Come."

They sped down the path to the clearing by the creek and pulled blankets they had tied to their saddles.

"Are you hungry?" he asked, his voice rough with the effort

to be a gentleman.

"Not for food," she answered, taking one of the blankets to lay it under the trees and tugging him near enough to untie his shirt at the neck and pull it from his shoulders. He needed no encouragement, making short work of her clothing so he could devour her with his eyes, food be damned. She shivered in the cool spring air, but he knew how to warm her.

Her inexperience proved to be no hindrance. They made love wrapped in blankets to the sound of flowing water, rustling leaves, and birdsong, their own murmurs of passion adding to a symphony of hope and joy.

NAN INSISTED SHE wanted to be wed in Saint Louis's big church with William Clark and the Chouteau brothers in attendance. It would, she explained, be good for his new business to have their support.

He didn't object to the formality, only the delay. He wanted to make her his immediately. Over the next few weeks, while she spent time with a dressmaker, spoke with church officials, arranged a wedding breakfast, and busied herself about mysterious female preparations that excluded her fiancé, he busied himself finalizing the purchase of their house, ordering furniture, and contracting to build his first boathouse, one for the construction of keelboats.

The first week, Jamie took Nate on a quick trip to the Kaskaskia land office while Luke took up the role of tenacious chaperone. Jamie returned a week later with news that the Archer deed was cleared of fraud. They'd also gone to check the farm and returned with the money he'd hidden and the news that the house still stood, though the inside had been trashed. Nate gleefully joined in Luke's game of keeping Phillip and Nan apart "until the wedding," while Jamie did his part by keeping Phillip busy about the boathouse.

Two days before the one designated for their marriage, a man barged into the Pride of the West and demanded to see Luke Archer. They heard his gravel-voiced shouts from the dining room where they sat eating breakfast. A moment later, he appeared at the door and surveyed the room, drawing frowns from the more fastidious diners.

Phillip gaped at the stranger, a buckskin-clad mountain man with grizzled hair sticking out under a fox fur hat, wearing knee-high moccasins covered in mud, and carrying a long gun. He stalked across the room to their table.

"I had devil of a time tracking you down, the lot of you. They told me in Cape Girardeau you'd come up here," the old man said.

"Pa!" Nan gasped, rising to her feet. "What are you doing here?"

"Luke there never came back. I got tired of waiting and decided I best come see about this farm business myself. I hear you let some squatters take our land."

"No, sir," Jamie said. "The deed is cleared and in your name at the land office. The damned Sullivan squatters are gone. They cleared out my furniture, but that didn't amount to much. The house is sound and the land is ours."

Amos Archer—for it must be him—peered around the table with a scowl. "Introduce me to your fine friend, Nan. Is this the one I heard you took in after he was fool enough to get robbed?"

Phillip grinned at the man. "I am indeed," he said.

"Pa, this is Phillip Tavernash, the Duke of Glenmoor, my fiancé," Nan said.

The old man didn't move so much as an eyelash at the duke, but his eyes flew open when she said fiancé. "You think to marry my girl?" he demanded.

"It is my honor. She has accepted my offer," Phillip said.

Archer glared at him for several moments. "You hauling her back east?" he demanded.

"We're going to live on Bonhomme Creek, Pa," Nan replied. That seemed to satisfy something in the old man. His posture softened.

"What about Archers' Roost?" her father asked.

"We're not selling that or the farm. We'll figure it all out," Luke said, standing to look their father in the eye.

"You approve of this?"

"Aye. Artie is a good man. She'd not likely do better," Luke said, holding his eyes.

The old man looked away first. He pulled a chair up to the table. "Fetch me some of those eggs," he said.

Two days later, scrubbed, trimmed, and in a clean shirt at Nan's insistence, with considerable help from her brothers, he gave the bride away.

Luke stood with Phillip at the altar while Nate and Jamie stood with Nan. There was a subdued, very formal breakfast at The Pride of the West Hotel, with the governor, his ward, and the elite of Saint Louis in attendance.

Phillip remembered none of it. None, that is, except his beloved's face, and their laughing rush up the stairs to share a bed at last.

Three days later, Phillip got his wedding wish, a bonfire on the lawn of Archers' Roost, with all their village friends in attendance, one that Amos Archer heartily approved of as, "Better'n that nonsense in Saint Louis."

They threw themselves into the dancing and imbibed of the passing jug Jolie generously provided. Fiddle music rang out far into the night, long after the newlyweds retired to make sweet love in Nan's room under the rafters in the Roost, the place he'd longed to be for weeks.

Luke and Jamie had insisted they would not sell Archers' Roost, but who exactly would manage it was left to be decided. One thing Phillip knew for certain. They would come back many times.

EPILOGUE

Ashmead, England, 1821

CLARION HALL RANG with unreserved laughter, animated conversation, and the antics of children echoing down the stairs. The Earl of Clarion, standing in the hallway, sighed with contentment. *Life as it should be.*

His entire family, home to Ashmead for the summer, had gathered to celebrate another christening. The newly blessed Grace Madelyn Frances Caulfield lay sleeping in the big cradle in her mother's bedroom—his bedroom in truth.

His youngest son toddled in the nursery, which rang with the voices of his older children and a bevy of nieces and nephews, Bensons and Morgans both, and also the stepchildren he had come to love, the Fitzwallaces. His sister Madelyn had invited her stepson Gideon Kendrick as well, adding his children to the fun, including his rambunctious year old son, John Phillip.

Yes, life as it should be. He smiled, stepping into the busy drawing room. "Tea will be served momentarily," he said. "And yes, my dear, before you ask, Grace is sleeping peacefully. The nursemaid is sitting nearby." He planted a kiss on his wife Delia's curly hair, oblivious to the audience.

He took a seat next to his sister, Madelyn Morgan, happy for her company. They spoke of children and country matters only briefly before a scratch at the door was followed by the entrance of his butler, Harris.

"You have a visitor, my lord. Shall I tell him you are occupied?" the butler asked. He held a card in his hand.

The earl rose, too full of joy to turn anyone away, and glanced at the card. "James Phineas Archer. I don't believe I know that name."

"I do!" Kendrick exclaimed, rising to his feet. "He must be looking for me."

Harris showed not one but two gentlemen into the room, both simply but respectively dressed. James Archer had the air of a barrister or steward, rather like the earl's own, Eli Benson, watching from across the room. The other, younger, stood just behind Archer's left shoulder.

"Oh, my goodness! Evan Fitzwallace!" The Countess of Clarion rose and, to the earl's surprise, engulfed the young man in a hug.

"Perhaps you could make introductions, Kendrick? Delia?" the earl said.

"David," the countess said, "may I present Mr. Evan Fitzwallace, a family connection of my late husband, and," she grinned at the blushing young man, "I believe, uncle to the children."

"Welcome, Mr. Fitzwallace," the earl said with a nod before glancing at Kendrick.

"This gentleman, Clarion, is Glenmoor's American brother-in-law." Kendrick—whom Clarion remembered was Glenmoor's brother—clapped the other man on the back. "Jamie, this is the Earl of Clarion."

Both young men made perfectly proper bows, and were soon being introduced to the entire room.

"Please come, sit. Make yourself at home," the earl said.

"And please, tell us how Phillip is doing!" Madelyn said. Phillip, Duke of Glenmoor, her stepson, remained dear to her heart.

"He and Nan are positively thriving. Susan started walking just before I left. I wouldn't be surprised to hear she's climbing trees by now," Mr. Archer said with a cocky grin.

Madelyn sighed. "I wish they would come to visit."

JAMIE GLANCED AROUND the room and wished Phillip had come as well. He'd learned to be the spokesman for business, but not for family. Not to this wealthy, well-dressed lot he was struggling to sort. "He suspected people would say that. He said to tell you all he loves you, but with the business to get off the ground, a little one, and settling matters with Archers' Roost and the Archer farm, it will be a few years before they're free to come this far." *Not that Nan is anxious to ever do it at all. I'll have to convince her otherwise.*

"You have a farm, Mr. Archer?" a young woman introduced as Lucy Benson asked.

"We do, small by your standards and mostly fallow at the moment," he told her.

"Small is still valuable," the woman said. "I have seven hundred acres at Willowbrook, and I love every one of them."

Encouraged by that, Jamie went on. "Artie, that is Phillip, insisted we not sell it when I moved to Saint Louis. He says, 'there is only so much land' and a family must hold on to it. Most folks in my country think land is abundant. He said to think of our grandchildren."

The earl and some others nodded. "You call the duke Artie?" Clarion asked with a laugh.

"He said he has no use for a title in Missouri," Jamie said.

"Nor here either," Kendrick muttered. Jamie had met Artie's brother Gideon in Wales when he first arrived. He'd spent several days with the family. "How did our business in Glasgow play out?" Kendrick asked.

Jamie brightened, on more comfortable ground now. Kendrick understood commerce. "Better than we anticipated. I was able to stretch our assets to four engines total and a healthy selection of parts."

"What is your business, Mr. Archer?" The gentleman, who had been introduced as the countess's brother, Jeffrey Graham, leaned forward, interested. He'd been sitting quietly up until then.

"I am Artie's assistant in the Duchess Boat Company. I was dispatched to Glasgow to purchase steam engines for our river boats," Jamie said proudly.

"*Duchess* Boat Company?" Madelyn asked, laughing.

"Yes, ma'am. He was going to call it the Glenmoor Boat Company or Tavernash, but he said he wanted to name it after my sister. She laughed mightily, but the name stuck."

"But steam, Mr. Archer! I'd like to hear more," Graham said. Soon Jamie, Graham, and Kendrick, who was a partner in the business now that he'd put up the stake for the engines, were deep into a discussion of river versus ocean crafts. Graham owned a fleet of merchant ships, as it turned out, and had a vested interest in steam.

The stiff old butler poked in and announced tea being served. Luckily, tea turned out to be more substantial than the beverage and some biscuits. There was coffee to be had and a spot of brandy as well. He confessed to hunger and no one seemed to mind when he wolfed down three sandwiches.

Evan, who'd been sitting in conversation with the countess, did the same with her encouragement. She told Jamie at least three times, to "tell Phillip thank you for everything he's done for Evan." Jamie suspected she didn't mean helping him sell his commission and offering him a job, but freeing him from his horrid half-brother. She apparently knew the Fitzwallaces well, and they were a nasty lot.

Not long after, a hoard of children were unleashed on the room, bringing noise and chaos. A cricket game had been promised. Jamie begged off, but Evan gleefully followed the crowd out to the front lawn of this great pile of a house.

Graham stayed behind, glad he said to spend time with a man

of business rather than a crowd of "worthless aristocrats." He said that last with a wink at his brother-in-law, Clarion, but Jamie suspected there was a grain of truth in it.

"I see your point about navigation and boats on those great rivers of yours," Graham said. "The size and distances are staggering. There's nothing like it here, or in Jamaica, my other base." That comment explained much. Both Graham and his sister the countess had the look of the Caribbean about them.

"You and your brother-in-law have a sound business plan," Graham went on. "Kendrick said you've yet to turn a profit, but it is early days yet. I'd like to invest."

Jamie shook his head. "Artie has been turning away folks in Saint Louis. He says he trusts only family." Pride at that lifted his chin.

"Where are those engines of yours now?"

"On their way to Bristol. I only came to report to Gideon. I need to hurry back to keep an eye on it all and get shipping arranged."

A wide smile blossomed on the man's face. "I can help you there. Graham Shipping can get that equipment safely to New Orleans. Perhaps in exchange for a small share? Ten percent?"

Jamie had learned a lot from Artie. "Three," he said without hesitation.

"Five might be fair," Graham said.

"It would be generous, but perhaps acceptable," Jamie said. "If Gideon agrees."

Graham's lips twitched. Jamie thought he saw approval. "I have every confidence in your business, Mr. Archer. Very well. Five."

"Perhaps you'd like to come along and see the river for yourself," Jamie suggested.

Graham, though clearly intrigued, shook his head sadly. "I'm fascinated and would love to, but not this year. I have business waiting for me in London." He didn't elaborate, but something in the faraway mist in his eyes hinted it might be more personal than commercial.

Jamie could only speculate what that might be before the earl popped in and positively insisted that they at least come out and watch.

"One other thing, Mr. Archer. Did I understand you to say Glenmoor has abandoned his title?" He leaned forward. The question obviously intrigued him.

Jamie grinned. "Not entirely. It may not define him, but he finds it useful now and then."

"Useful," Graham murmured. "Interesting thought."

The End

Author's Note

Those of you who've read my previous books will recognize the folks gathered in the Epilogue. Gideon Kendrick and Phillip were both introduced in *The Defiant Daughter*, which is Madelyn Morgan's love story. Gideon's own story is *Duke in All But Name*. The Earl and Countess of Clarion's story, *The Upright Son*, introduced Jeffrey Graham as well. His story comes next. He, it turns out, is the unlikeliest aristocrat of them all, in *An Unlikely Duke*.

As always, I've attempted to be careful in my research and accurate about the history of the era. The vastness of the North American continent, along with rapidly changing settlement patterns, road conditions, and technology in 1818, made estimating distances and travel times a particular challenge. I spent considerable time working out how long it took Phillip to travel from Philadelphia to the Mississippi, and then didn't use it! I believe my times and distances are mostly accurate, but I fear the story underestimates travel back and forth between Kaskaskia and Cape Girardeau. I apologize for the liberty.

All place names are real and as accurate as I could make them. Geography can be a challenge because the big rivers change shape. Kaskaskia, for example, described in this story as being on the east bank of the Mississippi, is now west of the river. The Illinois border jogs around to include it.

The older, settled French towns on the upper Mississippi were easy to track down. Sainte Genevieve and Cape Girardeau thrive as historic treasures. Kaskaskia, alas, suffered repeated catastrophic floods and faded in importance. The parish there, however, has been in continual existence since 1640, though successive buildings have suffered from the floods. A bell presented to the parish in 1741 by the king of France still exists.

Unfortunately, Kaskaskia has a dark history. The Jesuit priests who founded it also introduced enslaved Africans into the area. While Illinois, as part of the Northwest Territory charter, became a free state, Missouri, alas, was admitted as a slave state after our story, as a result of the so-called Missouri compromise. I like to think Phillip and Nan advocated fiercely against it.

The stretch of the Ohio River south of Illinois was a wilder country. Many towns now on the map either didn't exist in 1818 or have changed their names. It is unclear, for example, when the place called McFarlan's Ferry became Elizabethtown. I elected to use the latter name. James McFarlan built his tavern there in 1812. Cave-in-Rock, the pirate den, is now a state park. Smithland, Kentucky, was indeed a brawling, lawless town.

"Mr. Madison's War" refers, of course, to the War of 1812. It was not universally supported. Indigenous people allied themselves with Great Britain and suffered greatly, losing vast amounts of land in the aftermath. British negotiators for the Treaty of Ghent attempted to resurrect the idea of an Indian Barrier State, but the Americans refused to consider it. The flood of settlement continued, pushing indigenous people north and west.

The first commercial steamboat was Robert Fulton's Clermont, which was plying the Hudson River from New York City to Albany, New York in 1807. By 1814, Fulton's company inaugurated service from Natchez, Mississippi to New Orleans. Two years later, boats were traveling from Louisville, Kentucky to New Orleans. The first steamboat to dock in Saint Louis was the Zebulon M. Pike, which arrived on August 2, 1817. Development was hindered somewhat by the bank failures and economic collapse of 1819, but by the mid to late 1820s, recovery was well on its way and steamboats were becoming common. Phillip's timing was fortuitous.

There are some historical figures in the novel. William Clark of the Corps of Discovery fame was indeed governor of the Missouri Territory. Earlier, he had been brigadier general of militia for the Louisiana (later Missouri) Territory and a federal Indian agent for western tribes when his friend Meriwether Lewis was governor of Louisiana. Clark's ward, Baptiste Charbonneau, the son of Sacajawea and Toussaint Charbonneau, a member of the Lewis and Clark's Corps of Discovery, was the youngest person to reach the Pacific Ocean during the expedition. He was, of course, an infant. He spent his formative years in Saint Louis where Clark saw to his education and upkeep.

Auguste Chouteau was fifteen when he and his mother's common-law husband, Pierre Laclède, set up a fur trading post at what was to become Saint Louis in 1764. Oblivious to changing European politics that caused that very land to change hands repeatedly, Auguste and his brother Pierre forged close ties with the Osage people and continued to foster close ties to New Orleans, their home of origin, enabling them to create a business empire stretched along the length of the rivers and across the Great Plains. With the arrival of the Americans, they handled the challenge to their stranglehold on the fur trade by forming a partnership with John Jacob Astor's American Fur Company. Emily Chouteau was sixteen at the time of the book. She later married a career soldier. Gabriel Chouteau, a veteran of Mr. Madison's war, was twenty-four.

Officials in Kaskaskia and the Sullivan brothers are entirely fictional, though in the latter case, they were inspired by some actual con men, the Sturdivant family, who were notorious counterfeiters, generally engaged in passing fake currency, in southern Illinois in the early nineteenth century.

Acknowledgements

This work comes to you through the good graces of Dragonblade Publishing. Working with them has been a great blessing in my life. I am particularly grateful for their patience and support this past year during a difficult time.

Never doubt that it takes a team to produce a book. In addition to the work of the editors at Dragonblade, this book is better for the insights and input of Jude Knight, Sherry Ewing, Judy Johnsen, Corinne Lehman, Carol Thomas, and Laurel Busch. Thank you all for helping my little book shine.

About the Author

Award winning author, Caroline Warfield, grew up in a peripatetic army family, and the need to travel never left her. After a varied career (largely around libraries and technology) she retired to the urban wilds of eastern Pennsylvania with her Beloved to be closer to family and to write. She remains a traveler and adventurer, enamored of owls, books, history, and beautiful gardens (but not the act of gardening).

Caroline calls her books family-centered romance, and this one is no exception. Family makes her characters what they are, for better or worse, engenders motivation, creates the hurdles they must overcome, and sets them on their path to their own happily ever after and families of their own. Phillip and Nan are no exception.

Website: www.carolinewarfield.com
Amazon Author: amazon.com/Caroline-
Warfield/e/B00N9PZZZS
Good Reads: bit.ly/1C5blTm
Facebook: facebook.com/groups/WarfieldFellowTravelers
Twitter: twitter.com/CaroWarfield
Email: warfieldcaro@gmail.com
Newsletter: carolinewarfield.com/newsletter
BookBub: bookbub.com/authors/caroline-warfield
You Tube:
youtube.com/channel/UCycyfKdNnZlueqo8MlgWyWQ

9 781960 184757